TAROT

TAROT

A NOVEL BY

MARISSA KENNERSON

RAZORBILL

RAZORBILL

An Imprint of Penguin Random House LLC
New York

Visit us online at penguinrandomhouse.com

LIBRARY OF CONGRESS CATALOGING-IN-PUBLICATION DATA
Names: Kennerson, Marissa, author.
Title: Tarot / Marissa Kennerson.
Description: [New York : Razorbill, 2019. | Summary: "Before the Tarot, there
was Anna. When she escapes the tyrannical Hierophant King, Anna discovers
she is destined to create a new world"—Provided by publisher.
Identifiers: LCCN 2018040893 | ISBN 9780451478412 (hardback)
Subjects: | CYAC: Tarot—Fiction. | Fate and fatalism—Fiction. |
Magic—Fiction. | Kings, queens, rulers, etc.—Fiction. | Fantasy.
Classification: LCC PZ7.1.K506 Tar 2019 | DDC [Fic]—dc23 LC record available at
https://lccn.loc.gov/2018040893

ISBN: 9780451478412

Printed in the United States of America

1 3 5 7 9 10 8 6 4 2

Interior design by Lindsey Andrews. Text set in Sabon LT Pro.

To Greg and Shepard
And to Xan—my favorite young adult

Nothing is written.

                    —T. E. Lawrence, *Lawrence of Arabia*

*The dream is the small hidden door in the deepest
and most intimate sanctum of the soul, which opens
to that primeval cosmic night that was soul long
before there was conscious ego and will be soul far
beyond what a conscious ego could ever reach.*

                                        —Carl Jung

You belong among the wildflowers.

                            —Tom Petty, "Wildflowers"

A nna worked at the cold stone floor of the Tower, using a tool she'd made from the handle of a lantern years before. The entire floor was scored with small, white lines the size of matchsticks, each set of four lines crossed through with a bold diagonal.

She struck another line, knowing the next day would be her sixteenth birthday. She clenched her teeth against the familiar feeling of gloom settling inside her.

Anna heard the sound of keys grinding their way into the Tower's immense stone door. She jumped up, expecting to greet her advisors, but the King's Guard entered, followed by the Hierophant King himself.

"Anna," the King greeted her.

"Father." Anna suppressed the urge to lunge at him and scratch his eyes out. He stood for a moment and looked around.

The Tower was a circular stone structure with narrow stairways, and Anna lived in the round room at its top. There was one window overlooking the castle gates and the forest that lay beyond. On a windy day, she could fool herself into thinking she smelled salt coming off the sea, though she had never glimpsed or heard it. But she'd been told of the ocean's existence by her advisors, and now she imagined that it was behind her, in a direction she had never seen.

Despite a modest stone fireplace, the room was terribly drafty. The King pulled his robes closer. A small bed sat along the wall, but the room was mostly taken up by a large wooden worktable covered in sketches and a weaving loom the size of a small horse.

The King was not looking at the room itself but at the elaborate tapestries that curved around it, covering every inch of wall space. His heart caught in his chest at the sheer beauty of the tapestries.

"Heavens, Anna!" the King said. "These are truly extraordinary, and to think you are self-taught. The work of the so-called masters would surely pale in comparison. The pure imagination of it! My walls will be the envy of all." He paused. "You've accomplished so much since I was here last. Why, they look as if they are nearly finished."

"A year is a long time," Anna said quietly.

The King rubbed at the silver hairs of his closely cropped beard and ran a hand over his shaven head. "Has it been a year?"

"It has, and we made an agreement. When I completed the tapestries, you would let me go."

"So I did. Are you finished?"

"I just need to put some final touches on the last one, bind the threads. But other than that, yes."

"Please, take me through them. One by one." He shook his head, his eyes scanning the walls. "How one girl could create all of this . . ."

I have a lot of time, Anna thought. She wanted to say, *Because you keep me locked up in here like I'm some kind of monster!* But she bit her tongue.

Anna pushed aside a tall ladder that allowed her to reach the top of her tapestries, and then beckoned the King forward. She dove right in, worried that he could change his mind and leave her again at any moment.

"This is the land of Pentacles," she said. The two looked up at the great tapestry together, nearly fifteen feet high and just as wide. It was one of four grand tapestries, her life's work.

At the tapestry's center sat a king on an immense throne carved into the trunk of a magnificent brown oak tree. The king's robes were purple velvet and shimmered with golden silk threads that matched a bejeweled crown. At the center of the crown a golden pentacle symbol sparkled. Baskets brimmed with glittering gold coins at the King's feet.

The Hierophant King wore a large silver signet ring on his index finger, with a pentacle etched into its face. He twisted the ring now, staring at the scene while Anna spoke.

"This tapestry depicts the entire court as I imagine it," Anna said. "You have a regal queen in a magnificent gown of powder-blue satin, handsome knights in battle regalia. I imagine even the pages of this opulent land are dressed in tunics and stockings of the finest silks."

"Is that supposed to be me?" the King asked, gesturing to the king on the oak throne.

"You're just my inspiration," Anna corrected, wrinkling her nose behind the King's back.

"There's so much detail," the King said. "I can almost taste the food."

A feast was set with a succulent, bronzed pig laid over bright red apples, all roasted to perfection. Tarts and cakes dripped with cream, and goblets overflowed with wine. The food was so bountiful, it was almost obscene. The King noticed a tray on the floor by the door where he had entered. Leftovers of a modest breakfast of toast and jam. The sight embarrassed him.

Heavens knew how she had survived all of these years locked up. The King himself would have gone mad. He looked at Anna. Her pallor had turned gray, no doubt from a lack of sunlight and fresh air, and yet she had grown into a beautiful young woman. Long black hair swung down her back, matching her impossibly big black eyes. The King remembered where those eyes came from, and any guilt or tenderness he had started to feel evaporated. He tilted his head back up toward the tapestry. "Go on."

"The land of Pentacles revolves around a luxurious and mighty kingdom built in the middle of a great forest." She motioned toward the blanket of hunter-green pines and the massive stone castle that erupted from their center. The King was astounded. To have such an understanding of perspective! The forest was bordered by an angry sea, waves of slate blue pounding against steep stone cliffs.

"It's as if I can feel the mist, Anna. I can almost hear the crashing of the surf. I ride out to the sea often, and I could never depict the scene with such clarity. And you have never been there." The King marveled at the depth and movement of the image. "It almost appears to be a living, breathing thing, this sea."

Anna bowed her head slightly and accepted the King's compliment. He nodded for her to continue.

"Below the castle, we have the home of the serfs and peasants," Anna said. For a moment she and the King could not stand side by side, their path obstructed by the large worktable and its proximity to the wall. He was a stocky man of six feet, so he stood back to let her pass in front of him.

The kingdom was dotted with guards, the castle itself decorated with turrets and flags that looked as if they could snap in the frigid wind blowing off the turbulent sea.

"It is uncanny how much it looks like the kingdom," the King said.

"My advisors have described it to me, and I read a lot of historical texts."

"Hmm." Once again the King began to twist the masses of jeweled rings that decorated his long fingers. Anna tried to move more quickly.

"Some of it I can see from my window," she added. "But you know this kingdom well, so let's move on." They stayed close to the walls, walking past the window, to the side opposite, where Anna's narrow bed sat. There was more room here, and now Anna stood beside the King again. He watched her while she spoke, absorbed in her description. Her hips had widened from her tiny waist, and he was reminded of her mother, his late wife, the Queen. How could this girl have matured so much in one year?

Anna sensed the King watching her, and wondered what he was thinking.

"Here is the land of Wands." Anna looked up at the next tapestry, bold and bright. "Where Pentacles is a land of nobility, Wands is a village of artists and free spirits set in the mountains of a desert land."

"Desert land?" the King said.

Anna nodded. She pointed out the soft orange sands that seemed to glow with warmth. "It's a retreat for artists and crafts-people. Here is their marketplace." Anna pointed to a large depiction of an open-air market with goods ranging from elaborately patterned textiles and pottery to baskets overflowing with fruits woven in bright yellows, greens, reds, and oranges.

"May I touch it?" The King reached toward the sand.

"Yes." Anna hoped that the passion in her work might leap

from the threads and soften his heart. The King ran his fingers over the warm orange and yellow threads that made up the desert land.

Cloaked figures sat beneath the shelter of white tents, heads bent in concentration. "Wands draws the most passionate and creative people." Anna smiled.

The King studied her, his eyes suddenly flashing with anger.

"Free spirits," he scoffed.

"Father." Anna forgot herself. "I dream of a world where people can create and invent and—"

"Don't be ridiculous, Anna. You dream of chaos."

"Why? I bet half of the peasants who serve you could write books or make great art."

"That's enough, Anna. People are born into their positions for a reason. Fates are a fixed thing, destiny preordained," the King said.

"But what about our imaginations? How can you put limits on that?" Anna shook her head. "There are things I think about that lie beyond my experience or even my comprehension at times. Pieces of dreams, unfinished thoughts—things I can't yet weave into my tapestries. But I know one day I will."

He squinted at her. "People need order, direction. They need to know their place. *That* is how they thrive." He paused. "You're young and have not seen what I have seen," he added.

"Whose fault is that? I have not seen *anything*!" Anna wished she could take her words back the minute they left her mouth.

"Watch your tone."

"I'm sorry," she said immediately. He held all the power here. There was no point in pushing him. "I really am. I don't want to debate. I just want to finish showing my gift to you."

"All right. But no more of that sort of talk. I won't tolerate it from you or from anyone."

The King tapped his foot and took a deep breath in, which Anna took as a sign of impatience. There was a lot more she wanted to say to him, but she swallowed it, fearing he would storm off as he had one year ago, when he last visited her. She simply could not wait another year. She couldn't stand it.

"Over here," she said, trying to make her voice softer. The King gathered the velvet and silks of his robes and followed her across the room, avoiding the loom.

As he squeezed past Anna's bed, he took in the austerity of the linens and felt a pang of remorse. Perhaps he had been too harsh with her just then. He thought about his own lavish quarters and wondered if he could somehow make her life of confinement a bit more comfortable.

The truth was, when he wasn't with her, he didn't think about her very much. He got caught up in court life, the obligatory viewings with the peasants and the farmers and their litany of complaints. He rode daily and took vigorous walks to keep up his stamina. Admittedly, he always rode out through the northern gates so that he wouldn't have to see the Tower. Out of sight, out of mind.

He had charged three of his best advisors with raising Anna, and from what he could tell, they had done a good job.

To see her, to stand in her presence, was painful. To witness her as a living, breathing girl twisted him up inside. He hated these visits and the hangover of guilt and ambivalence they left him with for weeks afterward.

"Swords. The land farthest to the North." Anna held both hands out, presenting the next tapestry.

The King was listening, but his mind drifted. Perhaps now he could bring her back to the Keep with him and raise her properly at court. Truly be a father to her. It had been sixteen years.

He looked up and studied her, but when his eyes wandered to the tapestry, he was once again filled with wonder. It seemed as if the entire thing were made of shining silver and bronze metal.

"Swords is a bustling city of trade, invention, and ambition."

"What are these?" The King touched the towering structures that looked like they were made of precious glass. They reached far up into the sky, touching the clouds.

"It's where people work and sleep in Swords." Anna took a step closer and ran her finger over the greenish threads. They gleamed with hints of purple and gold, like blown glass.

He raised his eyebrows in question.

"They're buildings."

"Such a thing could never actually exist," he said, fascinated.

"It's just a tapestry." Anna shrugged.

"There are so many people. They look like ants."

"Yes, it's the most populated of all the lands." Anna wanted to say more about how the huge population of people brought vast ideas and talent, but she held her tongue this time.

He wondered if it would be blasphemous to hang these in his halls. They were so beautiful and unique, but they represented fantastical possibilities that opposed his ideologies. And yet, he wanted them. He felt an almost irresistible pull to them.

"Ready to move on?" Anna asked.

He nodded. They only needed to take two steps to reach the final tapestry, raw and unfinished at its borders. He ran his eyes over it and stopped suddenly.

"What is that?" The King could not believe what he was seeing.

"What?" Anna said. She moved closer to him.

"That." The word sounded like a door slamming shut. He jabbed his finger into a glowing white orb that hovered over the land of silky white beaches lined with tall, swaying palms. People Anna's age, young people, twirled throughout the tapestry, splashing in a calm, glittering sea. Others tended to small farms or napped in hammocks.

"The Moon," she said plainly.

"The Moon?" The King looked dumbfounded. "What do you know of the Moon?" He narrowed his eyes. "It certainly has never graced these lands, so you couldn't have seen it out that window of yours," he said.

Anna took a step away from the King. She looked from him to the Moon and back again. "The Moon has visited me in my dreams since I was a child."

"Has it?" The King's eyes bulged and his face turned an angry red. "Really?"

Anna paused, trying to explain. "Sometimes I feel like the Moon is guiding me. I know it's not real, but it's always there, somewhere between dream and waking."

"Did your advisors tell you about the Moon?" The King tugged at his collar.

"No, we've never talked about it," Anna admitted.

"You never asked them why there is no moon here? In this land?" he demanded.

Anna shook her head.

"Damn him." The King pressed his lips together. "Guard! I am ready to leave!" The guards, who had been standing at the doorway, snapped to attention.

"Where are you going? Damn who?" Anna tried to think of what she might have missed, but everything was happening so quickly.

The King leaned in close to Anna. "I had a feeling about you. I was right to keep you locked up here, and here is where you'll stay." He jabbed his finger at her.

"You don't even know me! You've never given me a chance!" Anna grabbed the King's arm. "You can't leave."

But the King shook her off and stormed past her, crossing the room in just a few steps.

"Father!" Anna pleaded, her voice dissolving into a desperate sob. "What's happened? Please stay and talk to me." But the King was already halfway out the door. His guards ran after him. "When will you return?" She was answered with the sound of the key turning in its heavy lock and then the stony, damp silence of the Tower. She pressed her head to the door and heard the echo of a guard's voice.

"I don't know why he doesn't just hand her over to us. We'd take care of her properly. Throw her in the real dungeons and teach her a lesson or two."

Anna stepped back, picked up a glass jar of charcoal sticks, and threw it against the door. "Damn you, Father! Damn all of you!" The jar shattered, glass cascading across the floor.

"You promised!" She shook her head. "And I was fool enough to believe you."

She turned and crossed the room to touch the unfinished tapestry—the tropical land, ruled by youth and passion. She pressed her palm onto the shimmering white threads of the Moon.

2

When her advisors finally arrived, it was dusk, and Anna had lit lanterns and candles to combat the coming darkness. Outside her window, the sky turned different shades of pink and violet as the sun set. She could hear the sounds of the day coming to a close: the loud creak of the front gates being drawn shut for the evening, the peasants yelling and corralling their livestock for the night. The hollow ring of the campanile's bells, signaling evening curfew. Anna could even smell the peasants' humble dinners roasting, the scent wafting through the evening air.

For the second time that day she heard keys grind in the lock of the Tower door. When it opened, a small white dog as fluffy as a perfect cloud came bounding straight for Anna.

"Hello, darling dog." She smiled for the first time that day and took him in her arms. The little dog launched an attack of unrelenting licks onto Anna's face, his small body trembling with happiness. She laughed and finally managed to duck away. "My little Bembo! What would I do without you?"

The dog was followed by Anna's three advisors: the Fool, the Magician, and the Hermit. They were called as such for the roles they served in the King's court. If they had other birth names, they had never revealed them to Anna. She let Bembo go, and he started exploring the room, sniffing everything he came in contact with.

"What took you so long?" Anna moaned. "I've been waiting for hours."

"We're so sorry, Anna. We didn't know how long he'd be here," the Fool said, fidgeting with his tall onyx staff.

"How did it go?" The Magician stepped fully into the room. She had silky brown hair, always in a long braid down her back, with one shock of gray woven through, making her look older than her thirty-five years.

"You haven't seen him? He didn't come to you?" Anna started pacing, nervous energy jolting through her.

"No." The Magician knitted her brows.

The Fool poured Anna a glass of water from a pitcher on the worktable and brought it to her.

"Thank you." She gulped it down and, taking a few breaths, walked over to the bench beside the worktable and sat down. Anna gestured for the rest of them to follow. Bembo took the opportunity to jump onto her lap, and she stroked his soft, downy fur, finding the motion calming.

"I was showing him all of the finished tapestries. He seemed very impressed, more so than he wanted to let on."

"That's great, Anna," said the Fool.

Anna looked at him. "He got angry for a moment, when I mentioned artisans and creativity." The three studied her, concerned. "But we moved on, and then—"

Anna stood up and walked over to the unfinished tapestry. Lantern light beneath it made it look as if the tide were ebbing, the tall palms swaying above it.

"What is *that*?" The Magician's voice was hard. Anna whipped around and faced her.

"*That* is what set him off." Anna looked closely at the Magician. "He saw the Moon, and he yelled at me and stormed out." Anna thrust her hands into her hair. "He said that he was right to keep me here and that here was where I was going to stay."

"When in heaven's name did you add this, Anna?" the Magician asked.

The three advisors stood up to examine the Moon, shining big and bright in the lantern's light.

"I did it last night. I was going to weave it into all of the lands."

"This is a disaster," said the Magician.

The Hermit, usually the image of calm, drummed his fingers over his lips.

"I think it's time we told her the truth," he said. He spoke slowly and not very often, so when he did talk, people tended to listen. He paused, always careful with his choice of words. "She needs to know who she is. It is the only way she can protect herself."

Anna's eyes widened. "Protect myself?"

"Maybe we can talk to him," the Fool offered. "He can be stubborn, but he's not a monster. Anna's just a girl."

"There will be no talking to him now. Not after this." The Magician lifted her chin toward the Moon. "We need a plan, and yes, Hermit, you are correct." She turned her attention back to Anna. "My dear, you and I are going to have a talk." She gestured to the seat next to her, and Anna came and sat back down.

"You're scaring me," Anna said.

"Frankly, you should be scared." The Magician placed a hand on her knee.

The Hermit cleared his throat, signaling for the Magician to be more sensitive.

"Anna, what we are about to tell you is going to change

everything." The Hermit looked at her, a calmness in his amber eyes. "But you are strong, and our hope is that it will set you on a new path."

Anna eyed the Magician, uncharacteristically harried and anxious. She fidgeted with the golden serpent belt that wound around her red velvet robes. The emerald eyes of the snakehead clasp gleamed in the candlelight.

"I'm not very good at this kind of thing. . . ." the Magician began, wringing her hands. "The King is not your father, Anna," she blurted.

The Fool and the Hermit looked at each other and shook their heads. The Magician really wasn't good at this kind of thing.

"What do you mean?" Anna said.

"Your real father was a great magician named Marco Russo. He was the most powerful magician that ever existed." She paused. "He was also the King's best friend since childhood. And my brother."

"Your brother? You are not my aunt?" Anna raised her brows in confusion.

"I am your aunt, but I am not the King's sister. I am Marco's sister. I *was* Marco's sister." The Magician stared down at her hands. She looked to the other two advisors for help.

"The Hierophant King is not my father?" Anna asked.

"No," the three advisors said in unison.

As her shock diminished, something like hope bloomed in Anna's chest. She stood up.

"Tell me the rest. I want to know all about my real father. Where is he now? How did I end up locked in this cell my whole life?" She started to pace. "Was my mother actually the Queen?"

"Yes!" the Fool said eagerly. "That is true!"

"Tell me more about Marco Russo," Anna said, turning to the Magician. "Your brother."

"Not now!" the Magician snapped at her. "Hermit, go to the kitchen and get two days' provisions. Anything from the larder you can manage. Tell them you're going on one of your silent retreats and you need supplies." The Magician looked up as if she were checking an imaginary list in her head. "Clothes too. A warm cloak, boots."

"Where can I get those *tonight*?" the Hermit asked, eyebrows raised.

"Steal them if you have to."

The Hermit nodded and pulled the hood of his own soft gray cloak over his head, covering his amber eyes and waves of prematurely gray hair. He motioned to the Fool to follow.

Anna looked on, shock taking hold once more. Her mouth hung half-open as she watched the scene unfold before her.

Anna and the Magician watched them leave, Bembo tucked into the silk handkerchief at the top of the Fool's staff. Then the Magician turned to Anna, who stared back at her like she was mad. "I know. You want answers."

"Why am I hearing this for the first time? Why now?" Anna's shock was turning to anger, but she wasn't sure where to direct it.

"When your mother died in childbirth . . ." The Magician paused.

Anna waved her aunt on to continue.

"The King hadn't recovered from her betrayal, and when she died, it was too much for him to bear. He was so full of rage, and you were just a baby. My niece, my brother's child, for stars' sake. I didn't know what the King was capable of. So I struck a bargain with him." The Magician peered at Anna now, her eyes filled with tears. Anna reached for her hand. The Magician let her hold it for a moment and then pulled it back.

"What sort of bargain?" Anna asked.

"I asked that he let me raise you. That I be responsible for you—for your education and upbringing. As long as I gave up my magic. I handed over my wand and my potions—everything."

"You gave up your magic for me?" Anna put her hand to her mouth.

"I never really thought of it like that. If I wanted to keep doing magic, I would've had to flee the kingdom. But I couldn't leave you. I don't think I would have gotten very far anyway. The King became especially vigilant after your mother's death."

"Vigilant how?" Anna asked.

"That's when he established his idea of *fixed fates*. He banned magic, as you've gathered. He became tyrannical. When a subject was born, he named their craft and even who they would marry one day. He closed the gates to trade, set rigid curfews, and—"

"He locked me in this Tower." Anna clenched her fists.

"He did. I was able to visit you every day, but I could not let you out." The Magician pulled her long braid over her shoulder and ran her hand over it. "But the Fool, the Hermit, and I were worried about the King snapping one day. I think in some ways we've been preparing for it all along. I never trusted him with your safety, Anna. This situation"—she gestured around them at the Tower—"always seemed precarious at best."

The Magician's chest rose as she took in a deep breath. "I have to leave you now. I should be at dinner, and I don't want to give him any reason to be suspicious." She patted Anna's knee awkwardly. "We'll be back at dawn, and we'll get you out of here."

"How?" Anna looked at her, incredulous.

The Magician lowered her voice and looked around. "The King took my supplies, but I have been practicing without them for many years in secret. I knew this day would come."

Anna bit her lip.

"My magic is significantly weaker without my wand and potions, but it's not useless. Performing spells just drains my energy."

The little spark of hope in Anna's chest grew larger. Something she hadn't felt in a very long time.

"We were forbidden from discussing any of this with you, Anna. But now I think we should have told you much sooner." She got up to go, but stopped and turned to Anna. "Now it's your turn to tell me something. How do you know about the Moon?"

"It has come to me in my dreams for as long as I can remember. It became my muse, my inspiration for the worlds I wove."

"And that is what you told the King?"

Anna nodded.

"When Marco died, the Queen was utterly devastated, and told the King that her love for him would never die. Your mother said that she and her unborn baby had a connection with Marco that could not be broken because he had taken the form of the Moon, and he was untouchable."

Anna's eyes sparkled.

"The Queen's assertion became a legend that swept through the entire kingdom. Marco was a beloved man. He was kind, and much better with people than I am. He would visit the peasant children and produce sweets and warm bread for them. No one would ever go hungry if he was near." The Magician wrinkled her nose and twisted her serpent belt. "He was a wonderful older brother. No one could make me laugh like he could."

Anna raised her eyebrows at the Magician.

"Right. No one else could even make me laugh." The Magician looked out Anna's window. Rain pounded against the walls of the Tower. "It's really storming now. Be sure to light that fire."

Anna joined the Magician at the window, watching the rain trickle down the glass. "So everyone believed the legend?"

"Yes. I think the people were so grieved by his loss, the story offered comfort. People told the legend to their children at bedtime. It made the King irate. He couldn't stop his subjects from looking up at night and saying a little prayer to Marco."

"But there is no moon here," Anna said.

"That was part of the bargain as well," she said. "I was to banish the Moon, and if I succeeded, the King would let you live. Here, locked away in the Tower, but alive."

"You were so powerful that you banished the Moon?" Anna gasped. "And I've just told the King that the Moon, *Marco*, has spoken to me in my dreams since I was a little girl." The realization slowly sank in.

"You're not safe here anymore, Anna. And there's one more thing." The Magician frowned. "We need to destroy your tapestries before you go."

Anna gaped at the Magician. "Destroy them?" Heat rose in her chest. "Absolutely not. You know how long I have spent weaving these worlds."

"That is exactly why you have to do it, Anna. You wove these tapestries into existence, and we have no idea how powerful they might be. You can't take them with you, and you can't leave them here with the King."

"I won't destroy my work. Could you hide them?"

"The King would find them. I know it's difficult, Anna, but it would be like leaving pieces of yourself in his possession." The Magician crossed the room to the door. "I'll see you in the morning. Try to get some sleep." She paused. "You'll make more, Anna. Trust in that." The Magician slipped out into the rain and locked Anna in for the night.

3

A great storm was raging outside the dining hall. The Fool could barely hear the pounding of the rain over the chatter of the King's court and the clanking of dishes, but he still jumped every time a flash of lightning lit the vast hall in eerie blue light. These were not good spying conditions. Despite being seated so near the King, he could not hear a word the man said.

A bubbling seafood stew was served, brimming with mussels, shrimp, crab claws, and whitefish. The crowd around the table, men and women alike, some noble, some cabinet members, decorated knights, spouses, and other hangers-on at court, tore huge chunks of warm, just-baked bread and dipped it into the stew's savory broth. Forty of them, loud and raucous, gulping down good red wine, happy to be indulging inside the great hall while the storm surged outside.

The King didn't touch his meal, though the stew was one of his favorites.

The Fool looked down the length of the spread and tried to catch the eye of the Magician or the Hermit. The table seemed to go on forever and ever, stretching across the hall. Tapestries that paled in comparison to Anna's, embroidered simply with the

King's purple-and-gold crest, hung from the giant stone walls. The Fool caught the eye of Drake at the other end of the table and gave him a small smile.

Drake was seated next to the other young squires and the knights they served. The Fool wished like mad that he were sitting with his friends or his lover. But that would never happen, not tonight or any other night. His job was to entertain the King after the meal.

Across the room, the Fool turned his attention back to the King, who had spent the entire meal speaking to Senator Bassett.

"Might I bring Bembo up for a brief visit before you sleep this evening, Sire?" The Fool held the little dog up and whispered in his ear. "Put on your cutest, most irresistible dog-face. This is for Anna, Bembo." Bembo lifted one paw up toward the King in a wave.

That did it.

Once in his private apartments, the King removed his rings and clenched and unclenched his fingers. His valet took his outer robes from his shoulders.

He started a game of fetch with Bembo, throwing a ball made from yarn for him to return. The Fool looked on while the Senator tapped his foot impatiently, his long, thin face pinched. Finally the King collapsed into a large oak chair, and Bembo jumped up onto his lap. Senator Bassett followed the King's lead and took a seat near him.

"That's it for tonight, little Bembo, my fierce beast." He held him up for the Fool to take. "Good night, Fool. You were right— that did me good. It's been a challenging day."

"I'm so glad he offered some comfort, Sire," the Fool said, meaning it. "I hope you have a sleep filled with peaceful dreams."

"All right," snapped the Senator. "We've got business to discuss. Leave us." He crossed his legs and waved the Fool away.

The Fool scooped Bembo into his arms and walked out of the room, but he did not leave. His heart pounded like a wild thing in his chest as he slid into the antechamber, hidden from view outside the King's sitting room.

"She's just a girl, Senator," the King said. The rain had let up a bit, but the Fool still had to strain his ears. Bembo snored softly, worn out from his play with the King.

"Yes, but she's also the daughter of your nemesis," answered the Senator.

"She has no power."

At this, the Senator paused.

"She's a gentle girl. I'm sure if I set her free, she would not seek revenge," the King continued. "That's what she wants: her freedom."

"She would be happy just to get out of the Tower," Senator Bassett said.

"But if she gets restless or bored, and she has any of Marco's powers, there will be trouble." The King thought. "Her imagination is the most fertile I've ever encountered. She's created lands that I could not dream up in a thousand years."

"But what about her use of the Moon in that tapestry?" urged the Senator.

Bassett, you snake, thought the Fool.

"There is no good explanation for it. Perhaps if she had read about it in books—"

"But, Sire," the Senator interrupted, "she said the Moon has spoken to her since she was a child."

"She did," said the King, growing more pensive. He'd wondered then and he wondered now if somehow Marco were communicating with Anna from beyond the grave. *Impossible!* And yet, the thought unnerved him.

The Senator was not deterred. "If she is the Queen's daughter, then we know betrayal is in her blood."

The King didn't appreciate the Senator's harsh words, but he spoke the truth. *Why did Anna have to mention the Moon today?* He couldn't let it go.

"Let me take care of the problem for you, Your Majesty," the Senator crooned. "Let me just make it disappear."

"Anna said she wants people to have more autonomy. She wants things to be like they used to be, but I'm not sure she understands what she's saying. She wasn't alive then." The King was vacillating, and the Fool was tempted to step out of hiding and help him along. "She spoke of artists and ambition and the freedom to become who you want."

"She sounds like Marco," Senator Bassett said.

"She does, doesn't she?"

"I'm afraid so, Your Majesty." The Senator stood up slowly.

The Fool wanted to wring Bassett's neck.

"It will be painless?" The King's voice was thick with grief.

"You have my word."

Anna stared at her tapestries. She held a pair of long, sharp sewing shears at her side. Her friends would be back at sunrise.

We need to destroy your tapestries.

The Magician's words rattled in her head.

Anna had a better idea.

She started with Pentacles. At first the fabric would not give in to the shear's blades. The threads were so tightly woven that they didn't budge.

Anna took a deep breath and stood back. She bent down so that she was at the bottom of the tapestry and turned the shears at a diagonal. At first it was slow going, but the threads began to give as she sawed the shears back and forth. She grabbed a hook from her sewing supplies and loosened the threads as she cut.

Once the threads were unraveled enough, she climbed up on the ladder and cut out the King in his throne. Next went the image of the Queen of Pentacles, and then the knights. She snipped the pages, the castle with its turrets, and pieces of the raging gray sea. Energy surged through her as the swatches of her work fell into piles at her feet.

When she finished with Pentacles, Anna moved on to Wands,

pushing the ladder with her. She looked around at her other tapestries, her arms already burning from the effort it took to cut through Pentacles. Fingers aching, she worked through the desert land, unbinding artisans and their wares from the tapestry. They would be liberated along with her.

She cut through Swords, the towering glass buildings, the inventors and their strange machines set free. She severed swaying green palms and sections of turquoise sea from the land of youth, cutting away the Moon and the young King and Queen.

When Anna looked out the window, the rain had stopped, and a light blue was beginning to dilute the deep black of the night's sky as dawn took hold. Anna's hands were cut and blistered, her neck stiff and aching when she heard the key turn in the Tower's lock. Her back throbbed from working ceaselessly through the night. She gathered her tapestry pieces and hugged them close to her chest.

"Anna!" Her advisors burst through the door.

"Oh my stars, what's she done?" The Fool gasped, taking in the mangled tapestries.

"I could not destroy them," she said in a sure and even voice. "They are as much a part of me as my hand or my heart. They are reduced to tattered landscapes, and these remnants, but I can bring the remnants with me, and that's better than nothing."

The Magician was impressed. "You will take them with you. Now come, we have a plan. The Fool has gathered some information, and it is not good."

"We have very little time, Anna," said the Hermit. The Fool, his blue eyes red-rimmed with misery, ran to her, pressing his face into her cheek and letting out a sob.

"Has he decided to get rid of me? Permanently?" Anna asked, knowing the answer by their faces. She shook her head.

"What does he imagine I am? There is no justice here! It's all because of things that happened before I was born that have nothing to do with me!"

"There's no logic to it," the Hermit responded.

Anna looked up at him. "I hope you've brought me warmer clothes, dear Hermit. This muslin frock and these woolen slippers will not get me far."

The Hermit nodded. "I have." He pulled a warm cloak and boots from a satchel.

"You can put your tapestry pieces in that bag," said the Magician. "But you must change, Anna. We need to go before the kingdom wakes."

5

Anna took one last look around the Tower. The scratches on the floor, her tapestries reduced to pieces hanging from the walls at odd angles. The Fool began to gather what was left of the tapestries, ripping them down from the walls. Anna looked at him questioningly. He shrugged.

"I'll hide them as best I can." He looked at the Hermit. "Help me?" They all pitched in, tearing down the large landscapes and rolling them up.

"Can you destroy this?" Anna said, twirling her finger in the air to show she meant the Tower itself. "I want this prison destroyed when I leave. Is that too much to ask of your magic?"

"That's a fine idea," said the Magician. "It would create a distraction big enough for you to get through the gates unnoticed."

"Could you really do that?" Anna's eyes were wide. The Hermit gave the Magician a warning look.

"If you fail, we could all be caught," the Hermit cautioned. "Let's just stick to the original plan. You can put the guards to sleep, and Anna can sneak out."

"I love it," the Fool said. "Knock it down, and go out with

a flourish." He stomped his foot and snapped his fingers above his head.

"But if I succeed, the King will think Anna is the great magician he has always feared she is." The Magician had a mischievous glint in her eyes.

"Is that a good thing?" the Fool asked.

"Beware your ego here," the Hermit said.

"It is a good thing." The Magician ignored his warning and turned to Anna. "He'll be terrified of you."

Anna did not look back as she walked through the heavy door and into the Tower's cold stone corridor.

The sprawling courtyard that lay between the Tower and the Keep was quiet with the early morning hour, and the air was frigid and still. The peasants had not yet stirred from their white clapboard cottages. Even the livestock were still asleep in their piles of dirt and straw.

"We have to say goodbye here," the Hermit said, his amber eyes misting as he and the Fool dragged out their large packages of Anna's tapestries. They needed to get back to their chambers before the chaos of her departure ensued. Anna nodded. Inside, she felt unspeakable sadness at this goodbye. She did not know if she would ever see her friends again, these two young men, and her aunt, the Magician, who had been her only lifeline since she was a child. The Fool sensed her worry and jumped in, pushing aside his own grief.

"Anna, darling, you are on a Fool's journey!" He smiled warmly at her, his eyes wet. "Think of this as an adventure. Have faith in your abilities. You are moving forward, and that is never a bad thing." Anna nodded, fighting back tears. The Fool embraced her tightly and kissed her cheek. "You're going to be okay. I promise." Anna held on to him, as if she could glean extra strength by staying in his arms just a few minutes more. She turned to the Hermit.

"You are ready," he said to her.

"I really wish I didn't have to do this alone. I wish you could come, all of you." At this point the tears came. "I'm scared," she whispered.

"I know," the Hermit comforted. "Remember how to quiet your mind? Remember our deep breathing in times of stress and how to cast out fear by finding your center?" He took both of her hands in his. His hands were always warm.

"I do," she said, trying to practice the exercise. She wiped at her tears and attempted a smile. "I'll miss you terribly. You've taught me so much. You taught me to weave, and it changed my life. I would have slipped into insanity a long time ago if not for that."

"But you didn't." He squeezed her hands. "Time to go." He hugged Anna awkwardly but held on an extra beat.

"I have to believe I will see you both again," she said to the Fool and the Hermit. They had no answer to that. "You'd better go before I lose my nerve," she choked out. "This isn't going to get any easier." She nodded at them, and they turned and ran toward the Keep. She watched them go, feeling her heart break inside her chest.

She turned to her aunt. "You'll go with me as far as the sea?"

"Yes. Of course."

"Can you really do this?" she whispered. "Maybe we should start running." But the Magician did not hear her. She was chanting now, and her face had a faraway look, the veins in her neck and temples straining.

Finally. How long she'd had to hold her magic at bay. How

good this felt. She poured every ounce of resentment into the spell. *This* was what she was meant for.

She held her hands above her head and threw them toward the Tower, mumbling an incantation and then finally shouting, "*Khatoszrophenze!*" Her eyes rolled back into her head, and the green stones of the serpent belt glowed and pulsed.

Suddenly a small cadre of guards came running toward the courtyard in a tight formation.

Anna and the Magician looked at each other in alarm. They ducked out of view and watched as the guards ran to the Tower and disappeared into its massive stone structure.

"They've come to escort you to the execution." The ground beneath them rumbled, and Anna stumbled backward, nearly dropping her satchel.

"Can you stop the spell?" Anna's heart beat rapidly in her chest, and her palms started to sweat.

"We have to go, Anna. We need to get to the gate. It's already happening; I can't stop it now." An earsplitting sound erupted from the Tower. Stone torn asunder.

"What about the guards?" Anna's eyes shone with fear.

The Magician shook her head and grabbed Anna's hand. Together they ran toward the castle gates. Sleepy-eyed peasants emerged from their cottages, their faces a mixture of confusion and horror. Large pieces of rock hurled from the sky, and flames hissed and crackled. The Tower was being destroyed from the inside out.

Just as they'd hoped, the sentries deserted their posts at the front gates. The air was filled with screaming as the guards inside the Tower flung themselves from the windows in hopes of escaping the devastation.

Filled with adrenaline, Anna and the Magician ran at top

speed through the gates. Anna barely noted the fact that she was free as they tore toward the forest that surrounded the kingdom.

Before long, the Magician's pace started to slow. They were still near enough to hear the screams and smell the smoke from the burning Tower.

"Come on!" Anna looked back at her aunt, who had turned deathly pale and struggled to stand. "What's happening to you?"

"It's the magic. I'm not strong enough for such a big spell yet."

Anna looked around. "You can't be caught out here. Come!" Anna hooked her arms beneath the Magician, struggling to hold on to her bag of tapestries and supplies.

Anna looked around, not knowing what to do. She needed to be running as far from the kingdom as possible, but she could not leave her aunt here. Not like this.

"This will pass," the Magician managed. "Anna, I'm going to need your help getting to the woods." She gasped for breath. "But you'll have to go on from there without me." She closed her eyes, and her head fell forward. "I'm so dizzy." She grabbed at her stomach. "I need to rest, and you need to keep going."

"By myself?" Anna said, glancing behind them, her body trembling with fear. She didn't like the idea of continuing alone, but she didn't have a choice. She had to get her aunt to shelter.

Together they stumbled toward the forest as the sun rose higher in the sky.

6

"This is as far as I can go." The Magician looked even more pale, and sweat beaded her brow. Several times she turned her head to the side and gagged violently.

"How can I leave you here?" Anna pleaded.

"The pain will pass. It's a debt I have to pay for the magic." She took a deep breath, and Anna knew how much it was costing her to speak. "I will soon be as good as new. I can sleep here and then return home. I'll sneak back through the gates unseen."

"Will I ever see you again?"

"I don't know, Anna," her aunt said plainly. "Take this." The Magician reached into the front of her robe and pulled out a long chain. At the end was an infinity symbol forged in gold. The Magician pulled the necklace over her head. "I wore one and your father wore one. They were given to us by your grandparents." The Magician stopped, gasping for breath. Her chest heaved up and down with the effort.

Anna took the necklace.

"It symbolizes so many things, but perhaps the most important is that our familial bond is endless—through dark and light, life and death." She looked at Anna with tears in her eyes. "Your father is buried with his. You have a family and you are loved, even if we cannot be together."

"Thank you for this," Anna said, clutching the necklace in a fist to her heart. "Can I give you some water before I—"

"Go!" the Magician barked.

Anna nodded and kissed the Magician's forehead.

"Forward," Anna said, repeating the Fool's advice.

"Forward," agreed the Magician.

Anna felt as if her heart were being ripped from her chest, leaving her aunt, her only family, behind, but she turned toward the woods and began to run, clutching the golden heirloom in her palm. She ran as fast as she could, fleeing from feelings of guilt and fear. Her aunt was no martyr. As Anna ran deeper into the woods, toward the raging sea that bordered the land at the north, she had to trust that the Magician meant what she said.

7

When the Fool reached his chambers, he found Drake, fully clothed and asleep on top of the coverlet. Bembo was fast asleep too, snuggled at Drake's side. The Fool carefully rolled the tapestries beneath the bed, taking care not to make any noise. When he was finished, he sat on the edge of the bed and gently woke his love.

"I'm so sorry. I must have fallen asleep." Drake pushed himself up onto his elbows and rubbed his eyes. He looked at the Fool's red-rimmed eyes. "Is it done?"

The Fool nodded, and Drake sat up to put an arm around his shoulders.

"I'll miss her so much," the Fool murmured.

"I know," Drake said, smoothing the Fool's head of blond curls. "At least now she has a chance at a life."

"I'm so glad I have you. That goodbye was the hardest thing I've ever had to do."

Drake rubbed the back of his hand gently down the Fool's cheek and pressed his full lips to his forehead. The Fool leaned into him.

"You do have me. Always."

Bembo, a little jealous, nosed his way between them.

"And him too," Drake said, making room for Bembo. "Are you going to be okay, my love?"

The Fool nodded. "Not much choice."

At that moment a giant boom seemed to explode from the sky, and the very ground shook beneath them. The two young men shot up.

"What was that?" Drake gasped.

"I think I know." The Fool's tears gave way to a cautious smile. Drake looked at him like he was a madman. "Come. You're going to want to see this."

8

The sun was sinking out of sight when Anna heard the horns sound. She'd been walking a full day, and she did not trust her ears. The sound was faint but clear. She was exhausted, her body horribly weak from a lifetime without proper exercise. Her lungs burned, her feet were blistered and throbbing, but she pressed on. She needed to get as far as possible before darkness took hold.

She looked up at the sky, which was quickly turning from swirls of hot orange into streaky light blues. She needed a plan for the night. The forest was thick with trees and rocks and uneven ground. She was already heavily scratched and bruised, even with the light of day to guide her.

Finding a rock, Anna sat down and let out a deep breath. She hoisted up her bag and dug through it, placing its contents on the flat surface of the rock. Cold chicken wrapped in cheesecloth, a large loaf of bread, and a generous hunk of a hard cheese. Her stomach rumbled as she tore off a piece of the chicken with her teeth and continued to dig through the bag with her other hand. The food tasted so good, the sitting such a reprieve, she almost forgot her plight.

"Oh!" Something hard and cold stabbed her hand, and she pulled it away. Anna put the chicken down and wiped her hands on the cheesecloth. Slowly, she reached back into the bag and carefully withdrew what had hurt her. It was the Hermit's precious star lantern. Anna shook her head, fighting back tears. She knew how much this lantern meant to the Hermit. It had been a gift to him when he was a boy from the Queen, her mother. He never went anywhere without it. He'd also supplied a small bundle of wax and flint. A tiny card fell from the package when she unwrapped the wax.

It won't last long; use it wisely. —H.

Anna marveled at her friends and what they'd done to help her. She thought of the Magician, so sick and alone when Anna had left her. The thought gave her resolve, and she packed up the bag and started out once again. At least with the lantern she'd be able to go a little longer. If she was being chased, she couldn't stop out in the open. She'd go a bit farther and find a place to hide, and maybe even sleep, for the night.

Darkness fell like a hammer.

Anna had never experienced such blackness. She couldn't even see her own hand in front of her face. She stopped and looked up.

"Father, if you are out there, and you are the Moon, now would be a good time to show yourself." She was answered with silence. "Thought so," she said, disappointed. She heard something rustle through the trees, and her breath caught in her throat.

She had no idea what kinds of animals lived in this forest. For a moment she missed the safety of the Tower. At least she had shelter there, a bed, friends, light.

She unclenched her fist and put the necklace her aunt had given her around her neck, tucking it into the front of her gown. She got down on her knees and felt through the satchel. She'd placed the lantern and flint near the top and found them easily. Anna was good with her hands from all the years of weaving, and was able to strike the flint and light the lantern on her third attempt.

The light sparked a feeling of hope in Anna's chest. It was such an exquisite lantern, with the perforated metal star swinging at its center throwing light and snowflake-like patterns around her.

She held the lantern up. She had to find shelter.

As she walked deeper into the woods, fatigue started to overcome her. Her thoughts clouded, and she wondered if she'd gotten lost or if the sea was really just a myth. She did not smell salt air or feel a mist. She stumbled and fell to the ground, scraping her legs even more.

She was dragging herself up, almost ready to sleep on the spot, but the ground began to vibrate with the sound of horse hooves pounding the earth. She couldn't hear them yet, but she could feel them. Heart racing, she held the lantern up, but it only lit the space directly in front of her.

Men's voices called to one another in the distance. This time she knew she was not hallucinating. What had she been thinking—a girl on foot trying to outrun an army of men?

Anna dropped to her knees once more, and put the lantern on the ground beside her. She opened the satchel and took out a few pieces of her tapestries. She always thought best at her loom; this would have to do.

She threw the pieces in front of her. The images stared back at her. There was a Page and a Queen and a King. There was a girl having a tea party and a boy swimming in a vast sea.

She studied them. There was no doubt in her mind that she was about to be caught, but maybe she could talk her way out of it.

Anna focused on the fragments again and wished a hopeless wish that she could dive into them—leave this world behind and go to a place like the one spread before her. She pressed her palms to the pieces and closed her eyes.

When she opened them, she was still surrounded by darkness, but she no longer heard the sound of horse hooves or the voices of men.

She gathered her things quickly and stood up. Perhaps they were farther away than she'd thought. Maybe she'd find the sea after all.

Anna's body pulsed with renewed energy, and she quickened her pace. Soon she came to a bridge.

It was built of stone and dripped with green moss. Anna stepped onto it, feeling the air change. The cold wet around her shifted to a dry warmth. She tossed back the hood of her cloak. When Anna reached the middle of the bridge, she tried to hold the lantern out to see what waters lay beneath, but all she could see was darkness. She found a rock at her feet and threw it toward the water, but she never heard a sound. The air felt warm but thin, giving her the sensation of being suspended at a great height.

Anna's fingers ached from gripping the lantern so tightly. Her next step landed her in something gelatinous and sticky. She tried to pull her foot back, but it was stuck.

She bent down to tug at her boot, and her head knocked against what felt like a wall of viscous sludge. Disgusted, Anna

put her arms through the muck to get at her foot, but instead of
more stickiness, her hands landed in warm water.

"What sort of trick is this?" Anna used her hands to part
the wall and gasped at what lay before her. Half of her was in a
shallow body of warm water, the sky above her full of stars shimmering like diamonds, and her other half was on the stone bridge,
stuck in the sludge. Frightened but also delighted, Anna grabbed
the satchel and lantern and pulled the rest of her body through the
sticky wall and into this other place, with its soothing water and
golden starlight.

She stared up at the navy sky with its twinkling lights. And
that was when she saw it, round and white and glowing: the
Moon. She thought of what her aunt had said about the legend of
her real father.

"Where did you come from?" a deep voice asked.

"Me?" she asked the Moon, placing a hand on her chest.

"Yes, you. But I'm over here."

Anna whipped around to see a boy about her age, shirtless,
lean chest gleaming in the moonlight.

"You seemed to come out of nowhere," he said.

9

Anna stumbled backward in shock. She expected to meet the cool gooeyness of the wall, but instead found herself in the water. She held up her bag, not wanting her tapestry pieces to get wet, and tried to push out of the shallow water with her free hand.

"I didn't mean to scare you." The boy crept toward her, holding out his hand as if approaching a frightened animal, which was exactly what Anna felt like. Her hair was a tangled mess, she was covered in scratches and bruises, and she was completely disoriented. She couldn't even get enough traction to stand up without dropping her bag into the water. Anna looked up at the boy, who stood above her with his hand extended. He looked at her warmly. Anna gave up and reached for his hand.

His grip was strong, and he pulled her up easily.

"Thank you," Anna whispered, her cheeks flushed with embarrassment.

"Are you okay?"

Anna turned around and looked for the wall, the bridge, any sign of the forest from which she'd just come. Aware that the boy was watching, she stopped herself from searching the open air for an entrance. On one side of her stood the boy and a long stretch of white sand. On the other was a tranquil sea, black beneath the moonlight and stretching as far as the eye could see. There was no wall or forest or bridge.

Suddenly Anna heard the clip-clop of horse hooves and braced herself.

"James, what's going on here?" A girl with waist-length white-blond hair and the longest legs Anna had ever seen pulled up beside them, splashing her with water. Anna blinked and hugged her bag closer.

"Ivy," James said. "I just found this girl. I think she's in trouble."

"Does she talk?" the girl asked, looking down at Anna from her horse.

Anna cleared her throat. As exhausted as she was, the girl's dismissive tone was not lost on her.

"Yes, I talk."

"Do you need help?" asked the boy. "I'm James, and this is Ivy."

"My name is . . ." She paused, wondering if she should tell them her real name. The King would be looking for her. "Anna." She was too tired to think quickly, but she was already weaving a story in her head. Next they would ask where she came from.

"Nice to meet you, Anna." James extended his hand once more. The gesture was so simple and kind that it made Anna smile.

"You too." Anna took his hand, and they shook gently.

"Do you need somewhere to stay, Anna?"

"James," Ivy scolded. "She's a stranger."

Anna felt her face go red again.

"Ivy, you take the horse. We'll walk back to the villa. Lara and Daniel will know what to do." James paused and looked Anna over. "Can you walk?"

Anna looked up at Ivy, who was glaring down at her. "I can walk," Anna said.

Snapping the reins and turning the horse around, Ivy looked back at them. "Suit yourselves. See you back there. I'll tell them to get a bath ready. I can smell her from here." Ivy tore up the beach on her horse.

"Ignore her," James said.

"Forgive me. I've traveled a great distance—" Anna began.

James gently placed his hand on her arm. "I like it; it's earthy."

Anna looked at him. It reminded her of a joke the Fool would make. She raised her eyebrows at him and smiled.

"You are too kind."

"Come on. Let's get you to the villa. Can I carry your bag for you?"

She hesitated, unsure if she could walk much farther.

"Thank you," she said, handing it over.

They walked in silence, and Anna, exhausted, took in what she could. The ground was sandy, and it sank beneath her heavy boots. The air was warm and moist and pleasant. Anna was over-dressed in the heavy cloak, but she kept it on for a layer of protection. The Moon, bright against the dark sky, seemed to follow them as they went. James would look over at her now and then, making sure she was okay.

She kept looking out at the sea, black and seemingly infinite to their left. The warm breeze lifted its salty scent and made a gentle swooshing sound as the tide came in and out.

Suddenly the ground beneath her felt as if it were turning to liquid, and a blackness closed in around her vision.

"I don't feel very good," Anna said. She wasn't sure she could take another step. James stopped and took her elbow.

"You need to get out of this. You must be burning up." He

unhooked the cloak and took if off her shoulders. "Now take a breath."

Anna did as he said, and she experienced a second of relief.

"I don't know if I can walk anymore."

"We're almost there," James said. "Look." He pointed up the beach.

Ahead was a giant white villa. Its shutters were painted turquoise, and warm yellow light poured from the tall, wide windows facing the sea. The Moon lit up the ceramic tiles of the shiny red roof. The villa was flanked on either side by tall, lush palm trees.

James guided her gently toward the house. When they reached the steps, the front doors flew open and a young man and woman rushed out.

Anna looked up and saw Ivy at the top of the steps, her arms crossed, leaning in the doorframe.

"Why didn't you tell us she was in such rough shape, Ivy?" Anna heard someone say. As Anna's legs started to give, she felt a pair of arms grab her. She watched Ivy shrug and walk into the house. Delirious, Anna turned to the young woman at her side. "I'm sorry about the smell," Anna said. "I think I'm about to faint. Your hair is so red." Anna slid into unconsciousness.

"It's okay. We've got you," the young woman assured her.

The two young men propped Anna up between them. "Lara, can we help her?" James looked to the young woman.

"She's probably just exhausted," Lara answered. "Let's get her inside and into bed. I'm sure she needs rest more than anything."

"Is she injured?" asked Daniel as they carried Anna up the stairs.

"No," James said. "She seemed . . ." He paused, thinking of the right word. "Lost."

10

The King flew out of the Keep, his guards marching behind him with heavy, syncopated steps. He took in the scene, the massive stone Tower now reduced to smoking ruins, his eyes burning with fury. Charred pieces of chain mail were scattered, still smoldering, evidence that members of his Guard had been killed. Had Anna burned along with them?

He walked the perimeter of the fallen Tower, his thoughts racing. This could be the act of Marco returned from the dead, or perhaps the girl had inherited his gifts after all. Maybe an enemy from afar had felled the Tower while they slept.

But there was no foreign attacker pounding at their gates. They were not under siege. This attack had been focused and singular.

The King whipped around, eyeing the throngs of peasants and members of court who had gathered. They looked to the ground to avoid the wrath of his gaze. His subjects followed his rules, and in return, he fed, clothed, housed, and gave them humble occupations. It was a regimented life, but a stable one.

"Who saw what happened here this morning?" he shouted.

The Fool and the Hermit were hidden among the crowd, each

holding his breath, while the King's question hung in the air. Anyone could have seen them leave the Tower, but no one spoke. Drake pressed his shoulder close to the Fool. He wished he could openly take his hand, but the relationship that existed between them was punishable by death. To outsiders—the Hermit, the Magician, and Anna the exceptions—they were simply the best of friends.

"No one?" the King asked again. He clasped his jeweled fingers together and brought them to his chin. "We'll see about that," he said to himself. At that moment Senator Bassett came running through the mob. He was still in his sleep clothes, and his thin black hair stuck out in all directions as he raced toward the King.

The Senator surveyed the scene before them, his eyes widening. "I . . . I . . ." he stammered.

"You what?" the King snapped.

"I ordered my Guard to keep watch at dawn, Your Majesty. The execution was set for this—"

The King held up his hand. "I want every person in this kingdom questioned. Find out what happened here," he boomed. "And find the girl."

The Senator nodded, but his eyes were filled with doubt. "I will open a full investigation, Sire." He hesitated, afraid to say more.

"You suspect magic," the King guessed.

"We must consider it, Sire."

The King felt a thin tug of dread. He looked back out at the people of his kingdom, only now processing their looks of fear and confusion.

"Look at them. They're terrified," the King said. "They need to know we have this in hand." The Senator nodded again and stepped back.

The King walked toward the crowd, his Guard moving with him seamlessly, their steps beating in unison, swords flashing at their sides. He wasn't sure how he would explain the accident.

But that was what it meant to be a king. To give the appearance of being in control at all times, no matter what the circumstance. He had learned this from his father and his father before him—each of them distant father figures to the people of this land. The men on the throne were duty bound to keep the people from harm and respond to their grievances. The common man was a sheep, the King his shepherd. That was the way it was and the way it must always be.

"Something evil has transpired here today...." he began. The people responded to his deep voice and looming presence, their eyes suddenly riveted on the King's face. "But we do not tolerate evil in this kingdom. We never have, and we never will." He raised his arms as if embracing them, and he let his words settle over the crowd.

The Fool, watching from the back, felt a familiar warmth stir in his chest. He didn't have a father, and the King's presence had always made him feel safe.

The Fool felt torn between his love for Anna and his loyalty to the King. Ultimately, his love for her had won, but it was not without cost to his heart.

The Hermit looked on from beside the Fool, feeling less emotionally conflicted, and wondering instead how the King was going to explain the Tower's destruction to his people.

"I will find out who or what did this, and they will be punished severely. They will wish for death when I am through with them. I will make an example of them, and when I am done, no one will ever dare threaten this kingdom again."

The Hermit felt his composure slip away. The King's threats

toward Anna made his stomach churn with worry.

The King walked back to the Keep among a chorus of cheering, but the sound meant nothing to him. He was consumed with the idea that he might have made a fatal error in not keeping his promise to the girl. Maybe if he had let her go, treated her with greater care, even love, the Tower would still be standing. Anna was alive. He could feel that in his bones. She was alive, and he had just committed to publicly torturing her when he found her.

11

The Magician listened to the sound of barking hounds and the pounding of hoofbeats. She had dragged herself into a dense copse of bushes, where she had fallen asleep against a rock. But no amount of twisted branch and bramble could hide her from the Guard's hounds. When she stood up, the forest spun around her. She took a deep breath and placed a hand on her stomach, waiting for the trees to steady themselves.

The Magician weighed her options. She needed to get back to the castle. The King would surely be calling a meeting of his advisors at any second.

Her magic was spent. In truth, she didn't know how long it would take for it to return. She'd been dabbling, retaining her skills by enchanting irritating guards and levitating objects in her chambers. Knocking the Tower down without her wand was something else entirely.

The dogs howled with more urgency, and their barks were growing louder.

The Magician dropped to her knees and started frantically scrubbing fistfuls of soft wet dirt and moss all over her body to cover her scent. She covered her hair in moss and pine needles, rubbing fallen leaves against her cheeks, hands, and clothing.

She stayed very still, holding her breath.

The dogs whined and whimpered in frustration.

"Did they lose the scent?" shouted a guard.

"It was probably just a rabbit," said another.

The first guard squinted into the brush. The Magician backed away from her hiding spot, treading carefully. The guard drew his sword and walked toward her hiding place, cutting away at the overgrown foliage.

"We're moving on, Aidrick!" called a guard. Aidrick hesitated. The dogs were running deeper into the wood. He crouched down and stared into the brush.

Suddenly the stillness and quiet was interrupted by a flock of birds erupting from a nearby tree, making a great commotion of chirping and rustling of leaves.

"Good heavens." Aidrick jumped up and grabbed at his rapidly beating heart. He looked up as the small cadre of birds swept through the sky.

The guards on horseback tossed their heads back in laughter. Aidrick turned and glared at them, returning his sword to its sheath as he walked back to his horse.

"Those little black birds looked very fierce indeed!" a guard teased.

"Quiet, then!" Aidrick growled, mounting his horse. "Let's go."

The Magician ran softly through the woods back to the kingdom, using the distraction to her advantage. Fear carried her forward as she clenched her teeth to stanch the pain in her throbbing head.

12

Anna lay in a bed, looking up at a sky full of pale-gold sunshine. She wanted to enjoy the feeling of warmth on her cheeks, but disorientation set in too quickly. She bolted upright, and her muscles tensed as she grabbed at her neck, relieved to feel the cold metal of the necklace her aunt had given her. She touched the charm to her lips before dropping it back inside her gown. Her hair was tangled and matted, her arms and legs covered with scratches and bruises. When her feet, sore and blistered, touched the floor, she was hit with a rush of memories from the day before. Panicked, she looked around for her satchel.

She found it on the floor at the foot of the bed, covered with her clothing, filthy but neatly folded. She took a breath, relief coursing through her. It was grounding having something from her old life to hold on to, even though everything else had changed. She decided to hide her necklace with her things to avoid questions about it. She carefully felt for the silk lining at the bottom of the satchel and placed the necklace there, beneath her tapestry fragments.

The room was modestly sized, with high ceilings. Everything was white, from the bedding to the painted walls. The large bed faced a window that spanned nearly the entire west wall, over-looking the bright sea. Where the room itself was white, the view was blue on blue. The blue green of the sea met the soft powder blue of the sky in a neat seam of horizon. A breeze tickled Anna's skin. She marveled at the beauty and the feeling of fresh air.

"Hey," Anna heard a soft voice call to her. A petite girl with closely cropped hair and an upturned nose stood in the doorway.

"Hi." Anna studied the girl. Had she met her last night?

"It's quite a view, isn't it?" The girl smiled.

"It really is," Anna answered.

"I'm Terra." The girl bounced up and down on her toes.

She gave Terra a small wave. "Anna."

"I'm supposed to take you down to breakfast." Terra crossed the room and sat on the edge of the bed.

"Would it be all right if I took a bath first?" Anna asked.

"Of course! The tub is outside on the first floor. I'll bring a clean dress." Terra jumped up and led Anna outside to a small patio decorated with two wooden chairs and a table covered with colorful blue mosaic tiles that matched the sea. To the right was a set of narrow wooden stairs.

Anna stopped and inhaled the salty air, feeling the gentle warmth of morning sunshine on the crown of her head. She looked out at the sea and was humbled by how vast it was and how it spread out beneath the sky. She listened to the gentle swoosh of the tide going in and out.

She followed Terra down the stairs, which led to an out-door bathing area. There was a deep tub enclosed by a round wall made of bamboo shoots, tied tightly together with twine. The ceiling was the cloudless sky.

"No one will come in." Terra lifted a large bucket of water

sitting over a flame and tipped it into the tub with surprising ease. "I hope I didn't let the water get too hot."

A small wooden shelf was built into the wall next to and level with the tub. It held glass jars of salts, creams, and a bowl of dried flowers.

"Thank you, Terra." Anna dipped her hand in the water. "It's perfect."

Terra beamed. "We're on the ground floor now—beach level. You can go back upstairs or just follow the rock path through the sand to the front deck. Everyone will gather for breakfast there soon."

Anna wondered what time it was. She looked up at the brightening sky.

"Late sleepers. Nearly all of us are." Terra smiled. "I'm hanging your dress here." She pointed to two hooks on the bamboo wall, above the silver tub. One held a plush white towel. "There's shea butter and a comb on the shelf next to the tub." Terra hung the dress, wiggled her fingers in a wave, and dashed outside.

Anna slid off the nightgown and stepped into the tub. The water made her scratches smart a bit, but it also soothed her aching muscles.

She wondered if this beautiful land was under the Hierophant's jurisdiction, and how she'd even reached this place. As she scrubbed under her arms, Anna considered whether these people might turn her in to the King.

She slid under the water, letting the otherworldly hum beneath the surface drown out the noise in her head. She came up and took a deep breath. Anna couldn't remember much from the night before, but Terra had been nothing but kind and helpful. Anna rubbed the shea butter into her hair and combed out the tangles.

After she was bathed and dressed, she twisted her long wet

hair into a bun. She took a deep breath and opened the door that led outside.

The door seemed to open onto the side of the villa. To Anna's right grew a lush green jungle. To her left was the beach and sea, a stone's throw away from where she stood. She followed a stony path to the front of the villa and, when she reached it, her mouth dropped open.

The villa was two stories tall and stretched at least two hundred feet. Small flowers painted carefully in yellows, pinks, and purples climbed up the walls. Surrounding the villa were tall palms and shorter palmetto trees with long green leaves and thick, knobby trunks. Tiny lanterns, now unlit, hung from their branches, and the trees were filled with the song of colorful parrots and kingbirds.

The front deck was raised up on stakes made of a rich dark wood. There were four long tables with benches for chairs, and giant white canvas umbrellas, opened up like lilies in full bloom, shaded the people who sat at the tables eating breakfast. The air hummed with chatter, and Anna had to stop herself from gawking at the large crowd.

A girl stepped down from the deck and approached her. "Wow! You look like a new person."

Anna's eyes widened at the girl's beauty. Her hair was a bewitching combination of flaxen and strawberry that fell in thick, long waves. Her arms were covered with bracelets made from tiny seashells and sparkling green sea glass.

"I'm Lara. You may not remember meeting me last night."

Anna shook her head. "Everything is really foggy," she confessed.

"Are you hungry?"

"Very, now that I think about it."

"Come." Lara held out her hand, her bracelets tinkling musically. "You can sit next to me." Lara took Anna by the hand. "Make some room, darlings. We have a guest today." The talking stopped for a moment, and everyone at the table looked up at Anna. She felt heat rise to her face.

"This is Anna. You'll have a chance to meet her later." She waved her arms. "You can go back to eating now."

Anna bit her lip and tried to force a smile, but her nerves made it difficult. She achieved something between a smirk and a twitch and managed to hold up her hand in a wave.

"Hi ho, Anna," said a boy with a mop of sandy brown hair. She lifted her chin in answer.

"That's Simon," Lara said.

They took seats beside him as everyone returned to their breakfast.

Anna, now shoulder to shoulder with Simon and Lara, took a deep breath. She'd never sat so close to anyone, not even her advisors. She swiveled her head, trying to not be too obvious, but she could not help but want to take in everything happening around her.

Anna watched a girl at a neighboring table with a halo of blond curly hair toss her head back in hoarse laughter. The boy next to her bit into a bright orange fruit.

She glanced down at her hands. The people around her were every shade of olive imaginable, and while Anna was ghostly pale in comparison, they otherwise seemed like people she might have encountered in the Hierophant's Kingdom had she been given the chance to explore it.

Each table seemed to hold about twenty-five people, and now that Anna was actually seated among them, she realized they all had one thing in common.

They were young, all about her age.

She turned to Lara. "Where do the older people eat?"

Lara blinked.

"Or the children?" Anna asked.

"We're the only people here, Anna."

"Oh. I'm sorry. I didn't mean to be rude. I just—" She thought of her aunt and the King—at least twice as old as anyone at the table.

"It's fine," Lara whispered, glancing around the table.

"What can I get you?" A boy with bright red hair and blue eyes stood up from the end of the table, wiping his face with a cloth napkin and dusting crumbs off his shirt. "Henry." He held his hand out to her, and Anna reached for it immediately, wanting to seem friendly. "Do you like coffee?"

"I've never had it," Anna admitted.

"It's good," Simon said, standing up from the table. "Here, you'll have a bit more room now."

"Oh, I'm okay," Anna said, looking from the seat beside her and up at him. She wondered if she had done something to make him leave.

He smiled and pushed his mop of hair to the side, revealing a high forehead. "I've got to go feed the horses, but I hope to see you again soon, Anna." He did a little bow, and Anna laughed. "Henry, can I raid the kitchen for carrots?"

"You may indeed," Henry answered.

"See ya, Lara." Simon winked at her and ran off.

"Now, back to coffee." Henry leaned down and reached across the table for a bright yellow ceramic pitcher and a cup made from what looked like a coconut shell. Anna watched as he poured hot brown liquid into the cup. "I suggest drinking it with some of the coconut milk."

"Some sugar too," Lara added.

Henry handed the cup to Anna. "Be careful—it's still hot."

Anna took a sip. It was bitter but sweet and creamy, too. Delicious. She took another sip and nodded. "It's excellent."

"Let me make you a plate, Anna. Is there anything you don't like?" Lara asked.

Anna shook her head. Lara handed her a plate made of wood and piled with eggs, plantains, black beans, and rice.

She'd never had food like this. Anna sat and chewed, letting the spice of the beans and the sweetness of the plantains dance over her taste buds.

Anna stole another glance around her as she ate. Everyone looked so vibrant and, Anna thought, so beautiful. They were freckled and sun-kissed and seemed to glow from within. Anna felt ashen and shy next to them.

"Do you like it?" Henry scooted in next to her.

Anna looked at him blankly, her thoughts interrupted.

"The food. Do you like it?"

"Oh." Anna smiled. "Very much. Thank you."

"I'm the chef." He winked at her. "Most jobs rotate each moon cycle, but if someone really takes to a particular task, Daniel and Lara will make an exception."

Anna nodded, shoveling another forkful into her mouth, when a boy with a shock of bright chestnut hair and light-green almond-shaped eyes sat down directly across from her.

His skin was bronzed, his beatific smile flashing a row of straight white teeth.

"Good morning." He glanced at Anna. "You clean up nice." He grabbed a coconut shell and filled it with coffee from the yellow pitcher. Anna swallowed her eggs.

"James?" she said tentatively.

He raised an eyebrow. "At your service," he responded playfully. "Morning, Lara."

"Good morning, James."

"Thank you so much for finding me last night," Anna blurted out, her voice trembling.

"You are quite welcome." James smiled at her warmly. "I'm glad I found you."

At that moment, Ivy strode up.

"Make room," she said to James, squeezing in next to him and taking a sip of his coffee. She eyed Anna over the steaming cup. "Look who took a bath," she said, reaching over James to grab a banana. Anna felt her cheeks redden.

"Ivy!" Lara said.

"Don't mind her," said James. "She has no manners." He winked conspiratorially at Anna.

Ivy broke off a chunk of banana and squished it into James's cheek.

"See what I mean?" James swiped a finger across his cheek and popped the banana into his mouth. "Mmm."

Anna studied her plate, avoiding Ivy's gaze.

"Really, Ivy?" Lara rolled her eyes.

"Here, have some more beans." Henry pushed a bowl of beans toward Anna, who had lost her appetite completely.

"Thank you, but I'm feeling pretty full." Anna smiled at Henry. "I will take some more of that coffee, though," she said, holding out her cup.

"How about a walk?" Lara offered. "You can take that with you." She gestured to Anna's cup. "I want you to meet Daniel." Lara looked at Ivy and James and admonished them with a shake of her head.

Anna stood abruptly, knocking her spoon off her plate and

into the sand. She felt both James and Ivy look her over as she crouched down to retrieve it. James cleared his throat and asked Henry to pass the eggs.

Anna threw the spoon onto her plate and turned to Lara. "I'm ready."

"See you later, Anna," James called after them. "Say hi to my brother for me." Lara tugged at Anna's elbow, leading her down the beach. Anna chanced a glance back at the table. James smiled broadly. Ivy rolled her eyes.

"Sorry about that," Lara said as they walked away.

Anna shrugged.

"How are you feeling today?" Lara asked, changing the subject.

She and Anna walked along the water, the sand velvety soft beneath their feet. Anna could see straight through the clear blue water as it ran over their toes.

"Honestly?" Anna answered.

"Of course," Lara said, grabbing her mane of strawberry hair and pushing it over one shoulder.

"Exhausted. Confused. A little scared." Anna stopped and looked out at the exquisite stretch of sea. "Exhilarated. I have no idea where I am, and I've already met so many new people. I've finally touched the sea and felt sand beneath my feet." Anna stopped herself. She was giving too much away.

"You've never seen the ocean," Lara guessed, studying Anna's face. "I wish I could see it again for the first time." She squeezed Anna's arm. "I don't want to overwhelm you. That's why we're going to go talk to Daniel. He's"—Lara paused— "good with these things."

"These things," Anna repeated. "Like strange girls showing up out of nowhere?"

Lara let out a warm, husky laugh. "You are a rarity for us. And he is very wise."

"He is James's brother?"

"Yes, and my partner."

"Oh!" Anna said. The only person she'd ever known with a partner was the Fool, but she'd never actually met Drake.

"There he is." Lara pointed down the beach. At the shoreline stood a young man. He was tall and broad-shouldered, with dark brown hair skimming his shoulders. He was casting a fishing net into the shallows. His shirt was thrown beside him in the sand, and his brow was furrowed in concentration. Lara let out a magnificent whistle.

"Hi, my love!" she called.

Daniel spun around and a big smile spread across his face. He looked from her to Anna and pulled his net out of the water. He came toward them and gathered Lara into a tight embrace. They locked eyes and he kissed her, running a hand through her rippling hair. Anna looked down at her toes, tracing circles in the sand.

"Official introductions," Lara said as she and Daniel broke apart. "Anna, this is Daniel, the king of our beautiful land. Daniel, this is Anna—mystery girl."

"Hello, mystery girl." Daniel extended his hand, and Anna noticed a goblet inked into the skin of his forearm. His handshake was solid, and he held her gaze in a way that would be intimidating if not for the softness around his eyes. Anna stole another glance at Daniel's tattoo. She'd heard about them, but she'd never seen one before. She imagined one of her tapestry needles breaking the skin, marking it with ink, and she shuddered.

"King. So does that make you the Queen?" Anna turned to Lara, who sighed.

"I am the Queen, but I know that word can be intimidating. I think of myself as Lara, not Queen Lara."

As Anna listened, she thought about the fact that she was a princess by birthright, a title she'd never been able to claim. She wondered how she might have seen the world differently had she been raised in court.

"Let's sit." Daniel nodded up the beach, pulling on his shirt. "There's some shade beneath those palms. It's starting to warm up."

"Good idea," Lara agreed. "Anna, you're so fair. We'll have to watch that you don't burn."

Anna's years of isolation had left her pale skin dull and ashen, and she knew she must look like an apparition compared to these tanned people.

Anna's eyes scanned the sea as she took cover beneath a large palm. "Are you the only king of this land?" she asked.

"That I know of," Daniel said, laughing.

Anna knew in that moment that she had traveled beyond the Hierophant King's jurisdiction. The Hierophant King would never allow another man to call himself ruler.

"Where did you travel from, Anna?" Daniel eyed one of the bruises on her arm. "You look like you had a long journey."

"I escaped from . . ." Anna began. "I was a great lady's maid, and she treated me very poorly." The story came to life as she spoke.

Anna could not tell them the truth when she barely understood it herself. She was the daughter of a great magician and a queen, and the man she thought was her father had imprisoned her. She came here by crossing a bridge that seemed to disappear as soon as she reached the other side. Then there was the worst of it: a very dangerous and powerful king was going to come after her.

She cleared her throat and thought of the made-up worlds of her tapestries. "I came from a land called Pentacles," she said.

"We know of Pentacles." Daniel nodded. Anna's head jerked up.

"You do?" Anna tried to keep her expression blank.

"Of course. It is the land to the east. We've never traveled there, but we've heard stories of it."

"Our friend Christopher should be in Pentacles right now actually," Lara said.

"Yes, Topper is the first of our people to make a journey to another land," Daniel explained.

Anna raised her eyebrows. Had her father whispered Pentacles's existence to her in dreams, like he had the Moon?

"It's a long trek. How did you get here, Anna?" Daniel asked, tearing her away from her thoughts.

"My friends, the ones who helped me, put me in a boat," Anna lied. She felt a sick sensation in her stomach. "I was so disoriented, I felt half-dead when James found me on the shore. I'm lucky he was there."

"You must have lost consciousness at some point," Daniel said.

"The voyage was arduous," Anna said, thinking of the Tower, her aunt becoming sick, the bridge. "What do you call this place?" she asked.

"This"—Daniel stretched his arms wide and turned in a slow circle—"is Cups." His voice was thick with pride.

"We're happy you're here now, Anna." Lara unclasped one of the bracelets on her wrist. It was a round piece of sea glass, teal green, tied to a band of thin leather on each of its sides. "A welcome gift." She held it out.

Anna had just lied to these kind people, and they were giving her a gorgeous gift in return. She hesitated.

"Take it, Anna. I want you to have it."

"It is so beautiful," Anna said, her eyes misting.

Lara smiled, reaching for Anna's wrist.

"I can sew! I can weave anything—clothes, tablecloths, whatever you need," Anna blurted out.

"That's a very kind offer, Anna," said Daniel. "I do want you to know, we all contribute equally. If weaving is your passion, then that's what you should do."

Lara added, "We all do our part, but that doesn't mean we don't also know how to enjoy ourselves." She winked at Anna, and then her eyes wandered over her shoulder. "Look who found us."

Anna followed Lara's gaze down the beach, back in the direction of the villa. James was running down the shoreline toward them.

"The most playful of us all," Lara said.

Anna watched James approach, hoping the little surge of excitement she felt was not apparent on her face. He bounded up to them, smiling broadly.

"Hey!" he said. "Anyone up for a swim?"

"I'm going to head back. I need to make sure everyone knows their jobs for tomorrow," Lara said.

Anna wanted to stay, but she didn't know the first thing about swimming, and she was embarrassed to admit it.

"I want to see if I can find that old loom and fix it up for Anna," Daniel said.

"Really?" Anna brightened.

"Let's see what we can find." Daniel nodded back toward the villa.

"Suit yourselves." James turned toward the water and pulled off his shirt, revealing a tan, muscled back. Lara caught Anna staring.

"James is great," Lara said. "But, as you witnessed this morning, Ivy is one to watch out for. She's a great friend of mine, but I wouldn't want to get on her bad side."

"Does Ivy love James?" Anna asked. She knew nothing of these things, save for what she'd read in books. Anna wondered whether they would make fun of her if they knew how truly naive she was.

"I don't know if I would call it love. I'm not sure what I would call it, but she can be as threatening as the plant she's named for if you cross her."

"You owe me a swim, Anna!" James called to her from behind before diving into the clear blue water.

"I don't know how to swim," Anna confided to Lara in a whisper.

"Oh, I'm sure he'd be happy to give you lessons."

Anna smiled at the thought.

13

Everyone was milling about the King's war room when the Magician entered. She had managed to reach her chambers unseen and had wiped herself down as best she could, exchanging her soiled robes for new ones. She knew she must look three shades of green, but she could explain that away as illness.

When the Hermit spotted her, she saw a look of relief cross his features, but he quickly hid his emotion. The Hermit nudged the Fool, and when he saw her, he ran straight for her.

"Are you okay?" he whispered. "What happened?"

"Not now," the Magician snapped. "I need to sit." The Fool's face fell.

They found their seats at the King's large oak table with the rest of the advisors, senators, and the Minister of War. Beneath the table, the Fool squeezed the Magician's hand, and she felt a pang of remorse for snapping at him.

The King stood up from the head of the table to speak. He looked almost dazed, and the Magician felt a knot inside her chest. She knew her actions were justified, but she still didn't like the deception. It was dangerous and exhausting.

"We all understand what a difficult situation this is. Clearly, I underestimated the girl."

"We all did, Sire," Senator Bassett offered. The King ignored him.

"I've sent my Guard out in every direction to search for the girl," the King bellowed, "but I suspect that, if she could level a stone structure, finding her will be complicated and potentially dangerous. She could be somewhere right now, planning a full attack on the kingdom." *She certainly has plenty of motive*, he thought.

The Fool cleared his throat anxiously. The King did not notice, but Senator Bassett did.

Across the table, he turned to the Fool, the Hermit, and the Magician, who were seated next to one another. This made the Fool clear his throat again. Beneath the table, the Magician nudged him with her knee.

"I just need some water," the Fool said, getting up to reach for a pitcher and a cup. "Bit of a tickle," he added, pointing to his throat. In his nervousness, he knocked the pitcher over and water cascaded down the table. The King halted his speech. The Fool's cheeks flamed red as a young servant girl came forward to wipe up the mess.

"Are you finished now?" the King asked the Fool.

"Quite," said the Fool, sitting back down. Senator Bassett clucked in disgust and turned his head back to the King.

"Can you use your magic to track the girl?" The King now directed his focus to the Magician, who was having trouble keeping her eyes open. "Am I boring you?" he snapped.

The Hermit squeezed the Magician's thigh beneath the table and she jumped out of her seat.

"Never, Your Highness," she said.

"Is there something wrong? You look terrible."

"Something I ate, I think," the Magician said, grimacing. The King nodded knowingly, as did others at the table.

"The worst kind of sickness," the King said.

"Indeed," agreed the Magician. The Fool stifled a giggle.

"Can I use my magic to locate Anna?" The Magician repeated the question. "I can certainly try. It has been a while since I was allowed to use magic."

The King waved a hand at her. "Right, right," he said.

"Who could have known, Sire?" Bassett shrugged.

The King whipped around to face him. "Stop doing that. I don't need your reassurance. My pride is not at stake here; our way of life is."

The Magician suddenly clutched at her stomach and covered her mouth. She started to gag and stood up from her seat. The King winced in disgust, leaning away from her despite their distance.

"Go and rest," he said to the Magician. "We'll reconvene this evening and try the spell. The Guard is out—if she's in the forest, they'll find her." The Magician feigned gratitude by nodding and then dashing from the room.

"I recall one time I ate a herring that was off," she heard the King say as she left the room.

"An absolute tragedy," Senator Bassett agreed.

"I swear, if you do that one more time," she heard the King admonish him, and the Magician managed a smile. Perhaps she'd bought Anna enough time to get far, far away from the kingdom.

14

"What else do you like to do? Besides weaving, I mean." Lara studied Anna. "Do you like farming or gardening? Or do you enjoy being in the kitchen?"

Anna was distracted. They had just returned to the villa, and, as Lara opened the front door, Anna got her first glimpse of the bottom floor.

It was stunning.

The ceilings were high and vaulted, supported with wood beams, and the walls were lined with floor-to-ceiling windows, designed to let in light and show off the view of the mountain ranges jutting out of the sea. Gauzy white curtains fluttered with the sea breeze. The walls were a bright white, and the floors, a dark wood polished to a shine, anchored the room.

"I don't know." Anna blinked. "I've never worked outside my chambers, so I'd like to be outdoors if I can. Maybe gardening?" Anna bit her lip. "I think I'd be a quick learner."

Lara beamed. "You can try anything! We trade off, but gardening sounds like a good place to start." Lara gave Anna's arm a light squeeze. "Oh, but I'm getting ahead of myself. Would you like a proper tour? You haven't even been here a day, and already

I'm talking about putting you to work." She giggled. "I'm sorry, Anna."

"No, I want to work," Anna assured her. "I'd rather keep busy. A tour would be lovely, though. I've never been anywhere like Cups."

Lara's eyes lit up. "Then let's go explore a little."

They climbed a large wooden staircase to the second floor of the villa, which was dotted with bedrooms. Each room had the same billowing curtains, giant windows, and open doorways facing the sea. There were several outdoor patios with places to sit and watch the large palms sway, or soak up the sun's warm rays.

After they toured the villa, Lara walked Anna out to the gardens that grew in the back of the property. A large plot of land had been cut away from the tropical forest, and the people of Cups had built an impressive garden. Lettuce, carrots, melons, squash, and plantains all grew in abundance in neat rows.

Three girls walked by carrying crates full of vegetables they had just picked.

"Hey, Daisy!" Lara waved them over. "Do you all have a minute?"

The girls set down their crates.

"Rebecca, this is Anna. She'll be staying with us for a while." Rebecca pushed back her heavy blonde bangs and smiled, holding out her hand.

"It's nice to meet you, Anna."

"You too." Anna smiled.

"This is Morgan." Lara gestured to a tall girl with dark brown hair piled on top of her head in a messy bun. Her cheeks were flushed pink from working in the garden.

"Pleasure, Anna," she said. Her handshake was firm and her

manner direct. She looked straight into Anna's eyes when they shook hands.

"Clearly, she's saved the best for last!" A shorter girl with a head of tight yellow curls smiled at Anna.

"You must be Daisy?" Anna said.

"The one and only. Coming to the race tonight?" she asked, reaching into her crate and pulling out a carrot. "Snack?"

"Thanks," Anna said, accepting her offer.

"I'm definitely going to win tonight," Daisy said, crunching her own carrot and staring down Rebecca and Morgan.

"You are too competitive," said Lara.

"I know. Thank you." Daisy flipped her hair over her shoulder. The other girls laughed.

"The race is tonight on the beach," Lara said, turning to Anna. "It's thrilling. You'll love it."

"Do I have to join in if I come?" Anna asked. "Or can I just watch?"

"Of course," Lara reassured her. "But you might change your mind once we get there."

The girls picked up their crates and hitched them onto their hips. "See you later, Anna," said Rebecca as they headed back toward the villa.

Lara placed her hand on Anna's shoulder. "You're going to make friends fast."

Anna nodded. She thought about her advisors, her oldest and dearest friends, and felt a stab of grief in her stomach.

She watched the girls walk away, and something struck her. They wore simple white dresses, yet Cups was so full of color—the water alone had been about six shades of blue in the little time she'd been there. There was the purple of the orchids and the lime green of the palms. She looked past the gardens into the jungle that bordered the villa and the beach; she'd never seen so many shades of green. She could weave some of this color into their clothing, bring a bit of the beauty of their land into what they wore to show her gratitude for how openly they had welcomed her.

But first things first, she'd have to see if Daniel had been able to locate the loom.

"Would you like to see West Farm next?" Lara asked brightly. "It's our smaller farm, where we keep the animals. South Farm is much bigger and too far away to go on foot. We'll have to ride out there another day."

Anna hesitated. "Do you mind if we end here for today? I know we've barely begun, but my feet hurt from yesterday's journey, and to be honest, I'm not used to being around so many people."

"Oh." Lara nodded. She pivoted back toward the villa.

"I love what you've shown me so far, and I can't wait to see more. I just have to . . ." Anna shuffled lightly from foot to foot, trying to think of the right word.

"Process?"

"Yes, perhaps while sleeping," Anna said, nodding sheepishly.

"Say no more, Anna. I should have thought of it myself. Do you want me to walk you back?"

"That's all right." Anna smiled.

"Why don't you rest until dinner? Then you'll have heaps of energy for the race tonight." Lara winked.

Even the few steps back to the villa filled Anna with wonder because she was taking them alone. For the first time in her life she was experiencing freedom, and it felt like she'd been gifted a pair of wings.

Moments later, Anna paced around her new room. She let her hair out of its bun and sat on the bed, bouncing up and down a few times, reveling in the softness of the puffy white covers. She stared up at the ceiling and watched how the fingerlike leaves of the palms outside her window cast strange shapes and moving shadows above her. She listened to the sounds of the sea and enjoyed the cool breeze moving through her hair. She felt thankful for the quiet time to collect her thoughts and process everything that had happened since she'd stumbled into this new world.

Her mind traveled back to her advisors. She had seen them every day for her entire life, and now she wasn't sure if she would ever be with them again. She wished desperately she could tell them she was okay, make sure the Magician had made it back to the kingdom, and talk to them about this world of Cups she'd landed in.

"Count your lucky stars, Anna." She took a deep breath and pushed herself off the bed. If it weren't for her friends, she would be dead by now at the hands of the King. She shook her head. She couldn't believe he would actually kill her.

But she knew one thing—her tutors would not want her sitting around by herself, moping. *Well, the Hermit might*, she thought, laughing to herself. But the Fool would not.

Her hands were itching to work. It was the best way she knew to quiet her mind. She started down the stairs to find Daniel and, she hoped, her new loom.

When she walked outside, a bead of sweat sprang onto her forehead. The afternoon air was thick with heat. Down at the beach, a group of people were swimming and playing in the sand. Her eyes widened, and she could feel the heat rising to her face. She'd never seen so much bare skin.

The girls were dressed in two-piece bathing costumes and

the boys were bare chested, their bodies bronzed, some curvy and solid, others lean and supple.

A smaller group was on the sand, batting a ball back and forth with their palms, their hands wrapped in cloth for protection. They were loud and uninhibited, yelling to one another as they hit the ball and laughing when someone missed.

Anna watched them. She felt compelled to join in, but she was afraid of revealing her inexperience.

"I'm going into the water. Do you want to join me?"

Anna's blush deepened, and she felt the little hairs on her neck rise as James ran up behind her.

"Hi," she said, recovering. "I was just going to go look for Daniel."

"I'll help you find him."

"I don't want to upset your plans," Anna said.

"We can go in after," James countered, not missing a beat.

Anna raised her eyebrows. "You're persistent."

"And you're avoiding. Lara told me you don't know how to swim," James teased.

Anna frowned at the small betrayal.

"Oh, don't blame her." James chuckled. "You have to learn how. It's kind of a requirement here."

"Later. I promise," Anna said.

"Let's go this way. I saw Daniel heading for the farm shed earlier." James put a hand on Anna's shoulder to steer her and she felt a chill run down her back. She kept walking forward, embarrassed, wondering if he could sense her reaction.

When they got to West Farm, James led her past chicken coops and a large field where cows and goats were grazing, to a large wooden structure painted a bright crimson red.

"I present the shed," James said, spreading his arms wide.

"That's a very nice shed," Anna complimented. When they walked in, they nearly stepped on a shiny, russet-colored hound, fast asleep in a pool of sunshine, its nose resting on its oversized paws.

Anna sucked in her breath. She suddenly thought of Bembo.

"Dragon, Daniel's right-hand dog," James said. "Are you afraid of dogs?"

"No, the opposite," Anna said. "I love dogs. I had one called Bembo, and I miss him terribly."

"Dan!" James shouted. "Where are you?"

They heard a loud clatter and walked toward the back of the large space, where old farm equipment, musical instruments, tiles, dishes, glass jars, and other discarded objects where piled high along the walls. Daniel emerged, his long hair tousled, a big splotch of dirt on his nose.

"Perfect timing. I found it."

"Yes!" Anna whooped, and Daniel broke into a grin.

It was dusty and needed some love, but it was a newer loom than the one Anna had used back in the Tower. Just like everything in Cups, it seemed better somehow, more modern.

"I don't know much about looms," Daniel admitted. "But I think I can tinker with it."

"I can help," Anna offered. "It looks like we'd just need to clean it and tighten the screws." Daniel walked over to a big wooden crate and came back with rags and tools.

The three of them set to work in comfortable silence, until Dragon stirred from his sleep and ambled over. When he saw the loom, he bared his teeth in a growl.

"It's okay, boy," Daniel soothed. "It's a loom. Anna's going to weave with it."

"May I?" Anna said, looking from Daniel to the dog. Daniel

nodded. Anna stuck out her hand slowly and waited for Dragon to approach. He narrowed his eyes and sniffed her hand tentatively. His low growl rose into a ferocious bark. Anna leapt back and fell into James, who propped her up until she found her balance.

"Whoa. Hey, buddy." Daniel cut in front of Anna.

"Take him out, Dan!" James yelled.

Daniel shook his head. "He's usually so mellow." He led Dragon outside, and when they were gone, silence fell over the shed.

"Maybe he's been talking to Ivy." Anna laughed nervously, feeling breathless.

"That's funny. You're funny, Anna."

"He hated me," Anna said, perplexed. "My dog never barked at me like that."

"He did hate you." James put his hand on Anna's arm and gave her a dark look that quickly dissolved into a grin. Anna felt a jolt go through her at his touch. "That was kind of intense, though. Are you all right?"

"I am." Anna leaned closer to James until their shoulders touched.

The feel of the loom beneath her fingers was like breathing. She and James had unearthed a crate of treasures in the shed after Daniel left with Dragon. It was full of thread, yarn, and all kinds of trinkets, from sequins to buttons and a rainbow of ribbons. She could hardly believe her good luck. They had created a workroom for Anna in a space at the end of the hallway, opposite her bedroom. It was half the size of her room, but it had a huge window with a view of the jungle.

First, she wove and sewed a sundress for herself, almost as

fast as she'd envisioned it in her head. Light blue to complement her dark eyes, with simple lines that drew in at the bust, inspired by the way the girls dressed in Cups.

When she finished, she held it, admiring her work. She had an extreme agility with a loom that she hadn't recognized before. She was *fast*. She had hours and hours, years upon years of practice, but her tapestries were so large and involved. The end result took time—lots of time.

The Hermit had taught Anna to weave when she was nine, and before long she had surpassed his skill. Her arms had pulled the loom's shuttle back and forth as if by memory.

Anna thought about her father, her *real* father, a powerful magician. Maybe there was something about her ability to weave so quickly that was a little magical.

Or maybe it was just the hours and hours of practice.

Anna sat for a few moments thinking about Lara and her gorgeous strawberry-blond waves, her tinkling, musical bracelets and anklets, the easy way she expressed herself with her body, her warmth and kindness. Anna rummaged around in her new stash of supplies and chose a collection of sea greens and shimmering gold threads to weave a dress for Lara, something for special occasions.

Anna pulled her hair over her shoulder and worked it into a loose braid before embarking upon the new project. She had woven this sort of dress for the queens in her tapestries, and Lara was a queen, after all.

The sun was setting when Anna heard Terra calling to her from the bedroom across the hall. *Perfect timing*, she thought when Terra bounded into the workroom. Anna was just sewing the bottom hem of a dress for her using a needle and thread. She tied the stitch off with a knot and then cut the thread closely.

"Think this will fit?" Anna held up a summer dress the color of the sea at midday, made of a light fabric smocked at the chest, with yellow ribbons for shoulder straps. It flowed out from the waist, hitting right at the knee.

Terra squealed. "Yes!" She held it up to her small frame and twirled. "Oh, thank you, Anna."

Anna grinned at Terra's joy. A warm feeling spread through her chest. She had dreamed of making new friends when she was a little girl, but she'd had to settle for the people she met in books.

"Oh!" Terra hugged the dress to her chest and put a hand to her head. "I'm supposed to get you for dinner. It's almost time."

Anna frowned. "Another meal has been prepared, and I haven't helped at all."

"Don't worry—you can help with cleanup. Loads of fun." Terra waggled her eyebrows. "What's that?" She pointed to the wrapped package next to her loom.

"It's for Lara. Want to deliver it for me?" Anna asked.

Terra's eyes widened. "Only if you come too." She grabbed Anna's hand and looked her up and down. "Is that a new dress too? You've been so busy!"

"Do you like it?" Anna swished the skirt.

"It's perfect! Like you." Terra twirled with excitement. She was effervescent.

Anna snorted. "I'm hardly that."

Terra led Anna down the hall to Lara and Daniel's set of rooms.

"Lara?" Terra called from the hallway. "Anna has a present for you." Lara came to the door, and Terra pointed to the package in Anna's arms.

"It's nothing," Anna insisted. "Just an offering of thanks for your kindness."

"How lovely." Lara smiled. "Let's have a look before dinner." She led them into her and Daniel's bedroom, which faced a side of the island Anna hadn't ventured to yet. The lilac remnants of dusk were fading away, and all she could really make out were the black silhouettes of moonlit palms against a darkening sky. A large bed sat in the center of the room, with the same kind of fluffy white blankets and plushy pillows that were in her own bedroom.

"Let's see what we've got here." Lara's bracelets jingled as she unwrapped the package and unfolded the dress. Her breath caught. "Anna, it's divine. How on earth did you create this in an afternoon?"

"She made three dresses, but that one is the fanciest!" Terra exclaimed.

Lara held the bodice up, a faraway look in her eyes. She set the dress down gingerly and wrapped Anna in a light embrace. "It's magic, Anna."

After dinner, Anna returned to her room, grabbing her satchel and going outside to sit on her patio until the race started.

She opened the bag and lovingly pulled out the Hermit's lantern, setting it on the little mosaic table beside her. Above her was a wood pergola that shaded the patio from the sun in the daytime, and when she lit the lantern, the little star in its center threw patterns of light onto the slats. She reached back in her bag and dug around until she found her aunt's necklace in the bottom lining. She took it out, placing it around her neck and tucking it into her dress. She smiled, wishing her advisors were there with her.

Along with weaving, the Hermit had taught Anna how to cope with solitude in the Tower. He showed her meditation and breathing techniques, how to close her eyes and count each breath. How to visualize a tiny, golden spark within and let it grow and grow until it covered her whole body, flowing through the Tower, over the Keep, and even out into the stars. This was how she'd fought loneliness when it had scratched and clawed at her all those years.

Now she found that a little solitude offered her solace.

She dipped back into her bag and removed her tapestry remnants. For a moment she was overcome with loss. What had felt like great pieces of art were now reduced to these haphazard squares. But as she started to examine them, shuffling through them in her lap and holding them up one by one, she changed her mind. She organized them by land, putting them in separate stacks on the table. She found that when she was able to hold them in her hands, turn them and view them at different angles, they transformed. She could hold and manipulate them, turn them upside down and watch them take on new meanings.

She took some shears from her workroom and began to clean the edges of the tapestry pieces until they formed a neat stack. She took a deep breath and smiled.

Sounds of laughter floated up from the beach. Race time. She marveled at the fact that she could just walk down the stairs and join the activity. How many times had she imagined people beneath the Tower, wanting to join them by their fires, to listen while they told one another stories and drank their mugs of ale?

Anna packed up her tapestry pieces and blew out the lantern. She was going out tonight.

15

When the Hermit reached the Magician's chambers, he found her up and pacing. He was struck by the beauty of her long hair, which spilled down her shoulders in waves of chocolate brown, and her skin, restored to its natural olive tone.

"There you are! What took you so long?" The Magician turned to him and immediately began winding her hair into a braid.

"The meeting went on after you left," he said.

"Did I miss anything? Sit." She pulled out two chairs from a small wooden table. A vase of fresh white and red lilies sat in the middle.

"No, not really," the Hermit said, taking a seat.

She squinted at him. "Did you stop to meditate on the way here?"

"I did. I am of no use to anyone if I am not centered."

The Magician stopped pacing and looked at her friend. "You know most of us are off-center for the majority of our lives."

"My point exactly," he said.

The Magician snorted. "Well, it takes all sorts."

"It does indeed," the Hermit agreed. "You seemed to have recovered."

"I'm getting there." The Magician looked around and lowered her voice. "I need some supplies for a tracking spell. The King has asked me to perform one tonight, but I want to try it here first. I'm worried that if Anna is still nearby, then the spell will lead him straight to her."

"Is that wise?" The Hermit furrowed his brow. "What if we get caught? What if it can only be performed once? What if you get all green and gaggy again?"

The Magician collapsed into the chair across from the Hermit.

"The King will lose his patience if you are not well by this evening."

"You might have a point." The Magician tapped her foot.

"You were quite ill before. So pale, you looked near death."

"Thank you for that," the Magician sneered.

"I just think you should rest and prepare yourself for tonight's spell. If Senator Bassett gets suspicious, he might connect your sudden illness with the Tower falling and Anna's escape," the Hermit said.

The Magician sat up. "But what if I *do* lead him right to Anna? What if she's hiding somewhere right under our noses, and I expose her?"

"Could you manipulate the spell? You'll have all of your supplies." The Hermit raised his eyebrows.

"Hmm." She smiled at him. "Might there be a little deception in your nature after all?"

"We all have deception in our nature. The best way to handle it—"

The Magician held up her hand. "I'm sorry, friend, but your philosophy is wasted on me."

16

The beach was alight with torches, their swirls of orange and blue flames dancing against the darkness. The light reflected cobalt and crimson on the sea's vast black face. Along the shore a horde of people whooped and hollered, barefoot in the cool night sand.

"It's about to start, Anna!" Henry beckoned for her to join him and Terra at the front of the crowd.

"Be quick!" Terra shouted.

Anna darted over to them.

"We start the race, and Daniel and Lara are down at the other end to mark the finish line." Terra heaved a huge yellow flag over her shoulder. "You can help me wave this thing. It weighs a ton."

Anna took a deep breath to settle her nerves and ran with Henry and Terra toward a small group on horseback at the starting line. James and Ivy were among them, their horses side by side, but their faces were tight with focus and neither of them noticed her. Anna felt a pang of jealousy.

"Okay, everyone!" Terra held out the flag, and together she and Anna raised it high above their heads. "When the flags go down, you take off!" Henry followed suit, hoisting his own flag above his head. The horses shuffled their hooves in the sand. "Anyone who moves early will be disqualified!"

Terra's voice boomed down the beach. Anna raised her eyebrows, impressed by her commanding presence.

"On three?" Henry whispered.

"On three," the girls answered. Anna's heart drummed in her chest. She held on tight to the flagstaff as Henry began the countdown.

"One, two, three!" Anna and Terra dropped the flag, and the riders rushed past them, kicking up sand and letting out a symphony of cheers. The hairs on Anna's arms and neck stood up, and she realized she was screaming along with the others. They watched the contestants disappear into the night as they stormed toward the finish line down the shore. Henry laughed heartily, breaking away from the group and falling down onto the sand. Anna and Terra joined him at a spot halfway between the villa and the ocean.

"I've got to learn to ride a horse. And swim," Anna stated. Henry and Terra studied her expression. She smiled back at them, but sadness glinted in her eyes.

"No time like the present," Henry said, looking out at the sea.

Anna shook her head and scooted away from the shore. She thought of how she'd rejected the same offer from James. Maybe she was avoiding the inevitable, but the sea looked terrifying in the dark.

"Let's just get your feet wet," Terra offered. "Let the water run over your toes."

Anna screwed up her face, eyes closed. She blew out a long breath and opened her eyes again. "Just the toes," Anna said, eyeing Terra and Henry.

"Just the toes," they agreed.

The three held hands. They looked at one another and approached the water. The riders were long gone. Anna couldn't even hear them anymore.

The sea felt like a warm bath on Anna's feet. She pressed her lips together and ventured a look at Terra. Her eyes danced with excitement. Terra smiled back, and Henry winked at her. A warm breeze picked up the hem of Anna's dress, and it fluttered around her knees.

Henry dropped Anna's hand. He dipped his fingers into the water and ran them through his fiery locks. "There is nothing as good as the sea, Anna." He paused. "Except maybe my bread. My bread is spectacular." He smirked at her.

Anna laughed. "I look forward to eating it!"

The three of them stood like that for a long time with their feet in the warm water, the Moon reflected on the ocean's surface.

They didn't speak, just stood in comfortable silence until James came pounding back down the beach, the moonlight gleaming off his horse's silky brown mane. "Victor!" he announced.

"Next time, James. Lucky ride!" Daisy called after him.

"What is this? A fair maiden in the sea?" James said as he galloped toward them. Anna felt herself blush and was thankful for the cover of night.

James jumped off his horse, patting the velvet of her muzzle affectionately. "Don't go too far," he whispered to her.

There were at least twenty competitors dismounting their horses and making their way back to the starting line one by one. Anna watched as they strode down the beach, scanning the group for familiar faces. Terra noticed Anna watching them. "You'll get to know everyone eventually." She pointed out a small group breaking away from the crowd of spectators.

"The one with the shaggy hair is Luke, and the guy next to him with the shaved head is Tanner. He's really quiet." Terra put her finger to her lips. "Oh, and the girl with the curly hair, the one who rode up with James, that's Daisy. She hates losing."

"So I've heard," Anna said.

Anna felt the water lap her calves as James splashed up behind her. "It looks like you're ready for a swim lesson." His voice was like warm honey, and she felt her stomach flip. Anna glanced up at Ivy, who was making her way down to the water.

"Tomorrow," Anna assured him. He was so close to her now, his suntanned skin glistening with sweat from the race.

He frowned. "Why not tonight?"

Ivy swept past them, taking off her dress in one fluid movement and revealing her lithe, slim-hipped body. Anna tried not to look, but Ivy made no effort to cover her bare copper back. She flipped her curtain of long blond hair.

"You seriously can't swim?" Ivy smirked and dove into the black water, leaving a wake of uncomfortable silence behind her.

"I'm going up to bed. It must be late." Anna turned away from the group, her face hot with embarrassment.

"I'll walk you," James offered.

"No, it's okay," Anna said. "Enjoy the water." All the other race contestants had joined Ivy, but Henry, Terra, and James stood there watching Anna, their eyes soft with sympathy. "I'll see you guys tomorrow." If she said any more, she knew she would cry.

"See you tomorrow, Anna." Terra squeezed her hand gently. James and Henry turned back to the water. Anna nodded and started to walk up the beach toward her washroom and the stairs to her patio.

"Is she all right?" she heard James murmur.

"She'll be fine," Terra answered.

"She probably just needs a little breathing room," Henry added.

Thank you, Henry, Anna thought.

Anna climbed the stairs and collapsed onto her bed. She struck a fist of frustration into one of her pillows, longing for the simplicity of the Tower and feeling sick at the thought of being back there. She wondered if isolation had ruined her chance at a normal life.

All she wanted was to hear the advice of the Magician, the Hermit, and the Fool.

She went to her loom, loaded it with yarn, and began to weave, starting with the Magician, recalling every detail she could of her aunt. At her feet, Anna wove a garden of white lilies and red roses, her favorite flowers. She pictured her red robes and the careful way she arranged her hair in a long braid down her back. Anna wove the shimmering gold of the Magician's belt and the green of the snake's glittering emerald eyes. She imagined what her chambers might be like and created the scene. A simple wood table would hold her few belongings. She added a sword, a cup, and a pentacle and depicted the Magician holding her wand up to the sky in a gesture of power.

Anna placed a hand to her chest and lifted out the infinity charm the Magician had given to her. She squeezed it tightly, wishing her aunt were with her. Anna returned to her loom and, above the Magician's head, she wove her own golden infinity symbol.

Anna bound the threads and placed the small likeness inside her satchel. She walked the perimeter of her workspace, blowing out the lanterns and shrouding the room in darkness.

17

"Anna, it doesn't have to be perfect."

Rebecca and Anna were knee-deep in dirt, planting a new crop of pumpkins in the garden. Luke sat shirtless on the ground, banging rhythmically on a drum while Morgan and a boy Anna had met that morning, Thorn, were lying on their stomachs nearby, painting tiny star patterns on rocks.

"Look," Rebecca said. She scooped a shallow hole with her spade and dropped the seeds in. "Then just throw a little dirt on top, and make sure it has enough water."

Anna took her cue and poured water from the can beside her over Rebecca's small mound of earth.

"Good?" Anna asked.

"Yes, that's great. Now you finish this row."

Anna dug another shallow hole, faster this time. She couldn't help but nod to Luke's drumming as she planted. "I really like your music," she said, tossing in another handful of seeds.

"Thanks, Anna." Luke looked up from his drum. "I think you might have a visitor."

Anna turned and saw James approaching from the villa.

"You all got started early this morning," James called as he walked up to them. He took a seat on the ground next to Luke. "May I?"

Luke nodded and handed over the drum. James tapped out a slow beat and Luke snapped his fingers in time. Rebecca started singing, connecting words that fell in with the rhythm. Morgan and Thorn moved their heads to the beat while they painted.

The sun is out and we are shining.

Her voice rose on the last word, and she held the note like a bell. The boys jumped in with their own lyrics, riffing off one another.

Shining so bright, feeling so strong and so light.
The sun is on my mind and my mind is on that
*   pumpkin over there.*
Your mind is in the dirt, that dirty mind of yours.

The words were getting sillier, but Anna marveled at the others' ability to keep up. Rebecca took her hand and, as Anna stood, Rebecca twirled her. Luke, James, and Rebecca looked to Anna for the next line.

She froze.

They were all bobbing their heads to the beat of James's drumming. Anna stared at them blankly, holding her hands out by her sides. She shrugged and smiled.

"I'm not sure what to sing." Anna moved her head to the beat as she spoke. James laughed and handed the drum over to Luke. He picked up James's beat.

"How about a break?" James looked to Anna. "Do you want to walk down to the water with me?"

Anna winced. "I said I would go in today, didn't I?"

James shrugged and raised his eyebrows. "You did. But I'm not going to hold you to it."

Anna looked to Rebecca.

"Go ahead, Anna," Rebecca encouraged. "I'll finish up here. We're almost done anyway."

"Okay." Anna sighed.

"Yeah?" James said, his lips turning into a hopeful smile.

"But I'll have to go borrow a bathing suit from Lara."

"Fair enough." James smiled. "Meet me where the race started?"

Anna set her jaw and nodded. She had escaped execution by a tyrant. She could learn how to swim.

Lara and Daniel were still asleep. Lara's beautiful hair spread out red and flaxen on her pillow like rays of sunshine at dusk. Daniel was shirtless, and his tattooed arm was thrown around Lara's waist. The image of the two lovers took Anna's breath away. They looked like a painting.

Dragon slept at the foot of the bed, his head resting on his giant paws. Anna looked at him with trepidation and tiptoed toward Lara's side of the bed. She didn't want to disturb their peaceful sleep, but James was waiting.

Anna gently shook Lara's arm and said her name softly. Lara woke easily, opening her bright green eyes and smiling at the sight of Anna.

"I'm so sorry to wake you," Anna whispered. "Can I borrow a swimsuit?"

Lara raised her light eyebrows and smiled. "Of course!" She

carefully removed Daniel's arm and planted a light, long kiss on his forehead.

"Do you have anything that would cover more?" Anna stood in front of a tall mirror in Lara's bathroom. "I feel like I'm showing so much . . . everything." Anna tried to pull the swim top down to conceal more of her stomach. "I'm not sure I can go outside like this."

"I'll find a dress for you, but wow, Anna," Lara crowed. "Maybe I should go with you. Someone needs to make sure he doesn't get distracted and let you drown." Lara grinned and ducked into her closet.

"Drown?" Anna mock-wailed.

Lara emerged, chuckling. "Okay, bad choice of words. Now go. Off with you." She tossed Anna a short green dress to wear over the suit.

Anna held it up and, where the light hit, she could see Lara straight through the fabric, grinning mischievously.

"Hey! You came." James's pale-green eyes twinkled.

Anna laughed, crossing her arms over the dress that was doing absolutely nothing to cover her body. "I did. You've asked me what, three times now? I suspected I was going to have to get this over with sometime."

James narrowed his eyes. "It might have been four. So let's go before you change your mind."

James led her down the beach toward the south end of the

island. Anna took deep breaths to slow her galloping heartbeat.

"Tell me about Pentacles," James said, breaking the silence.

"Pentacles?" Anna repeated, buying herself time to think of an answer.

"I've never been anywhere else besides Cups. My friend Christopher is the only one who has ever left here to explore another land."

"Lara and Daniel told me about him. Why is that?"

"He's the one person who thought to do it, and Daniel let him go. This is his first journey." James moved closer to the shoreline, the waves lapping over his feet wet as they walked.

"Did you think about going with him?" Anna had to quicken her pace a little to keep up with James.

"He didn't ask. Maybe next time," James mused.

"He just went off alone?" Anna asked.

"That's Topper. You'll see when you meet him," James said.

Anna smiled. James expected her to be there for Topper's return. She followed suit and walked a little closer to the water, but she jumped when the tide reached her feet. James laughed.

"How did he get there?" Anna studied James.

"He sailed." James looked out at the ocean. "Topper sent us a letter describing the place. It came to us on the leg of a small gray bird." He turned to Anna and smiled. "We nearly missed it actually! So clever. He said it's a very wealthy land of noblemen and noblewomen."

Anna thought of her Pentacles tapestry.

"It is. Pentacles is an opulent kingdom full of riches." While she didn't like the idea of lying to James, the words came easily, and what else was she going to do? James looked at her, waiting for her to continue. "See, everything here is of the land, right? The farms, the sea, the beaches. There it is all man-made, but glorious." For Anna, Pentacles was like the Hierophant's King-dom, but with joy and abundance and magic.

James nodded for her to go on. He trailed his hand through the water and came up with a fistful of stones. He picked one up with his other hand and skipped it over the water. James handed Anna a few stones.

"There are castles with walls eighty feet high, and turrets and flags made of the finest silks," she continued. She threw a stone into the water, and it immediately plopped down into the sand.

"It's all in the wrist." James tossed another stone and it bounced lightly four times before disappearing into the sea. "Pen-tacles sounds very grand," he said.

"That is a perfect way to put it. The castles sit on rolling hills of green, emerging from a vast forest of the tallest pine trees you can imagine. And the smell! A scent so green and fresh, it clears the head and the heart." Anna could almost feel the land coming to life as she spoke.

"It sounds amazing," James marveled.

"It is. For some," she added, remembering her lie about be-ing mistreated by a great lady.

"Oh, I'm sorry," James said, his voice faltering. "You don't have to say more if you don't want to."

"I don't mind," Anna assured him. There was something comforting about describing her tapestry of Pentacles and sharing this piece of herself with James.

"The kingdom is flanked by great rocky cliffs the color of a storm cloud and a violent gray sea. Very different from this sea," she said, and nodded to the calm and translucent body of water before them. "The sea that borders Pentacles to the north is cold and angry and has taken the life of many sea captains and their crews."

"No wonder you're afraid of the water." James shivered. "It sounds so cold there."

"It can be," Anna agreed, getting more and more caught up in her tale. "But fires blaze in stone fireplaces the size of small oak trees in nearly every room. Blankets are made from the softest, thickest wool, and rugs from faraway lands warm the cold stone floors. There's always something wonderful cooking in the kitchens and wafting through the drafty halls."

"But you were not happy there?" James asked. He had stopped throwing stones and was studying her as they walked.

"No." Anna shook her head. "I was a servant. My room was cold and damp, and I did not have freedom to roam or explore. It was work and not enough sleep and more work." She felt a tug at her stomach as she told this half-truth to James. He looked at her with an open, curious expression.

"Topper should be back soon. He's been gone two moon cycles already. You can compare experiences when he gets back."

Anna blinked. Or Christopher would catch her in a lie.

"Look, we're here!" James exclaimed.

Anna gasped. In front of her stood a cove, where a tall wall of jagged black rocks formed a perfect half circle around bright white sand and the smooth deep-green sea. Palms stood like centurions at either end of the sheltered bay.

But it was not the beauty of this place that had stopped Anna in her tracks. It was the black stone wall, the perfect half circle, the grouping of gently swaying palms, exactly seven of them. She had woven this very spot into one of her tapestries. Seven palms framing a lush, sparkling cove. She was sure of it.

Anna turned to James, her eyes wide. "James, tell me about the night you found me."

"You'll really do anything to get out of swimming, won't

you?" He cocked his head at her and arched an eyebrow.

"No, I promise, I will. I just have this feeling as if I've been here before," Anna said. She looked behind them, in the direction they had come from. The villa was a small dot in the distance.

"I found you on the other side of this cove," James began. "Ivy and I were out messing around." Anna wondered what that meant. She brushed the thought away, frustrated at these new, recurring feelings of jealousy.

"You were just standing in the shallow end of the water, which terrifies me now that I know you can't swim." James looked at her, wondering if he should continue. She nodded for him to go on. "There's not much more to tell. It was like you came out of nowhere." He paused. "I could tell you'd been through something pretty intense. You were all scratched up, and your eyes were wild. You looked terrified."

"But there was no boat or horse or anything?"

"No, just you and your bag, which you refused to let go of. Are you remembering it differently?"

Anna thought of the green bridge and the sticky sludge. She remembered that moment of feeling like she was suspended between two worlds—the Hierophant's Kingdom and, she now knew, Cups.

"I don't remember anything," Anna lied.

"Can I make a suggestion?" James smirked. "One you might not love?"

"Sure."

"Swim. It will take your mind off things. I can tell it's getting crowded in there." He tapped his head. "It always helps me to move." James held his hand out to her.

"Okay," she said, taking it and letting him lead her toward the water. Maybe he was right. Her fear of the water would overpower the questions that had started firing from her brain. Anna decided she would come back later to examine the spot where James had found her. For now, she would swim.

"Ready for this?" James asked. Anna managed a weak smile in response. "I brought you here because it's shallow. You can walk out for a while before the seafloor drops. It's the perfect place to learn."

James led her into the water. As it touched her feet and then rose up over her ankles, she held his hand tighter.

"I've got you." He turned around and smiled, his eyes crinkling at the corners. "You're not in danger—remember that. It's just new." They walked out farther, the water rising over Anna's calves and knees. They stopped when it hit her thighs. Lara's dress billowed around her.

Anna was starting to feel like she might run for the shore at any moment. She looked up to the sky and closed her eyes against its bright rays. She took a deep breath. "The water feels so good."

James squatted down and reached his arms in front of him, pushing off the sand and paddling forward.

"Do I have the option of keeping my feet on the ground?" Anna asked.

James flipped over onto his back. "We're going to start with floating, so that might be difficult. But it feels unbelievably freeing."

"Floating," Anna repeated. Her whole body trembled with fear.

"Breathe, Anna. It's really important." James stood up. "You're going to lie on your back, and I'll place my arms underneath you for support," he instructed. "May I?" He held his arms out, and Anna nodded as he gently rested them on her back.

"Now lie back like you're going to fall into the water. I've got you."

Anna eyed him. "You're sure?"

"I've got you," he repeated.

Anna leaned back, letting him lower her into the ocean. She bent her knees and, feeling the water wet the back of her head, kicked her legs up awkwardly. She felt sure she'd sink if not for James's arms supporting her.

"I'm going to walk out a little." James smiled. "You're tall." He carried her out deeper, and Anna felt her hair spread around her. She let her muscles relax, losing herself in the warmth of the water and the sun beaming on her skin.

James looked down at her and their eyes met. She stared back up at him and smiled.

"You're floating," he whispered.

Anna realized she no longer felt James's arms against her back. She took a deep breath, her heart beating fast. She was sure she could feel herself sinking, and kicked her legs.

"Can we go back to where I can stand?" she pleaded.

"Whoa," said James. "If you kick, you'll sink. Just put your legs down. It's shallow here." James held her as her feet found the soft sand.

"Better?" he asked.

"Yes." They stood side by side, the sea stretching out before them, calm and dark teal.

"I think you're ready to try paddling," he said.

"Could we stop for the day? I'm scared."

"Do you know the best way to conquer fear?" James turned to face her in the water.

"Deep breathing?" Anna suggested, thinking of the Hermit.

James laughed. "Well, yes. But another way is to keep doing what you're afraid of. If you run away now, it will be much harder to get into the water tomorrow. So I'm going to push you." He paused. "But only if you're okay with it."

"Well, you are very pushy, James," Anna teased. She thought of Ivy and her competence on a horse and in the water. Anna pictured what she would look like flailing around in the sea and groaned. "Let's get it over with," Anna conceded.

"I'll hold my arms out again, but this time in front. You're going to lie down on them and put your feet up and your arms out to the sides," James directed.

He walked out farther into the water until it came up to his chest and he bent his arms, palms up. Anna followed and when she felt the water rise over her belly button, she grabbed James by the shoulder. Anna could feel the ripple of his muscles beneath her hand and willed herself not to let her hand travel farther down his arm.

"Okay, breathe." He pulled her fingers from his shoulder and grabbed her by the waist. His hands were sure and strong, and she felt her stomach flutter pleasantly at his touch.

James helped Anna glide onto his arms. The feel of his skin beneath her stomach made everything in her stir, despite her fear. She took a deep breath.

"Now what?" she asked.

"Now paddle with your arms, like I was doing earlier, and kick your legs as hard as you can."

Anna waved her arms through the water and kicked her legs violently while James held her in place. She giggled to herself thinking of how she must look, and was thankful for the seclusion of the cove.

She kept going until her muscles burned, and she collapsed onto James's arms.

"Okay, that's enough for today," James finally said.

Anna held on to James's forearms as they walked back to the shallows. Standing in the water, so clear that she could see her feet and the tiny brightly colored fish swimming around her ankles, felt easy. Even pleasant.

They turned toward the cove and waded out of the sea side by side, hair slicked back from their faces, dripping with seawater.

James gazed at Anna. "You did great."

She raised one eyebrow.

"You did!" he reassured her. "Same time, same place tomorrow?"

"Yes," she said reluctantly.

James smiled. "It's going to get easier, I promise."

"Stars, I'm so hungry," Anna said, tearing into an egg-and-vegetable pie that Lara had placed in front of her. They were sitting at a round table in the villa's huge, bright kitchen. The table sat in front of a large sea-facing window, and Anna and Lara sat beside each other, enjoying the view.

Anna licked her fingers.

Lara raised her eyebrows. "So, how was it?"

"Hard. Salty. I sort of hated it."

Lara chuckled. "I mean with James, not the swimming."

Anna took a sip of a pink frothy juice. "Mmm. What is this?"

"Guava juice." Lara smiled. "I'll whip some up for you anytime. You make me feel like I can actually cook!"

"You can!" Anna said through a mouthful of pie.

Lara laughed. "Not like Henry, but I do okay. I think you might just be really hungry."

"The food I am used to . . ." Anna paused. "In Pentacles, I mean. It was bland and always the same. I had come to think of food as merely sustenance, really."

Lara wrinkled her nose in sympathy. "That sounds awful." She took a sip of her own pink juice.

"It was nice with James," Anna said, returning to Lara's question. "I really liked talking to him."

Lara eyed her. "Did he like the suit?"

"I don't know," Anna said. "I kept the dress on."

Lara laughed. "You're so modest, Anna." She looked thoughtful for a moment. "But I guess if I hadn't lived my whole life in bare feet and a swimsuit, I might be more modest too."

Anna shrugged. "Can I have one of those dates?" She pointed to a bright orange ceramic bowl filled with them. Lara passed them over.

"You should only do what you're comfortable with," Lara assured her. "I think it's very sweet how James has gone out of his way to be with you."

"Maybe he just feels responsible for me since he found me. And what about Ivy? You said to watch out for her when it came to him."

"I think that's over." Lara sighed. "They're kind of on-again, off-again. Either way, he is clearly taken with you." Lara popped a date into her mouth. "I think she and James have messed around because it's easy, but I don't think she's exactly his soul mate."

"Oh. I get it." The thought of James and Ivy *messing around* made Anna's stomach clench. Why did she care so much? She had only just met him. But that smile. He was gorgeous and strong and so sure of himself. And *kind*. He'd found her and brought her home with him. He'd persisted in giving her swim lessons and helping her acclimate to life in Cups.

Anna looked up at Lara. "It's nice to be able to talk with you like this." Anna grinned. Lara reached for her hand. "I never got to know my mom, and I feel like—I just wonder what she would've taught me, what she would've shown me, if she'd had the chance."

Lara tucked her legs up under her skirt and hugged her knees.

"Well, that makes two of us. No mom for me, either." She smiled sadly. "You can always ask me anything."

Anna squeezed Lara's hand. "Where are they? The parents and the babies?"

Lara shrugged. "They're just not part of our culture. No one really knows where we came from. Some of us believe in a Goddess creator; some think we were just born of the earth. So I get what it's like not having a mother. I think I'm the closest thing to a mother any of these kids have."

"It's strange." Anna rested her chin on her hand. "If not for the simple clothing and the warmer weather, I might have thought I was just in another corner of Pentacles. I had read about people from other lands looking different from the few people I knew back home, but maybe the inhabitants of Pentacles originally came from the Goddess as well. In any case, I think the people of Cups are very lucky," Anna said sincerely. "To have you."

"That may be so, but sometimes it feels like an enormous pressure. On Daniel too. Sometimes things go wrong here; people get into fights or someone doesn't do their share. As free and unrestricted as life is here, there are still consequences to people's actions. I think people forget that, and it's really fallen upon Daniel and me to remind them." She threw her hands up. "Keep order, if you will."

That sounded like an immense responsibility to Anna. She had never been responsible to or for anyone. Lara and Daniel had an island full of young people looking to them for guidance, and they could hardly be considered their elders.

Anna thought about the Hierophant King and his fixed fates.

How he always claimed that order and rules kept the peace. There was no doubt in her mind that the people of Cups would feel absolutely choked under his rules.

But maybe nowhere was perfect.

"One more date. I think dates and coffee are my new favorite things," Anna said, breaking their thoughtful silence.

"That woman in Pentacles kept you pretty isolated, didn't she? No dates? No coffee?"

"You have no idea," Anna said, chewing.

Lara dropped her knees and leaned across the table, resting her chin on her hands. She narrowed her eyes conspiratorially at Anna. "How would you like to help me plan the Full Moon Festival this month?"

"Full moon? That sounds magical." Anna swallowed the last of her juice.

"It's how we celebrate the twelve cycles of the Moon. A giant party with an equally giant feast." She pointed at Anna. "You are going to love it!" Then she took Anna's shoulders and shook them lightly. "We eat on the beach beneath the stars. There's music and dancing and we paint our faces and bodies, like we're creatures who live on the Moon."

Anna sat up straighter. "That sounds amazing." Chills erupted through her body, and the hairs on her arms stood up. "Maybe I could weave costumes," Anna said, feeling inspired.

"Of course!" Lara looked out the window over the ocean, at the blazing midday sun. "I'm so glad you're here, Anna. I don't think I realized it until now, but I needed someone to talk to too." The girls squeezed hands and smiled at each other.

18

The Minister of War was an intimidating figure. He was a pale, hulking man named Barda, who stood at a solid six feet two inches, with a barrel chest and not an inch of fat on his frame. He had short white-blond hair, and his eyes were such a light shade of blue, they almost looked clear.

Now he stood in the King's meeting room, towering over the Magician's wand and a large crate full of her supplies as if he were guarding a lit cannon. The crate contained glass jars of powders in every color of the rainbow, along with vials of liquids, firmly corked and thick with dust after being locked up for sixteen years.

It was early evening, and darkness had fallen outside the windows. The room was dimly lit with candles.

The Magician stood in the doorway, watching him.

"Enter," he said to her without looking up.

The Magician walked toward him, nearly salivating at the sight of her things, *her most precious things*, just sitting there on the table, unlocked.

"That's close enough. Sit." Barda motioned to a chair across the table from him, and the Magician pulled it out and sat. "The senators and His Majesty will be here soon, but I wanted to take a moment to explain how this will work."

The Magician nodded.

"The King has put me in charge of your tools. When we decree that you need them, we will give them to you. You will do whatever we have asked you to do, and only that."

The Magician nodded. It took all her strength not to grab her wand and turn him into a rat.

"You will have use of your wand and whatever all of this is." He waved a hand over the crate dismissively. "And then they will be locked up again, hopefully for good."

The Magician's heart dropped. She silently admonished herself for thinking the King would do otherwise.

"Understood?" he asked, as if he were talking to a small child.

"Understood." She pushed her chair back and stood up. "I'm going to need them now to perform a tracking spell for the King."

"Of course." Barda stepped back and gestured for the Magician to approach the crate. As soon as the Magician stood, the King swept into the room, his cloak trailing along the floor behind him.

"You're looking much better," he said to the Magician.

"Thank you, Sire." The Magician smiled wearily.

"Are you ready for this? I'm counting on you." The King gave her a warm smile.

"Yes, Your Majesty. I just need to gather some supplies."

"Good." He walked over to Barda, and the two men became engrossed in conversation.

A small group of people filed into the room, seating themselves around the large table.

Senator Bassett entered, followed by Senator Terrin and Senator Gorvenal and each of their attendants. It made the Magician nervous to have these men so close to her treasures on the table, but they barely seemed to notice them.

"I need a large ceramic bowl filled with water," the Magician whispered to Senator Terrin's young attendant, who nodded, eager to please.

"I'll be right back with it," the young boy said, and dashed out of the room.

The Hermit and the Fool arrived together.

"How are you?" the Hermit asked the Magician, regarding her with a pinched expression.

"I'm all right," she whispered.

"And Anna?" the Fool spoke in a low whisper.

The Magician nodded darkly and walked toward her wand and powders. The attendant came rushing back in, sloshing water from the large bowl he carried. He looked to the Magician and waved her over.

The Fool and the Hermit took seats at the table.

The Magician stood at the head and took several jars of powder and a rack that contained vials of fluid in colors ranging from the deepest black to the yellow of a chrysanthemum. She put the rack back into the crate and took out another that held vials filled with matter in various states. One looked like it held smoke, another was completely clear, while yet another looked like silty water.

She chose the silt water and a jar that held a powder of similar color. Finally she gingerly removed a tiny vial that shimmered with golden sparkles.

The Magician cleared her throat loudly, and the men stopped their chatter. They all turned to look at her.

"Ready?" the King boomed.

"I am. This spell will show us a moment in time. From there we'll have to infer her whereabouts."

Barda and the King walked over and stood on either side of her.

"Might we get a look too?" asked Senator Bassett.

"Certainly," said the King. The men pushed their seats back from the table and shuffled over, crowding the Magician in a half circle. The Fool and the Hermit joined, but they were pushed toward the back.

"More light!" the King ordered his servant, who came at once, lighting the unlit lanterns on the table. The servant was tall and slim, and the men watched her as she walked between them. The girl ignored their stares, and when she finished lighting all of the lanterns, she stood back in the corner of the room.

First the Magician picked up a jar that looked like it contained dried mud. She tossed a few pinches into the bowl of clear water. The Fool and the Hermit inched closer, desperate to see what had become of Anna.

Next, the Magician chose the vial of murky water, and poured half of its contents into the bowl. As it splashed the surface, a loud crack rang out. The men jumped.

The Magician could feel their delight at the sight of real magic, but so could the King. He scowled at the bowl of water, which was now turning a milky white.

Now the Magician grabbed her wand. It was like taking the hand of an old lover. The King fingered his dagger, prepared to act if she became overeager.

She unscrewed the little golden vial and used the tip of her wand to scoop out the slightest bit of the sparkling powder.

"Fool, come help me." Barda made room for the Fool to move through the throng, pressed shoulder to shoulder in the small space. "Screw this back on as carefully as you can. You must not spill a drop." The Fool cautiously took the vial from her and did as she asked, then gently placed it back into the rack on the table.

The Magician began to stir the water with the golden-tipped

wand. She uttered an incantation, closing her eyes and carefully stirring the milky water.

Suddenly the surface of the water shimmered and everyone gasped, including the Magician. There was Anna, standing on a bridge.

"I don't recognize that place," said Senator Bassett, pushing his chin over Barda's shoulder. Barda winced. "Do you, Sire?" Bassett looked to the King.

"No, I don't," the King said, stroking his beard in thought. "I have explored every inch of these woods, and I have never seen a bridge like that."

"She's looking for something." Barda brushed the Magician aside. The room watched in awe as Anna looked around, then threw a rock off the bridge. She took a few steps across and then seemed to disappear.

"Where did she go?" The King gave Barda a sharp look, and he moved aside. He stared into the water.

"I don't know," the Magician answered. The image of the bridge was still before them, but Anna was gone. Then the bridge itself evaporated, leaving only an image of the woods and its towering pines.

"Can't you do it again so we can see where she went? Stir the water more?" Senator Terrin suggested from behind the King.

The Hermit, who had inched closer, noticed the Magician was growing pale again. A thin sheen of sweat glistened on her brow, and the color was quickly draining from her cheeks.

"It doesn't work that way. The magic has its limits, and I am not practiced enough to push them."

The room was silent, taking their cue from the King. The Magician slumped into a chair, feeling like she'd betrayed Anna. The King placed a hand on her shoulder.

"You've done well." He looked at his advisors. "Call back the Guard. I believe she's crossed over into another place. The bridge, the way she just disappeared . . ."

"You mean she's dead?" the Fool blurted out.

"I can't say for sure, but I don't believe that bridge is of this world," said the King. "We're going to have to use other, stronger means to find her." He eyed the Magician, then turned back to Barda. "Get the soldiers ready. When we figure out where she went and how to get there, we're going to go in with the full strength of my army."

The King stared down the Magician. "In the meantime, you are to practice your magic," he commanded. The Magician's heart fluttered as the King gave his orders. "Hone your craft and do it as fast as possible, because I have a feeling that each minute that passes, Anna is doing the same. She will be a formidable opponent."

The Magician stood up and began to gather her things.

"Wait," Barda said, barring her way with his arm. "You'll be supervised while practicing. We'll start tomorrow at dawn."

The Magician looked to the King. "Sire, surely you will not bind me with such restrictions in these circumstances."

"I'm afraid he's right," the King said as he started to leave the room. "Barda's in charge. But don't worry," he called back to them. "You're in good hands."

The Magician squeezed her fists at her sides and clenched her teeth. It took everything she had not to show her anger. The senators were leaving, but Barda stood guard over the table, elbows crossed, a smirk on his face.

"I've never trusted your kind," he said.

"How dare you," she answered back. "I could say the same about you." She felt a hand on her elbow and whipped her head around.

"Let's go," the Hermit said gently.

She gave her tools one last longing look and then nodded, letting the Hermit lead her out of the room. The Fool followed close on their heels.

The three of them walked the large stone halls in silence until they reached the Magician's chambers.

"She's all right," the Fool said. He collapsed onto the Magician's bench. "I'm so relieved!"

"And your spell did not give away her whereabouts," said the Hermit.

The Magician unclasped her belt and placed it on the table next to the Fool, his eyes level with the green eyes of the serpent. The Fool slid down the bench a bit to avoid its beady emerald stare.

"That was yesterday," the Magician said. "I was able to cast the spell so it showed Anna twenty-four hours ago. Just to give her some more time in case she was still in the wood."

"But she's not in the wood!" said the Fool. "Or she wasn't. That bridge was huge and dripping with green moss—like something out of a fairy tale. We would have noticed it before."

"I wasn't lying when I said that I don't know where Anna is." The Magician sat down across from the Fool. "I believe the King is right. She's crossed over to another world." She paused. "I just hope it's a friendly one."

19

Anna struggled to climb up the mountain alongside the others. She slipped on the rocks while everyone else scaled them with the ease of the monkeys watching from the trees. But when she got to the top, out of breath, her palms hot and nearly blistered from the effort, she saw that the trek was worth it.

The small mountain flattened out into a perfect plateau with a panoramic view of Cups. The water sparkled hot pink and orange, reflecting the colors of the setting sun. Henry, Morgan, and Daisy stood in front of a small cottage, handing out coconut shells filled with cool tea. The whole of Cups was there, which seemed to Anna to be about a hundred people. Most milled about, drinking and talking.

Anna caught her breath and thanked them for the tea. She found herself scanning the crowd, hoping to catch a glimpse of James.

"Hey!" Terra bounded up behind her.

"Hi, Terra." Anna smiled, happy to have found a friend in the crowd.

Rebecca, Luke, and Simon followed behind Terra. "Want to sit together?" Rebecca asked.

"Sure," Anna said.

The beat of a drum filled the air. They quickly seated themselves cross-legged on the ground while people around them also sat, creating several neat rows in front of the cottage. Daniel and Lara emerged from the small bungalow, and the crowd whooped as they smiled down at them. Lara wiggled her hips and spun around, clapping her hands. The people of Cups loved it, whistling and shouting even louder.

"All right, everyone." Daniel held his palms facedown in front of him to signal it was time for quiet. "We've got a lot to discuss today, so let's start with some exciting news. We've received word from Topper." The crowd went silent. "And he's arrived safely in the nearby land of Pentacles!" A cheer erupted.

Anna shifted her position and cast her eyes to the ground.

"Yes, he's a brave soul, that one," Daniel said. "If you'd like to read the letter he sent to us, come visit me after the meeting." He smiled at the crowd. "Before we get to official business, we'd like to take a moment to welcome Anna. Anna, can you come up here? Where is she?" Daniel shielded his eyes and scanned the group. Anna's eyes widened, and she ducked her head.

"It's okay. It'll be quick." Terra squeezed Anna's shoulder and stood up beside her. She rummaged through a cotton bag slung across her chest and pulled out a small wreath made of tiny white flowers. She gently placed it on Anna's head.

"Thank you," Anna said, surprised. "It's beautiful."

Terra smiled at her and motioned for Anna to stand up. She gave Anna a small hug before gently pushing her forward. Anna tiptoed her way through the rows of people, toward the front, where Daniel and Lara stood waiting.

"Here she is," Daniel said, gesturing to Anna. The group clapped, and Anna smiled awkwardly at them. "We're so happy to have you here, Anna."

"I'm so happy to be here." She was overwhelmed by her

emotions, missing her friends from home but knowing that she really meant what she said. Anna felt more at home in this enchanting land than she had all of her years in the Tower. These people welcomed her into their community without question, and Anna had already met so many confident, unique, and kind young people—the types of people Anna had always dreamed of having as friends.

"For any of you who don't know, Anna came from Pentacles, where Topper is visiting now." Anna stared out at the small sea of trusting faces, and that was when she spotted James. He was standing at the edge of the crowd against the trunk of a palm. He nodded at her, and she nodded back. "If you haven't met her, please do introduce yourselves," Daniel continued.

"We have discovered that Anna is a very talented seamstress," Lara added. She turned to Anna. "On behalf of the people of Cups, we'd like to ask you to be our new seamstress and dressmaker."

"As you all know, we trade off jobs, but if someone is especially gifted in a specific area, we like to give them the opportunity to share their gifts with all of us." Daniel pointed at Henry. "Like our favorite cook."

"And then that person can share their talents with others," Lara continued. She slipped her hand into Anna's and squeezed it tightly.

"We think this role is a good fit for you, Anna. But only if you agree," Daniel added.

"If you'll have me, I'll do it." Anna turned to the people seated, squeezing Lara's hand back and then letting it drop. She took a small step forward. "Just let me know what you need. You've all been so welcoming." Anna's voice caught, and her chest swelled with emotions she couldn't express. They were giving her an official role in their family. She brushed her sudden tears away and smiled.

"Thank you," she went on. "Really. I can't say how much I appreciate all you've done for me." Anna found James in the crowd, his eyes twinkling as he met her gaze, the light from the setting sun sending waves of gold through his chestnut hair.

Daniel tapped Anna's arm and nodded in the direction of the crowd. Then Terra raised her arm and patted the place beside her while the crowd parted to let Anna return to her seat. Upturned faces, tan, young, and full of energy, smiled at her as she passed. Anna sat back on the ground and hugged her knees under her dress. A soft breeze blew off the sea, rocking the palm trees as the last rays of sun warmed her back.

"Gosh, Anna, you were awful," Rebecca said.

"Very awkward." Luke winced.

Anna's face dropped.

Rebecca giggled and patted her arm. "We're joking with you! You were glorious, of course," she said.

"Exquisite." Luke winked at Anna, and she laughed. Terra wrapped one arm around her and kissed her cheek while Simon gave her a thumbs-up and a smile.

Anna beamed and turned her attention back to the front of the crowd, happiness threatening to overwhelm her again.

Lara held a clipboard from which she called out jobs for the next moon cycle rotation. Kitchen duty, animal care, garden maintenance, fishing—every task that had to be done for Cups to run smoothly. As Lara shouted names, each person waved their hand in happy acceptance of their new role.

When Lara was finished handing out jobs, Daniel stepped forward. "Are there any grievances before we end?" Someone handed Anna a small square of paper and a writing instrument. She noticed people were passing them down every row.

"What is this for?" she asked Terra.

"You'll see in a minute." She smiled, her violet eyes sparkling.

"It's my favorite part of these meetings."

"No grievances?" Daniel's eyes swept over the crowd. Anna turned around, curious to see if anyone would respond, and she locked eyes with Ivy, who was staring daggers at her from a few rows back. Ivy rolled her eyes and turned away.

Anna felt her joy begin to wither inside her, and she tried to remind herself that Ivy was just one out of a hundred people.

"Write your wishes, the things you are grateful for, your deepest darkest secrets, and then fold them up tight." Daniel clapped his hands together. "When you're ready, tuck them into the mountain's face."

Two wishes immediately came to Anna's mind. That the Magician was well and safe back in the Hierophant's Kingdom and that the King would never find her. This land of free will and choice went against everything the King believed in, and she hated to think of the acts of violence he would commit if he ever found it.

Anna first chose to wish for the safety of her aunt, the only family she had left. She folded her square tightly as Daniel had instructed, and followed the others as they walked down the mountain face on the opposite side from where they'd climbed up. There were steep stairs cut into the rock, for which Anna said a silent thank-you. She had dreaded the thought of getting down the way they'd come, especially with the purple sky quickly fading to an inky black.

The wall of rock sat opposite the lush jungle, and was so shaded with trees that Anna had no sense of the sea or the emerging stars. The air was cool and fragrant, and the canopy of green and the orange glow of lit torches made the site feel mystical, a quiet place of peaceful reflection.

The people of Cups collectively wedged their pieces of paper in the side of the mountain—any space in the rock that they could find, and Anna marveled at how many slips of paper were already tucked away. It looked to Anna like years and years of wishes, gratitude, and secrets.

Anna stood on her toes, wedging her wish in a high-up gap.

"Was that a wish for another lesson?"

Anna spun around. James stood behind her, his arms crossed.

"What else would I possibly wish for?" Anna questioned. "Gulping seawater, burning muscles, hunger that can't be satisfied."

"Hunger that can't be satisfied?" James raised his eyebrows.

Anna coughed, feeling the heat of a blush crawling up her neck.

James cleared his throat. "I have something to ask you." He stood up straighter and uncrossed his arms. "Would you have a meal with me? Just the two of us?"

Anna brightened. "That sounds much more fun than swimming." Something within her stirred, and Anna wondered if Lara was right about James's interest in her.

James wrinkled his nose in mock disappointment. "Then you might be devastated to hear that we have to skip our lesson tomorrow. I'm helping plant this season's coffee crop." James ran a hand through his hair and looked up at Anna. "So how about dinner instead?"

Anna stiffened. "Yes," she blurted, too stunned and, she admitted to herself, too utterly delighted to say more.

"I *knew* he liked you!" Lara squealed. She was poking around Anna's new sewing room after dinner. "Can I try it?" Lara pointed at Anna's loom.

"Of course," Anna said, eying her. "You really think he does?"

"Almost certainly," Lara confirmed. She took a seat in front of the loom. "Are you coming out for tonight's ride? Or are you weaving something for your dinner outing with James tomorrow night?" She waggled her eyebrows.

"Well, since I don't know how to ride a horse, it's probably weaving for me." Anna picked up a nearby spool of thread and began to unwind it.

Lara looked down at the loom and screwed up her face. "This looks very complicated. How does it work?" She ran her hands over the warp beam and lightly touched her fingers to the harness.

"This longer piece here . . ." Anna walked over to Lara and pointed to a wooden part toward the center that ran the length of the loom. "See how it's cylinder-shaped?"

Lara nodded.

"The warp ends are wound here for weaving," Anna explained.

"What is a warp?" Lara raised her eyebrows.

Anna reached for a nearby piece of fabric and held it up to Lara. "If you look very closely, you can see the lines where the fabric interlocks."

Lara squinted. "Oh, I see it!"

"When I weave, the yarn is interlaced in two different directions. The one that runs down the fabric is the warp." Anna ran her finger down the length of the fabric. "And the one that runs across the width of the fabric is the weft." Anna looked up at Lara. "Does that make sense?"

Lara stood up. "I think it does, but the fact that you can do *this*"—Lara took the piece of fabric from Anna and scrunched it in her hand—"and actually make something . . ." She shook her head. "It makes riding a horse seem so easy." Lara looked back down at the loom and let out a low whistle. "You just hop on it and tell it to go."

Anna laughed. "I'm sure it's more complicated than that. Weaving just takes practice."

"If you say so," Lara demurred. "I could stay up here with you tonight. We could do something besides riding a horse for the first time in the dark, which I'm guessing you're probably not too keen on."

"Definitely not," Anna agreed. "But I liked your idea of staying in and making something new for tomorrow night. I found a metallic thread in the box of supplies Daniel gave me, and I've wanted to try it out."

"I love metallic colors." Lara narrowed her eyes. "But I wouldn't go too fancy," she suggested.

Anna scrunched her nose, realizing she had no idea what to wear for the occasion. "Am I hopeless?"

"No," Lara backpedaled. "You're just new to the ways of courtship in Cups. If you haven't noticed, we live and breathe the ocean, so the less restrictive the clothing, the better." She knitted her eyebrows. "Then again, you just witnessed my complete lack of weaving skills, so what do I know?"

"No, I think you're right," Anna decided. "What about a small top—something cropped—and a short, flowing skirt?"

"Yes." Lara glowed. "I'll take one of those too, when you have the time." Lara grinned mischievously.

"My first official order as seamstress." Anna beamed.

"I'm going riding now, but don't work too hard, my little hermit. I'm coming to get you early for the crop planting tomorrow."

As Lara walked through the door, Anna called to her. "Thank you so much for today, on the mountain."

Lara poked her head around the doorframe. "We're glad

you're here. You're like the missing puzzle piece we were wait-ing for."

Anna stood up from her loom, stretching her fingers and bending her wrists up and down. Her new, and decidedly casual, outfit hung on a chair next to her.

Anna focused on her most recent work—a woven version of the Fool in his best tunic, velvet and covered in moons and stars, holding his onyx staff with its crimson feather. She depicted him nearly walking off a cliff to show how he traveled through the world with such complete faith, but little Bembo was there at his feet to shepherd him to safety.

The Fool had given her a bit of that faith. She didn't even know she had it in her until she thought of all the risks she'd taken. Leaving the Tower. Running through the woods on her own while the King gave chase. Stepping into the water with James. Accepting the job as seamstress. Creating a new life in a new land, knowing that, should the King find her, it could all come to an end.

20

"I really wish I could take your hand right now." The Fool and Drake sat on a thick wool blanket, watching the Magician from their perch on a small hill overlooking a shallow valley of snow-covered grass. The three of them had ridden out earlier that day, under the watchful eye of Barda, until they found a large, flat expanse of land where the Magician could practice her magic.

"You know that's not possible." Drake cast his eyes toward Barda, who stood at the top of the field, arms crossed, eyes glued to the Magician. The air was wet and cold, and a layer of fog hung thick over the horizon.

"Of course," said the Fool.

"It makes me nervous when you speak like this outside of our chambers. We could be put to death. We *would* be put to death," Drake pressed. He sat up a little straighter and moved farther away from the Fool.

"I understand," the Fool said. "It was just a wish."

Drake turned to face him. "You're my everything," he said in a tight whisper. "You do know that."

"I do," the Fool said. "I'd like everyone else to know it too." He reached into the picnic basket they'd brought and grabbed an apple. "In a perfect world." He stared down at the fruit, not the least bit hungry. "And you should have worn a hat. Your head is going to freeze." The Fool glanced at Drake's shaved blond head, closely cropped to mimic the King's signature style.

Drake admired the King. All he had ever wanted was to be a knight in the King's Guard. Growing closer to the Fool complicated these ambitions and had broken Drake's focus.

He wished he could grab the Fool, hold and reassure him, but he couldn't change the laws of the kingdom. He loved the Fool with all his heart, but sometimes he wished he would just accept the way things were.

The Fool took a hard bite into the apple and turned his attention back to the Magician, who was swirling her wand around as Bembo chased the blue light crackling from its tip.

"He thinks it's a game of fetch," Drake called to the Magician, trying to lighten the mood.

"I'm going to turn him into a cat for my first trick!" the Magician yelled back.

"Don't you dare," the Fool warned.

"Why don't you make him a little friend to play with?" asked Drake.

The Magician nodded. She pointed her wand at a snow-dusted boulder and muttered an incantation.

A silver wolf emerged, taking the rock's place.

"Stars!" the Fool said, jumping up and sliding down the icy hill in his attempt to reach Bembo.

"Oh my!" The Magician grabbed the little dog and waved her wand at the magnificent wolf, who transformed into a boulder once more.

"That was not funny!" the Fool yelped, wrenching Bembo from the Magician's arms.

"That's not what I meant to do. I'm a little clumsy right now," the Magician apologized.

"Well, I'd rather not be eaten while you're figuring it out," Barda grumbled.

Unbeknownst to all of them, the King was watching from the wood. He hadn't set out to spy; he was on his morning ride and had happened upon the Magician's practice. When he saw the silver wolf, he remembered a night long ago, a night he had tried to bury deep in his memory.

The King had awoken in his chambers and the Queen was not there. She was a restless creature, often wandering the castle, but the King was not a stupid man and this absence was not merely restlessness.

He put on a robe and went to find her.

In those days, he was not so heavily guarded, so he roamed the castle halls by himself, searching for her. His heart beat rapidly in his chest, the way it did when his intuition got ahead of his consciousness.

The King rounded the corner to where an eerie blue light swirling with tiny stars spilled out of the doors to the great hall. He tiptoed through the entrance, feeling like a snooping child. It was a large, rectangular room, narrow and much longer than it was wide. And it was filled with giant beasts. Coarse-haired golden lions, black bears, and silver-haired wolves. Beasts conjured by magic.

Snow fell in giant diamond-like flakes throughout the great hall, despite the warmth of the fire that roared on the stone hearth.

Then the King saw them. They were sitting in front of the massive bay window overlooking the gardens. She sat on his lap, her hand in the air, trying to catch the snowflakes. Marco's skin glowed white against his black shock of hair, and he gazed up at her, blue light reflected in his giant black eyes.

He whispered into her ear, and she threw her head back in laughter.

Perhaps they're just having a bit of fun, the King lied to himself.

But then Marco took the King's beloved in his arms and kissed her passionately, and to the King's horror, she kissed him back.

The King felt stripped of his skin. Betrayed by his best friend and his wife. His hands clenched in fists of anger. Hurt and humiliation hit him so hard, he stumbled backward.

"Okay, we'll call things out, and you conjure them!"

The King unclenched his fists as Drake called out to the Magician.

"Some wine to go with our picnic," suggested the Fool, who had settled back down on the blanket. "I'm getting thirsty." The Magician frowned, pointing her wand at the edge of the Fool's blanket, where a cask of wine materialized.

"Ha!" cried the Fool, delighted.

The memory of Marco's betrayal hung heavy in the King's chest, squeezing his lungs. The King observed Barda, who did not take his eyes off the Magician.

Good, he thought. Here was Marco's sister, and the King was encouraging her to hone her magic. But what if she, like her brother before, betrayed him?

The King turned his steed around. He'd seen enough. The Magician had a long way to go before she progressed from wolves and wine to entering another world. But she was his only hope.

21

"Too fancy?" Anna stood before Lara with her arms spread wide. Lara let out a low whistle. "James will be speechless."

The light in Lara's bathroom glowed a brilliant orange as the sun set over the ocean and illuminated Anna, who turned to face the mirror, studying her appearance. She raised a hand to her head, stroking the long, neat braid Lara had given her.

"Thank you for doing my hair. It's beautiful."

"Anytime, Anna. It was like plaiting silk." Lara tugged lightly on the end of Anna's braid. "Did you have fun today? I was over at South Farm for most of the afternoon—I hope Rebecca and Daisy took good care of you."

"I learned so much. They put me in charge of herbs, and I am proud to say I planted cilantro—which I didn't even know existed—and basil." Anna scrunched up her face, looking toward the ceiling and counting on her fingers. "Lemon balm and calendula as well. I can't wait to see them bloom!"

"And I can't wait to smell them." Lara closed her eyes and took a deep breath in. "Those are some of my favorites."

The light in the room was quickly disappearing as the sun became a thin line of pink on the horizon. Anna shivered with nervousness. "The sun is setting. I'm supposed to meet James down at the beach." She set her shoulders and sighed.

"Off with you then." Lara shooed Anna toward the door to the patio stairs, smiling wistfully.

New love, she thought as she watched the sun vanish into the sea.

"Wow." James had combed his hair into submission and was wearing a light-blue shirt that Anna hadn't seen before. He almost looked nervous.

Anna bit her lip. "You don't look so bad yourself."

"We're riding tonight," he declared.

"Only if I am riding with you." Anna frowned. "I can't hide it any longer. I am no horsewoman."

"Yet," James corrected.

"Yet," she conceded. His eternal optimism was infectious.

James stuck his fingers in his mouth and let out a piercing whistle that made Anna jump. Luke emerged from the shadow of the palms, leading James's giant black horse by the reins. He handed them over to James.

"Thanks, Luke."

Luke dipped his head. "Anna, you look positively ravishing tonight. You two have a good evening."

James gave a sly smile and Anna giggled. He had obviously put some thought into this night.

Anna scrambled onto the horse behind James and delicately placed her arms around his waist.

"You're going to have to hold on a lot tighter than that, Anna," Luke warned from the ground.

She grasped James's waist tighter and looked up at the night sky, where the sun had been replaced by a glowing half-moon. Anna thought of her father's legend and imagined him seeing her off to dinner.

James spun his head around and followed Anna's gaze skyward. "I don't think I've ever seen it that bright. And it's not even full."

When Anna and James reached their destination, they dismounted in front of a ramshackle fishing cottage painted powder blue, the eaves strung with small metal lanterns. It was the most charming house Anna had ever seen. Like the villa, the cottage faced the sea, but it was much smaller and flanked by shorter, fuller trees that led into the jungle. A hammock hung between two palms to the right of the dirt path they had ridden in on.

"Do the wonders of this land never cease?" Anna marveled. She walked over to a small copse of trees with small fruits nestled among wide, yellow-green leaves. "What are these called?" She pointed to the fruits. "They look like little grapes."

"Sea grape trees. The birds love them," James said, pulling off a small bunch and popping a grape into his mouth. He tossed one to Anna.

She ate it immediately, and her face lit up, enjoying the burst of flavor as she crushed the grape between her teeth.

James reached for her hand, and Anna paused. For a second she considered what her hand might feel like. Sticky from the grape? Clammy from nerves? She hoped James wouldn't notice the heat rising to her face as she took his hand.

He led her behind the cottage to a lush green garden blooming with colorful plants and flowers, illuminated by the flickering lanterns.

"Did you plant all of this?" Anna asked. They were still

holding hands as they walked through shorter pigeon plum trees and wild guava bushes decorated with fruit the color of red wine and small pink flowers with thick, waxy stems.

"I did," he answered. He rubbed his neck, and a lock of brown hair fell into his face. "This is my . . . escape. When I just need time to myself."

James dropped Anna's hand and motioned in front of him. Anna moved forward, picking her way through purple orchids and shrubs of firebush, bright with the pinky orange of coral. She fingered the strange, bright fruit.

James knelt beside her on the ground. "That's the hummingbirds' favorite," he stated.

Anna spun around. "What you've created here . . ." She paused, searching for the right words. "It's magical."

James let out a sigh of relief and stood up straight. "Thank you, Anna."

They kept walking, and Anna discovered that tucked among the rows of colorful plants were wooden statues of animals she hadn't seen in Cups—elephants, bears, tigers—creatures from all corners of the world that she'd read about in her favorite childhood books.

"How did you make these?" Anna asked, tilting her head as she ran her hand over one of the statues.

"Can you keep a secret?" James asked.

Can I? Anna thought. *All too well.* She nodded.

"First, dinner." James pulled a mango from a nearby tree and peeled the skin with a wooden knife. He sliced it into pieces and offered them to Anna.

The flesh was velvety soft, and her mouth watered at the sweet taste of the fruit.

James motioned for her to follow him into the cottage, where he had laid out a small feast on a long wooden table just inside the door. There were skewers of grilled chicken, plantains—roasted and laid on their long deep-green leaves—a plate of leafy greens, bowls of coconut pudding, and two goblets of wine.

"This is so beautiful," Anna said breathlessly. "Thank you, James."

"You like it?" he asked, looking uncharacteristically sheepish. "I have to confess, I had a little help."

"It's incredible," Anna assured him. "My compliments to your team." She reached for the goblet first, feeling bold. James followed suit, and they both took a sip. Anna had never had wine before, and at first she winced at the tangy taste it left on her tongue. But after another sip, she felt a pleasant warmth begin to spread down her throat and into her chest.

They stood awkwardly and Anna scanned the rest of the room, waiting for James to break the silence.

The whole cottage was one open space, the front walls made up entirely of windows that faced the sea. In the corner sat a small kitchen comprising a long, thin counter, a washbasin, and a woodstove. A neatly made bed was pushed into another corner, and a table with a few mismatched chairs sat in the center of the room. It was much cozier and more rustic than the sprawling bright white villa.

James reached for a book from a shelf above the bed and held it a moment before offering it to Anna.

Her eyes flashed with surprise when she saw that it was the book her three advisors had read to her over and over as a child. The pages were filled with animals said to walk the fabled lands that lay across the sea from the Hierophant's Kingdom.

It began with the battle between a great magician (who Anna now knew was her real father) and the Hierophant King. Their war had left a great crack in the land. Without magic, the fissure could not be repaired, and many animals were left stranded on the other side. After months of torrential rains, the crack filled with water and transformed into an angry rushing river. Some of the animals attempted to cross it, but none succeeded. From then on, those left roamed the land alone, never to be seen by a human in the King's land again.

The book was full of fantastical and wonderfully detailed illustrations that Anna had loved as a child. She wondered how such a book had come to be in James's possession.

Anna ran a hand over her favorite page. Large gray elephants with wrinkled skin and flapping ears tramped through a flat yellow field. "The pictures are lovely." Anna passed the book back to James. "Where did it come from?" She scrutinized his face.

"Topper lent it to me from his library." James carefully placed it back on the shelf.

"Library?" Anna perked up at the idea of browsing a room full of books.

"I'll take you there when he returns," James said. "But for now that feast is calling, and it won't stay warm forever."

James took a seat in the middle of the long table. Anna looked at the book for a moment longer before she turned to join him.

"I think you just snorted," James teased. They had opened the front door, and a warm evening breeze blew in. Their plates and wine goblets were empty, and Anna found that everything James said sounded like the funniest thing she'd had ever heard.

"I did not!" Anna insisted, though she had definitely let out a small snort in a fit of uncontrollable giggles just seconds before.

She grabbed James's arm across the table, feeling emboldened by the warmth of the wine, which had made its way down to her toes. "James, why don't you have a tattoo?" Anna stared at the place on his forearm where she had spotted Daniel's inked cup.

"I do," James said. He considered Anna through narrowed eyes. "Hidden from view."

Anna's mouth opened. "It's on your bottom, isn't it?"

"Ooh, close. Do you want to see?" James raised his eyebrows.

Anna's cheeks reddened. "No. I mean, I'm sure you have a wonderful bottom, but—"

"It really is wonderful, Anna," James said with mock seriousness. They both erupted into giggles, and Anna snorted again. James sat up and pointed his finger at her, which only made them laugh harder.

When they recovered, both wiping tears from their eyes, James stood and waved for Anna to follow. His face relaxed into a soft smile and his eyes locked on Anna. She made her way around the table, her heart racing. They faced each other, and James swept back a stray hair that had come undone from her braid. He ran the tips of his fingers down her cheek and smiled at her.

Anna could barely breathe. She closed her eyes and felt his lips, soft and gentle, on hers. As James ran his hand lightly over her stomach where her top stopped, she drew in a sharp breath.

He pulled her close to him, and Anna stumbled. He caught her and smiled. "Bed?" James nodded toward the corner. "More comfortable."

"Bed," Anna said. She twirled across the room, the breeze lifting her skirt above her knees. James sat down, and Anna landed in his lap. He ran his fingers down her neck and over her collarbone while his other arm wrapped around her waist. Anna squeezed his shoulders in response. They stared at each other for a moment. He leaned in and kissed her, and she kissed him back, exploring the feel of his full lips. James ran his tongue lightly over hers and moved one hand down her body to stroke her calf. She thought he tasted like wine and coconut.

Anna pulled away gently, shifting off him and onto the bed so that they were seated side by side but facing each other. She stood up.

"Are you okay?" James looked up at her, surprise on his face.

She grabbed for his hands. "I'm good." She meant it. "It's just a lot all at once."

He stood up, still holding her hands, and leaned in close. "Do you want to spread it out a little?"

Anna nodded and pressed her lips to his softly, holding them there for a few moments before pulling away.

"I can certainly live with that," James said, nuzzling his nose into her neck. She shivered with pleasure.

They rode back to the villa beneath the light of the Moon, and Anna held on to James tightly, her head leaning against his back. When they reached the beach in front of the house, James pulled the reins.

"Ho!" James said. The horse stopped, and he got off and then helped Anna down. "Are you okay to get in by yourself? I need to put her back in the stable, but I can tie her up and come back later." He had one hand on his horse, and the other was gently rubbing Anna's arm.

"I think I can make it back from here." Anna laughed. James put his hand around her waist and pulled her to him one more time. "Goodnight," she said, and began to climb the villa's front steps without looking back.

When Anna reached her room, she found she was singing softly to herself. It was a song about spring blooming and people falling in love, a tune the Fool had taught her many years ago. She was surprised to find she remembered the words. She hugged herself, giddy from her night with James, and spun over to her satchel, lifting it with a grand sweep of her arm. She retrieved her stack of tapestry squares and did a few small pirouettes out onto the patio, still humming.

She lit a lantern and stretched out on the patio's cushions, staring out at the ocean, listening to the waves gently roll in, kiss the shore, and roll out again. The Moon cast a pearly sheen on the black water. Anna tossed her tapestry pieces out in front of her and then closed her eyes tightly, letting her hand travel over them until she suddenly stopped and grabbed the tapestry beneath her outstretched fingers.

Anna opened her eyes and studied the image. It was two people drinking from the same golden goblet. A rainbow of butterflies burst from the cup, tangling in the girl's flowing hair and landing on the boy's shoulders. The rest of the scene had been cut off, but Anna remembered weaving this tapestry in the Tower, back when she'd dreamed of love but never thought she'd experience it. She held the piece to her chest and thought of James. A quiver of euphoria, warm and golden, snaked through her spine, causing the thin hairs on her arms and neck to stand up. She couldn't wait to see him again.

The sun was rising, casting streaks of blue and pink through the sky. Anna was grateful to be sitting on her comfortable bed, knowing that, at any moment, she could run outside and greet the dawn. She ran her fingers over her lips, remembering her evening with James.

She quickly bathed and put on Lara's swimsuit. She was going to surprise James by finally being ready for their lesson. This time he would not have to chase her down.

Anna wrapped her hair in a bun, threw on the green cover-up, and crept down the hall, looking for his room. She knew it was on the first floor somewhere. She made a few wrong guesses, opening doors and finding bodies splayed out on beds, lost in dreams and early morning slumber.

She came to the last door at the end of the hall and quietly opened it, her heart thumping with the anticipation of seeing James.

It took a moment for her to process what she found on the other side.

A slim, tanned leg stuck out of the covers, and piles of white-blond hair spread over the pillow.

Ivy.

On the other side of the bed, James slept soundly. Anna's heart caught in her chest.

She started to back away, but she collided with a stool, and it fell over with a loud thump. James jumped up. "Anna?" His face broke into a smile, but it faltered when he noticed her horrified expression. "What's wrong?" He glanced at the space next to him on the bed where Ivy was sleeping soundly. "Damn it, Ivy," James mumbled, throwing the covers off him. "Anna, this isn't—" But Anna was already running down the hall.

Shock and disappointment tore at her insides. "How could I be so stupid?" she berated herself, dashing out of the villa and down the stairs to the beach. Her lungs burned and her legs ached as she pushed herself to run as far as she could down the beach, finally stopping when she reached the swimming cove.

Out of breath, she stared at the sea, anger and embarrassment threatening to spill the tears that brimmed in her black eyes.

The water around her started to ripple, and the wind picked up, slowly at first. Anna squeezed her eyes shut against the hair whipping at her face. The ripples offshore gained momentum and turned into waves that surged up the beach and crashed onto the sand before being pulled back out to sea. A buzzing sound permeated the air.

"Anna! Get back!" James was calling to her from down the shore, but she could barely hear him. The waves were building up and cresting before cascading down and leaving a white tuft of foam at Anna's feet. James cupped his hands and screamed, "Anna!"

Anna's eyes flew open, and she saw with horror the rushing sea in front of her. James sprinted down the beach, grabbing Anna by the waist and pulling her away as a massive surge of seawater struck the sand.

22

The King was playing chess with Senator Bassett in his chambers, while outside, a light snow fell onto the grounds of the Keep. He pressed the heels of his palms to his eyes and inhaled deeply. Bassett had just bested him and taken his bishop.

"Someday I am going to beat you," the King said.

"Of course you are, Sire." Senator Bassett did not take his eyes off the board.

"I appreciate that you never let me win." He struck his fist on the table and swept the pieces to the floor, eyeing Bassett.

Bassett, immune to the small tantrum, looked directly at the King. "I know. And that is why you never do," he said, his crooked smiled revealing a row of yellow teeth. "Sire, may I broach something with you? Something delicate?"

"When you've just beaten me again? Coming at me from both sides, are you?"

Bassett waved a hand over the board. "It's important. Or, at least, it could be."

The King gestured for Bassett to go on.

"I keep thinking about the girl's escape. She must have gotten word of the execution." Bassett put a finger to his lips. "It's quite a coincidence that she decided to run away only minutes before she was to be put to death."

"I broke my promise to free her. I imagine the disappointment pushed her over the edge. You don't see it the same way?" The King began to twist his pentacle ring, his attention fully on Senator Bassett now.

"I've been combing over the details of the night before," Bassett said. He leaned in toward the King. "The Fool was here."

"No," the King stated. He cleared his throat and pushed himself back from the table, standing up. He didn't like where this was going.

"But he offered to bring that creature up to play with you."

The King gave him a warning look. "I see where you are going with this, but it is not his nature," he batted back. He twisted the giant silver ring on his index finger, feeling the heat of anger stir in his chest.

An awkward silence fell over the room, and the King looked out the window at the snow, falling harder now, blanketing the grounds of the Keep in soft white.

Senator Bassett got up. It felt disrespectful to sit while the King stood. "But is it his nature to blindly protect the person he loves most?" the Senator ventured.

It was like a key opening a lock. Something clicked inside the King, and the Senator stood by, watching, a smug look of satisfaction spreading across his face.

23

James peered out at the thrashing sea. Anna wiped her tears and stared at him, wide-eyed.

"Is it supposed to do that?"

"I don't know," James answered honestly. "We've never had waves crash this close to shore before."

They watched the sea slowly calm again until the last of the waves were ironed out and the water was once again a flat expanse of blue. Anna's heartbeat slowed. James took her in his arms, and she fell into his embrace, too spent to resist.

"That wasn't what it looked like," James said, seeming to forget the storm that had just stopped as quickly as it had begun. "Ivy and I have had a complicated relationship for a long time. She used to sleep over." He hesitated.

Anna broke away from James's grasp. "It's fine," she said. "I'm too innocent for you."

James furrowed his brow. "That's not fair. And it's not true."

"I just found you in bed with a naked girl who hates me," Anna retorted. "How do you think that looks?"

Anna stood with her arms wrapped around herself while James mulled over her question. She wanted to walk away, make a dramatic exit, but she was rooted to the spot, awaiting James's explanation.

"We're not together anymore. But I think it's hard for her. I know it's hard for her. She didn't want it to end."

Anna wondered if they'd ended things because of her, and James seemed to read her mind.

"It's been over for a while now, but when you came—that settled it for me. And it's probably why she came into my bed last night. A last grasp at what we used to be." James sighed. "Ivy's confident and she knows what she wants, and maybe I could've been clearer about what *I* want and don't want from her." He ran a hand through his hair. "But nothing happened. I swear. I didn't even know she was there until you came in this morning."

Anna looked at him closely. "I'm not sure if I should believe you."

"I don't want to hurt you, Anna, but I also don't understand why you're so upset. It's scaring me a little." James shuffled his feet in the sand. "We just met." He grabbed Anna's hands and squeezed.

Anna ripped them away, the color in her face deepening, anger searing through her. She wished she'd walked away before, in the silence before James spoke the embarrassing truth.

"I'm sorry I don't have as much experience as you." Anna gestured at James. "I was so isolated, you have no idea. So if I'm too *intense* for you—"

"You're not, Anna. I shouldn't have said that." James put his head in his hands and took a deep breath. "Will you forgive me? I guess I would be pretty upset if I walked in on you this morning and someone was in your bed."

Silence again. Anna had no idea how she was supposed to respond to James's vacillating excuses.

"I'll have to think about it. And in the meantime, you should think about getting a lock for your door." Anna sat down on the sand and crossed her arms over her knees. She squinted out at the water, now bright and green as if nothing had happened. "A big one."

Later that morning, after a breakfast that she barely touched, Anna went to work at the stables, her assigned task for the day. She was surprised to find Daniel there when she arrived. Her first instinct when she saw him was to tell him about the waves that had almost crushed her at the cove just a few hours before. But the power and speed with which the storm came and went had unsettled her, and the idea of broaching the topic with the king of Cups was daunting. She was sure James would tell him anyway.

"Why do you do this job?" Anna asked Daniel, distracting herself from thoughts of her strange morning. "You could have other people take care of the animals." She couldn't imagine the Hierophant King caring for his own horse.

Daniel glanced up from the glossy brown steed he was grooming. "I like their energy. If you're patient enough to bond with an animal, it lasts for life. And the way they communicate is fascinating." He gently patted the horse. "They say so much with their eyes and their movements."

Anna was brushing a big white mare with long lashes and dark, serene eyes. The horse's ears twitched and her tail swished as Anna dragged the brush across her back.

"I also believe physical work keeps you grounded." Daniel tucked a lock of shoulder-length hair behind his ear.

"But you and Lara have so much responsibility."

Daniel nodded. "Everyone does. Responsibility should be shared." Daniel tossed the brush into a nearby bucket. "Ready to ride?"

They saddled up two horses, and Daniel helped Anna climb onto hers.

"Let's ride over to South Farm today and check on the new crops. We'll take it slow until you feel more comfortable. She's a gentle horse, you'll be all right."

Anna's thighs trembled against the horse's sides. She watched Daniel hop onto his horse with ease.

"We'll take the path through the jungle over to the other side of the island."

"Are there parts of Cups you haven't completely explored?" Anna asked as they began walking the horses. She tried to steady herself on the saddle, but her body rocked forward and backward with every step.

"Topper and I have explored every inch." Daniel steered his reins to the left and nodded at Anna for her to do the same. "Sit up straight and keep your thighs firm, Anna. You're doing great." He gave her a smile of encouragement.

"Did you want to go with him when he left for Pentacles?" Anna asked. If she kept talking she wouldn't have to think about all the things that could go wrong being up this high on a large animal she didn't know how to control.

"You're full of questions," Daniel said, not unkindly. "Let's pick up the pace." He pressed his legs into the horse's sides, pushing down and forward with his hips. In response, the horse began to trot.

Anna hesitated, holding tight to the reins. Then she mimicked Daniel's movements and, to her surprise, her horse broke into a light trot.

"Wanted? Maybe. But I needed to stay here and look after my people," Daniel said, glancing back at her.

Neither spoke as they continued on. Daniel wasn't much of a talker, and Anna was concentrating on riding. It seemed less complicated and potentially less life-threatening than swimming, but she still had to control her fear by breathing deeply and reminding herself that, if the King's witless guards could ride a horse, then so could she. She found herself wondering about the idea of exploring, a possibility that was never offered to her until now. She thought that she, too, would like to see every inch of Cups and maybe beyond. Perhaps she had this in common with Topper.

Their horses slowed as they came to a spot in the forest where a tightly interlaced canopy of green obscured the bright blue sky. Anna's horse kept pace with Daniel while her eyes wandered around the vast expanse of lush trees. She was barely aware of the huge creature beneath her, or the fear she had felt only moments before.

Anna was startled from her peaceful observation when an eerie whooping noise began to emanate from the trees. She pulled tight on the reins, reminded of the King's Guard and their signaling horns. The horse skidded to a halt, and Anna whipped her head around, frightened.

"Howler monkeys," Daniel called over his shoulder.

They let out another ominous call. Anna jumped. "Are you sure those are monkeys?"

"The sound is a bit unsettling if you're not used to it, but they're harmless." Daniel smiled warmly.

"When I left Pentacles, I was chased," Anna blurted. "They sound like the horns from the kingdom."

Daniel rounded back to join her, casting his eyes upward. "Look there." He pointed into a tree above them, and Anna saw a large, fluffy monkey the color of butter sitting on a high branch. He batted his eyes and swung his tail back and forth languidly.

"Oh, he's cute," Anna said, laughing as she looked up into the trees. The monkey responded by opening his mouth into a wide O and calling out. "There's another one," she said, her eyes fluttering around the jungle. A furry black howler swung down from the treetops.

"See? They're not so scary," Daniel reassured her. He squeezed his legs again, directing his horse back down the trail. "The path gets wider up here, and it's a great place to run the horses."

Anna blanched.

Daniel snickered. "It's a lot more comfortable than trotting."

When the canopy of trees opened back up, the sun flooded the widened dirt road and the warmth offered them relief from the cool damp of the jungle.

"Hang on and hug with your thighs, Anna." Just like James pushing Anna beyond her comfort level in the water, Daniel didn't coddle her when it came to horseback riding. He dug in his heels and cracked the reins. The horse took off at a run. Anna paused for a moment, nervous about giving the wrong signal.

"Sorry," she whispered in her horse's ear. Anna pressed her heels into her sides, and the steed cantered after Daniel's horse. Anna marveled at the freedom she felt—the two horses running in tandem while a steady breeze flowed through her hair and broke the relentless warmth of the sun.

Too quickly, they came upon South Farm, which was triple the size of West Farm. Daniel took her through the long aisles of green, pointing out plantains, large bushes of coffee with their bright red berries, and rows of sugarcane and cacao plants.

"This is where most of our food comes from," Daniel

explained. "We did a huge planting the other day."

Anna's eyes lit up. "Can it grow on its own?" she wondered, noticing that no one else was at the farm.

"We elect a few people to help out during the harvest and planting, but I manage it in the meantime. I can always pull some folks assigned to the villa garden or West Farm when I need extra hands. This is my personal project. I come by every few days to make sure the soil has enough moisture, and that the animals aren't eating more than their fair share." Daniel plucked a berry off a coffee bush and rolled it between his fingers.

"I'd never had coffee before I came here," Anna said lightly. "I was missing out."

Daniel smiled at her. "This is where it comes from." He walked his horse between the crops, and Anna followed beside him. "Speaking of where things come from, I'm curious to know more about you."

Anna halted. "What would you like to know?" She tried to keep her tone even.

"How did you come to live with the noblewoman?" Daniel pressed as they walked toward the farm's entrance. "We can head back to the stables; I'm satisfied," he said. They mounted their horses again and directed them back toward the jungle.

Anna decided to begin with the truth. "My mother died in childbirth."

Instead of running their horses down the wide path leading to the trees, Daniel and Anna allowed them to amble along at their own pace.

"She was the lady's maid, and I guess it was a big scandal that she was pregnant out of wedlock." Anna wove what she hoped was a convincing story, stringing together half-truths and things she'd learned about life in the Hierophant's Kingdom. "No one knew who my father was, and the noblewoman loved to always remind me that I was a worthless bastard."

Daniel's face fell. "You don't have to talk about this if you don't want to," he said.

"The lady had the other servants raise me until I was old enough to hold a broom, and then she put me to work." Anna hadn't even heard Daniel's offer. She continued, her voice tight with emotion. "But it was worse than being a servant because they had families of their own. I had no one, and she knew it."

"I'm—" Daniel paused, cocking his head to the side. "Do you hear that?"

Anna strained her ears. A low rumble hummed through the jungle.

"The monkeys?" Anna asked. They pulled their horses to a stop. Anna's snorted and tossed her head, eyes wild.

Daniel held up his hand. The rumble grew louder, and the wind picked up, lifting the leaves off the jungle floor and rippling through the trees. A strange buzz pierced the air. Anna clapped her hands over her ears, trying to hang on to the reins as the wind whipped around them.

"What's happening?" Anna yelled to Daniel. "Is it a storm?" She could barely hear herself talk above the rustle of the trees and the piercing buzz.

"Follow me!" Daniel shouted to her.

Anna tried to pull on the reins, but her horse was taking sporadic backward steps. She fought to keep her on course as the buzzing grew louder and the earth began to shake. Daniel's horse reared up on his hind legs, but he clutched his neck, managing to hold on. Anna's horse shook her head violently and whinnied in distress. She tried to grab on to her mane, but the silky hair slipped through her fingers and Anna slid off, hitting the ground hard. A sharp pain shot through her tailbone, making her eyes tear. She yelped as the steeds continued to stomp above her.

"Tuck your arms in and roll!" Daniel shouted, directing his horse away from Anna. He pulled the reins so vigorously that the leather ripped into his palm, splitting the soft skin open. "Damn it!" he yelled, wiping the blood on his pant leg.

Anna followed his instructions and rolled out of the way just as her horse reared up and her hooves pounded back down to the ground.

Then, as suddenly as it had come on, the shaking stopped. The wind died completely and the buzzing sound was reduced to a hum once more. Daniel jumped off his horse, holding his injured hand to his chest, and ran to Anna.

"Are you hurt?"

"I think I'm fine." Anna put her hand to her lower back and tried to stand up slowly. Her back was tender, but the shooting pain she had felt when she hit the ground was gone. She looked at the blood saturating Daniel's clothes. "You're bleeding!"

Daniel glanced at his hand. "It's worse than it looks." But his face was drained of color.

Anna ripped a strip of fabric from the hem of her dress. "Here." She took Daniel's hand and wrapped the fabric tightly around it. "What was that?"

Daniel shook his head. "It was as if the land itself were trembling."

Anna tied off the fabric. "That will have to do for now."

Daniel took his hand back and nodded to her. "Thank you."

Anna looked up at the still trees. "Does that happen here? Does the ground tremble like that?" Anna asked. The forest was eerily quiet. Even the monkeys had ceased their howling.

"We need to get back to the others." Daniel stroked his

horse's muzzle lovingly with his good hand. "I'm sure they felt it too."

Daniel held on to Anna's shoulder as she awkwardly helped him mount his horse one-handed. "Good thing you're tall," he muttered breathlessly once he was up. He took the reins in his good hand and glanced back at Anna over his shoulder.

"And no, that never happens here."

24

When they reached the beach, the sun was high in the midday sky and it seemed like all of Cups was there, swimming and sunning themselves. Thorn, Ivy, Daisy, and Luke were on the shore, playing the game with the ball and the hand cloths. Lara and Terra were floating in the water. Daniel and Anna stared at each other, perplexed.

"Did it really happen?" Anna wondered out loud.

"It must have," Daniel said.

They rode through the gardens and West Farm, but there was no sign of any disturbance. Anna helped Daniel put the horses back in the stalls and walked back toward the beach, Daniel a few steps ahead.

"It's like the ocean this morning," Anna mumbled.

Daniel whipped his head around. "What was that?"

"Oh." Anna flinched. "I went out to the cove early this morning with James, and there was a storm surge."

Daniel's mouth fell open.

"But we're fine," Anna assured him. "It was gone as soon as it had come."

He narrowed his eyes, studying Anna's face. "Anna, is there

something you're not telling me?" Daniel stepped closer to her. "These are dangerous events. You almost just got trampled, and you're telling me you nearly drowned this morning?" Daniel pointed his finger toward the ocean. "The entire population of Cups is out on the beach today. What if it happens again?"

Anna shrank beneath Daniel's unwavering gaze. "It came on so fast, I didn't—"

Daniel held up his non-injured hand, holding the other to his chest. "You can't hide things like this from me, Anna. Lara and I, we have a duty to protect Cups from outside forces that would harm us. We've worked hard to build our people's trust and respect."

Anna's lip trembled. *Outside forces.* For the first time, she felt isolated from the community that had so openly embraced her.

Daniel sighed. "James should've told me the second it happened," he said to himself.

"We had a fight. Don't blame him," Anna whispered.

Daniel wiped his brow. "I need time to talk this over with Lara. Truthfully, I don't have an explanation for what happened today, and that distresses me more than anything."

"Please, let me go get her. Your injury." She nodded to his hand, wrapped in her dress fabric, which was now soaked with blood. He nodded back, pale, a sheen of sweat covering his forehead. Anna turned on her heel, her lower back throbbing dully as she ran toward the water.

Anna had spent several quiet days working in the stables when she decided to join a small group on a trip out to sea. They were gliding along on a fine wooden sailboat built by the people of Cups.

"Thanks for coming." Lara looked back at Daniel, who was operating the boat, his injured hand now properly bandaged, with Luke at his side. "I needed to get him away. He's been so anxious since you two experienced that quake in the jungle."

"But nothing has happened since." Anna bit her lip and glanced at Lara. "It's been so calm."

Lara patted Anna's arm. "He just worries. I could barely get him out here for the morning. I wanted us to go for an overnight on one of the south beaches, but he refused."

James stepped onto the deck and plopped down behind them. "I can believe that," he said. "He wouldn't sleep a wink, so what would be the point?"

Anna threw a glance over her shoulder at James. He caught her eye and gave her a small smile, but she quickly looked away. She hadn't spoken to James since their argument at the cove, and she couldn't decide whether she was still angry with him.

"He's not sleeping as it is." Lara glanced back once more.

"How are you doing?" Anna asked carefully.

Lara wrinkled her nose. "It's hard to see him so anxious. I wish I could just make it all go away." She put up her hands and spread her fingers wide.

James and Anna nodded sympathetically.

"How's your back?" Lara asked. She picked up the hem of Anna's top and revealed an ugly cloud of purple-and-gray bruising.

"Anna!" James gasped.

Anna pushed her shirt back down. "It's fine. Just a little sore."

James looked at Lara, his brow furrowed with concern, but Lara shrugged.

"Let's moor at that cove!" Luke shouted, the wind sweeping his mop of blond hair from his face.

"We can have lunch there before we head back," Henry chimed in. Anna, James, and Lara stepped carefully to the back of the boat to join the others.

Lunch was crab sandwiches, fresh fruit, and cold wine. It was divine. The boys tossed a ball around while Anna sat on the sand with Lara, Terra, and Rebecca, letting the tide sweep over their toes. Even Daniel was not immune to the warm sunshine, salty air, and delicious food. Anna watched as he threw the ball to James, higher and farther each time despite having to play one-handed. She laughed as James jumped and dove, skidding through the sand to catch it.

After a particularly close catch, a very sandy James bounded up to Anna. "Join me for a walk?" he asked.

Anna looked at Lara, who gave a subtle nod and shooed Anna off with her hands. She stood up and wiped the sand off the backs of her legs.

James tossed the ball to Terra and gestured for Anna to walk with him down the beach. "It's a perfect day," James commented. The sky was a brilliant powder blue and the crystalline sea stretched out for miles in front of them.

"It is," Anna agreed, avoiding James's eyes. She worried her voice might betray her nerves if she said more. They walked in awkward silence until the rest of the group were just specks in the distance.

"Have you thought any more about what happened the other day?" James blurted. "I don't know how much time you need, but not talking to you is killing me."

Anna stopped and placed her hands on her hips, finally ready to look James in the eye. "I don't understand what you want from this." She gestured between them. "Things are over with Ivy, but I'm too much for you right now. It's confusing, James."

James placed a hand to his forehead. "I shouldn't have said that about you, Anna. I've liked you since the first moment I saw you. Poking around at the air like some kind of carnival mime."

She cocked her head.

"You know." James pushed an invisible wall with his hands.

Anna clapped a hand over her mouth, unable to control her giggles. She took a deep breath and set her shoulders. "Why didn't you tell Daniel about the storm at the cove?" Anna asked.

"I should have," James answered. "But you see how he is now. This is all Daniel will think about for months." He frowned. "I was going to wait until things cooled down, then talk to you first. I thought maybe we could figure it out together, if there was even anything to figure out." James smiled his warm smile, the one that made his eyes crinkle at the edges.

Anna was finding it harder and harder to stay mad at him.

"And another thing." James placed his hand lightly on Anna's shoulder. "Daniel takes his role very seriously, but sometimes it can cloud his vision. Whatever he made you think, Anna, none of this is your fault. He just likes to explore every angle of a situation."

She dropped her arms and took a step toward James. As he moved his hand from her shoulder to the small of her back, she jumped.

"Ouch!" She winced, gently touching her bruise.

"I'm sorry! I forgot," he said, pulling his hand away.

"It's all right." She moved closer to him, pressing her chin to his stiff, salty shirt and focusing on his sparkling green eyes.

James leaned down and gently pressed his lips to hers. Anna felt like she was melting, engulfed in his warm cedar-and-salt smell, tiny sensations of pleasure spilling down her sun-warmed shoulders. One of James's hands found the soft skin of her stomach beneath her shirt while the other found her outstretched fingers and they intertwined tightly. Anna kept her eyes closed as James's lips touched her cheek, then her jaw, then her neck.

His hand was sliding farther down to Anna's leg when someone shouted their names from down the beach. They broke apart, giggling and shuffling their feet in the sand.

"Race you back?" James narrowed his eyes at Anna.

Anna frowned and pointed at her bruised back.

A wide grin spread across James's face. He leaned down, scooped Anna up in his arms, and tore off down the beach.

25

The Fool sat at a small writing desk in his chambers. He had lit a fire and wrapped himself in a thick wool blanket to combat the cold. Bembo sat at his feet, head resting on his little paws and providing the Fool with some much-needed companionship while Drake was off training with the other squires and their cadre of knights.

He was attempting to write a new poem, and it was not going well. Ever since Anna had left he'd felt a giant space in his heart, in his day, where she had always been. The Fool tapped his feathered quill on the depressingly blank sheet of paper. He was stuck.

Suddenly Bembo let out a low, rumbling growl.

"What is it?" the Fool asked, leaning down to stroke the fluffy dog. Bembo shot to his feet and ran to the door. It was then that the Fool heard the heavy footfall of boots approaching his room.

"Bembo, go hide!" the Fool hissed. "Visit the Magician later. She will keep you safe." Bembo obediently jumped into the bed and burrowed under the covers just as the chamber doors burst open.

Two large guards stomped inside and grabbed the Fool by his arms. They dragged him from his chamber in his stocking feet, the wool blanket falling to the floor in a heap.

"Can I at least put on my shoes?" the Fool pleaded, but the guards ignored him, continuing to drag him down the cold stone hallway. They pulled him roughly down several flights of steep stairs as they traveled into the bowels of the kingdom. It quickly became clear to the Fool where the guards were taking him—the castle's dungeons. He wanted to scream, but he knew that, deep underground and surrounded by feet of stone on all sides, no one would hear him.

The guards finally stopped in front of a cell and shoved the Fool inside, slamming a heavy metal door behind them, leaving the Fool alone in the dark, dank cell. He crumpled to the floor and hugged his knees to his chest. Freezing, wet, and unable to see a way out, the Fool cried softly.

"Magician, if you can hear me, come get me," he whispered. The Fool concentrated on the thought, but his heart fell as he was hit with the realization that perhaps she, too, was being dragged down to the dungeons. Their plan was falling apart. He wondered if the Hermit had managed to escape, and how they were ever going to save Anna if they were all locked away.

The Fool heard faint voices outside, and for a moment he allowed himself to feel hope, but when the door clanged open, it was Senator Bassett, standing alongside a guard.

"Hello, Fool," he said with a wicked smile. "We have a few questions for you."

"And you had to ask them here?" The Fool's words came out in a strangled sob. "I need to see the King, you awful snake!"

Bassett chuckled. "Oh, he knows. He's the one who gave the

order." The Senator's expression turned sour. "Get him up," he snapped to the guard. The Fool scurried backward, but the guard was twice his size. He grabbed the Fool by the elbow and stood him up. The Senator delivered a brutal slap to the Fool's face.

"Just in case you're thinking of lying to us," the Senator said. "We will not tolerate anything but the truth."

The Fool gritted his teeth. "Can you at least give me the courtesy of explaining what this is about?" He wrenched his elbow from the guard's grip and shook out his hands, trying to think of what Drake would do if he were in this position. *He probably wouldn't have gotten himself into this position in the first place*, the Fool thought.

"This is about your colluding with the girl and helping her escape."

The Fool gasped and put a hand to his chest. "I did no such thing."

Bassett sneered. "Before this night is over, I will know the truth." He waved to the guard. "Bring them in."

The guard leaned out the door and signaled to someone in the hallway outside. Two more guards appeared, pulling off their close-fitting hoods.

"I want you to see how much I am going to enjoy this," one guard snarled.

The Fool felt his stomach churn with fear. "Please!" he yelped. "I can't believe you would suggest such a thing. Just let me see the King."

"The King is too soft and too quick to believe your lies. You'll deal with me." Senator Bassett stuck out his thumb. "After you deal with them. When they are done with you, you will tell us how the girl escaped and where she went."

"But I have no idea how she escaped." The Fool rushed

toward Bassett, and a burly guard pushed him against the wall.

"What a lovely boy," the guard jeered. "It would be a shame to ruin such a pretty face."

"Perhaps he's ready to talk. Look at him." A shorter, stockier guard jammed a finger at the Fool's chest. "He's already pissed himself."

"Nah, I think he needs a little more incentive." And with that, the bigger of the two men delivered a crushing blow to the Fool's stomach. The guard dealt another blow to the side of the Fool's head, knocking him off his feet. He felt his teeth tear at the soft skin of his cheeks and tasted the metallic tang of blood on his tongue.

Sprawled on the floor and unable to move, the Fool nearly nodded off into the sweet escape of unconsciousness. But before his eyes could flutter closed, the short guard dumped a pail of frigid water over him, forcing him to stay awake. The Fool curled into a ball, sure he was going to die from the kicks to his small, delicate frame, the jabs to his stomach with the guard's heavy boot, the strikes to his shoulders. He rocked on the floor, humming to himself, thinking of his little dog and his sweet face, wishing he could disappear into his silky white fur.

The torture went on for what felt like hours, and finally the Fool fell into a heavy black sea of oblivion. He floated free of his broken body and looked up at his old friend the Moon, Marco.

The Fool had helped a friend, an innocent. He had done the right thing.

He opened his eyes to a rough tugging at his scalp, disappointed to find that he had not truly left this land. Bassett crouched down over him.

"I'll tell you what you want to know." The Fool's voice was barely a whisper. "Then please, just kill me."

The guards lifted the Fool and carried him as one would a small child, winding back through the tunnels and up to the King's chambers.

"What have you done?" The color drained from the King's face when he saw the Fool. A look of horror and regret flashed across his features. "Was this necessary?"

Senator Bassett stood silent, arms crossed, flanked by the two guards from the cell.

The King knelt down next to the Fool. "Look at me, son. Will you tell me the truth?"

"She was brilliant," the Fool began, his eyes darting around the room, his speech slurred. "She created a world, a magnificent world. A place to escape from you and your rigid rules." Tears fell down the Fool's cheeks, and while his words ran like water, he kept the truth of how the Magician had helped Anna locked deep inside.

"I spied on you, and when I found out you were going to kill Anna, I told her." The Fool looked the King straight in the eye.

The King sucked in his breath. Senator Bassett clucked, unsurprised.

"How could you betray me?" the King demanded. "Have I not loved you like you were my own son?"

The Fool shook his head. "You were wrong. You were wrong to lock her up, to call for her execution. She is just a girl—an innocent." He spoke freely, knowing he would probably not live to see another day.

"How did she destroy the Tower? Where did she go?" the King pressed.

"I've no idea," the Fool answered honestly. "I warned her, and then I left the door open."

Bassett rushed toward the Fool, but the King held his hand up.

"Do you believe she is a powerful sorceress? That she destroyed the Tower with her magic?" The King tenderly pushed the Fool's blood-soaked blond curls away from his face.

The Fool thought of the Magician. "I'm sure she is the most powerful sorceress that has ever lived." His head lolled onto his shoulder.

The King took the Fool's limp hand in his own. "Just tell me you are sorry." His heart ached to see the Fool so weak and so broken.

"You had all the power in the world and no idea how to use it," the Fool whispered.

"You truly are a fool," the King said, letting the Fool's hand fall to the floor. "Take him back to the dungeons where he can rot."

"You said you would kill me," the Fool muttered. "Have mercy, Sire." The waves came, black and strong, and the Fool slipped away into darkness once more.

26

It rained every day and every night for nearly a week. At first the people of Cups were excited by the novelty of the murky gray sky, the nearly black sea. But then everyone began to grow restless.

"I feel like I'm going to jump out of my skin." James drummed his fingers on the table, and Anna gritted her teeth. She shot him a look and he paused mid-drum.

"Sorry." James winced.

Anna shrugged. While everyone around her was going nearly mad with cabin fever, she tried to remind herself that confinement could be much worse.

"Let's play a game," Anna suggested.

James looked at her warily. "I can't imagine anything we haven't already played. I don't see why Daniel won't let us go outside."

"The sun is about to set anyway. Maybe tomorrow," Anna said.

Anna looked out the rain-streaked windows of the common room and listened to the drops pounding on the roof. Dreary weather was common in the Hierophant's Kingdom, and while it had gone on long enough, Anna had found it strangely comforting when it started a few days back. The unrelenting sunshine of Cups made her feel like she was missing out if she rested.

"What's the game?" James asked.

Anna sat up and crossed her hands on the table. "I'll say something, and you have to tell me the first thing that comes into your head—no thinking. Then I'll say what comes to my mind from your answers."

"Fine, I'll play." He sat back up.

"Rain," Anna said. James rolled his eyes at her. She held her hands up. "I'm kidding." He cracked a smile. "In all seriousness— kissing." Anna raised an eyebrow.

James paused.

"No thinking!" Anna shouted.

"Touching," James said, leaning forward.

"Touching," Anna repeated.

"No thinking," James admonished her.

"Okay, okay." Anna scrunched up her face. "Feeling." Anna slid her clasped hands across the table.

"Skin," James asserted, reaching forward, his fingers grazing Anna's.

Anna was about to answer, when they heard a loud banging on the villa's two giant front doors. Everyone in the room went silent, and Daniel leapt up from a cushion on the common room floor. His hand was no longer bandaged. The healing wound ran down his palm in a puffy line of yellow and purple.

"Everyone is here, aren't they? Everyone's been accounted for?" He looked to Lara. She nodded, eyes shining with worry.

Anna felt a chill. Had the King finally caught up with her? She stood up and, without thinking, marched toward the front doors. James ran around the table and caught her hand, stopping her.

A deep voice shouted, "Anybody in there? I'm completely drenched!" Followed by more pounding. James dropped Anna's hand and rushed for the doors, a look of relief spreading over his face. Anna looked to Lara for an explanation, but she, too, was heading toward the villa's entrance behind Daniel. Anna followed closely behind them, hoping to get a look at the stranger. James reached the doors first and thrust them open.

A tall, painfully thin young man with nothing but a rucksack stood on the threshold, drenched.

"Topper! You made it home." Daniel ushered him inside and pulled him into a bear hug.

Anna's heart caught in her chest. Topper, the traveler who had actually been to Pentacles. She slowly backed away, hoping to get lost in the small crowd that was gathering around the front door.

James and Topper embraced, laughing and clapping each other on the back.

Topper shook out his wet yellow-blond hair. "I nearly didn't. The seas were rough, almost more than my boat could take. I don't think I've ever seen it rain this hard in Cups."

"You have no idea," Daniel said gravely, rubbing a hand over his face. "I'm so glad you're back."

As Topper walked farther into the room, Anna kept her head down, hoping he wouldn't identify her as a newcomer. But he was quickly descended upon by familiar faces in the crowd and showered with offers of baths, dry clothes, and a hot meal.

"Traveler," Anna whispered.

Trouble was the first word that came to mind.

27

"What's happened?" the Hermit asked, his eyes shut tight. He was sitting cross-legged beneath a large silver birch in the garden. The Magician shivered against the biting cold.

"The Fool is missing," she announced.

The Hermit's eyes flew open. "What do you mean, missing?"

"I found Bembo in his chambers barking his head off, and his staff was leaning in the corner. I did a few laps around the Keep, but I couldn't find him anywhere." The Magician covered her face with her hands. "This is all my fault."

The Hermit jumped to his feet and grabbed the Magician's shoulders. "Where could he be? Have you seen Drake?"

The Magician dropped her hands and sighed. "No, I haven't, and I have a very bad feeling. I've looked in the dining room, the library, and the kitchens. The Fool's not in any of his usual spots." The Magician bit her lip. "And he would never go for a walk without his staff, not to mention Bembo."

The color drained from the Hermit's face. "Do you think they know what we've done?"

The Magician huffed. "This worrying is not like you. You have to . . . get centered, or whatever it is you're always on about."

She pulled away from him and straightened her robes and cloak. "We'll make our morning rounds to the King as usual, and we can find out what's going on."

The Hermit took a deep breath and, as he was pulling his cloak over his head, something whizzed near his ear and then exploded in the birch's trunk with a loud thwack.

"What in stars' name was that?" The Hermit put a hand to his ear, which buzzed with heat, and whipped around to face the tree. An arrow had lodged into the trunk with a piece of parchment wrapped around the shaft.

"A message?" the Magician wondered, looking around suspiciously as she walked toward it.

"It almost took my ear off," the Hermit mumbled.

The Magician pulled the parchment off the arrow and unrolled it. The Hermit read over her shoulder.

> *Meet me in the beer cellar below the old buttery.*
> *NOW.*
> *—D*
> *Make sure you are not seen!*

"Drake?" whispered the Hermit.

The Magician nodded. She crumpled the parchment into a ball and threw it into the air while muttering, "*Fotayah!*" The piece of paper burst into flames and disappeared.

The Hermit stared at her.

"What?" The Magician cleared her throat.

"With no wand? No potions?" He raised his eyebrows.

She shrugged. "I've been practicing."

"And you don't feel sick?" He put his hand on her shoulder and eyed her closely.

"No, but I will start to if you don't remove your hand." She squinted at him in warning. "We need to go now."

The old buttery was tucked into the abandoned great hall, Whitehoof. A new facility had been built, and no one ever entered the neglected space, except for occasional servants looking for a quiet spot for a tryst.

The long narrow room was dusty and dark. The Magician and the Hermit walked side by side as they entered the quiet old hall.

"It's so eerie in here," the Hermit said.

"Supposedly this is where the Queen and Marco used to meet." The Magician raised her eyebrows.

"Oh." The Hermit nodded in understanding.

The Magician stopped at a door that seemed to appear out of nowhere halfway down the length of the massive room. She turned a dusty brass handle and it gave right away.

They found themselves in pitch-blackness.

"*Spatitha!*" the Magician hissed. A glowing ball of blue rolled in her hand, lighting up the windowless room.

"The beer cellar should be underground. Let's look for a stairway," suggested the Hermit.

The Magician held up her glowing ball and illuminated shelves filled with old wine barrels covered in dust. She waved her hand around until the light rested upon a set of old, rickety steps that led to an even deeper darkness.

"You go first; he likes you better," said the Magician, nudging the Hermit forward.

"But you're the one holding a glowing orb!" the Hermit argued.

The Magician handed the Hermit the ball. It was warm, and when the Hermit gripped it, he felt a little bolt of electricity prick his skin.

"Please go. You know I don't like the dark," the Magician pleaded.

The Hermit frowned. "For someone so powerful, you're awfully—"

A voice floated up the stairs from the darkness, making the Hermit and the Magician jump. "Would you two stop arguing and get down here?"

Drake appeared at the foot of the stairs with a lit candle. The flame flickered, casting wavy shadows on the staircase.

"Give me that." The Magician took her ball back and closed her fist over it. When she opened her hand again, the ball had disappeared. She pushed her way past the Hermit and hurried down the stairs to Drake.

Drake set the candle on a shelf in the small beer cellar as the Magician and the Hermit crammed into the small space. The stale smell of ancient beer and dust hung thick in the air.

"The Fool was taken by Senator Bassett this morning, and"—Drake's voice caught—"and he was tortured." He hung his head. The Hermit patted Drake's shoulder, but Drake shook him off. He took a deep breath. "He was severely beaten for information about Anna's escape."

The Magician clapped a hand over her mouth. "Is he alive?" she asked. She tried to make her voice even, but she was clenching her teeth against the tears that threatened to spill from her eyes.

"He is," Drake said. "Or he was this morning." Drake collapsed onto the dusty floor and gripped his hair with his hands. The Hermit and the Magician looked at each other in the flickering candlelight. "At target practice today I heard a guard bragging about how much he'd enjoyed beating the"—Drake sobbed—"'little, pretty Fool.'"

"I'll go to him," the Magician said. "I'll sneak into his cell tonight and take some of his pain."

Drake looked up from where he sat on the ground. He wiped the tears from his cheeks. "You can do that? But how will you get in?"

"You just leave that to me," the Magician assured him.

"Thank you for telling us, Drake," the Hermit said. "Now we all must get back to our respective posts. Act as if nothing has happened."

Drake stood up and cleared his throat. He wiped his eyes with the sleeve of his tunic and nodded. "Whatever you think we should do, I'll do it. Just get him out."

28

Anna was frantic. She ran upstairs and paced the length of her room, thinking of her inspiration for Pentacles. Had she dreamed of it? She must have heard or read the name in her studies, and had thought it was her creation.

She took a deep breath, trying to calm her nerves. What was the worst thing that could happen? Topper would expose her as a lunatic. Or a liar. A liar who had put an entire land at risk by letting them hide her while a tyrant pursued.

For a moment Anna considered running, but where would she go? The only person with any knowledge of how to leave Cups was the very person she was trying to avoid.

Anna ran to the foot of her bed, grabbing her satchel and pulling out her growing stack of tapestry pieces. She rifled through them until she came to the Hermit, whose likeness she had woven during the first day of unrelenting showers, completing the depictions of her three best friends and beloved advisors. She could really use the Hermit's guidance right now.

Studying the image of the solitary figure, she tried to interpret it through the mind of the Hermit himself. Perhaps his lantern was lighting a path to her inner self. If she closed her eyes and pictured that path, it led to a warm light emanating from her center. Her thinking mind was giving way to something bigger. She didn't have a name for it—maybe intuition? It was a place beyond thought, where spirit and instinct took over, and in this place she found a great sense of peace. Her mind became quiet.

Was this magic? Anna had never felt anything like it before.

She took in her surroundings as she shifted out of the almost trancelike state—the sound of the rain tapping at the windows, the smell of something sweet baking downstairs. Her eyes fluttered open, and the peace that had overcome her immediately evaporated as she thought of Topper and James and Daniel. Anxiousness crept back in. She padded across the floor to the door of her workroom, wrenching it open and marching to her loom.

Anna considered how she might represent the magical tranquility she'd felt in an image. In that moment Anna understood where her strengths lay—in her fortitude and resourcefulness. Whatever happened next, she would find a way through.

She chose a golden ball of yarn and set to weaving a lion with a mane that curled bright and orange like flames. There was a story about the strength and courage of a regal lion in the book that James had shown her in the cottage. She had loved the tale as a child.

While the other animals wept for what had been and the loss of home, the lion warned that their tears would cause another flood. He gathered all of the animals and gave them tasks. The zebras were to gather hay for shelter, the hippos were to carry the injured animals to safety, the rhinoceroses were to stand guard, the dolphins were to find sea plants in the floodwaters for them to eat, and so on. Soon the animals were too busy rebuilding a comfortable home for themselves to remember their sadness.

Next to the lion, she wove a young woman in a simple

frock. One of her hands sat gently upon the lion's massive head, while the other scratched under its chin. Anna wanted something of the Magician's unwavering confidence in the image, so she wove the infinity symbol above the woman's head. The Magician's gift to Anna, her necklace, had reminded Anna of her own strength in times of sadness and stress. The Magician once explained that strength traverses two worlds, the inner and the outer. Sometimes it meant drawing on intuition or instinct; sometimes it meant physical displays of power, and other times, it meant asking for help from others.

As Anna was binding her final thread, a sharp ray of sunlight fell across her loom, making the lion's mane shimmer. Anna looked behind her to find that the rain had finally stopped.

Anna ran down her patio stairs and out through her bathing room. The beach was crawling with people playing in the water, frolicking in the shallows, and tanning on the sand. She stepped onto the shore and looked out over the water, drawn to its glittering surface after being cooped up for so many days.

She took a deep breath and waded in carefully. The water was still and comfortable, so she tried to paddle, knowing she could stand at any moment if she needed to. Feeling emboldened by the fact that no one was watching her or judging her or pushing her, Anna walked out farther and slid on her back to float.

Her hair spread out in all directions like a glossy black starfish. The sun warmed her legs, her tummy, her eyelids. She silently thanked the Fool for his gift of spontaneity, which had pulled her into the water today. Anna let her mind wander, relishing how much she was changing now that she had the freedom to pursue her potential as a human being, as a woman, a friend, an artist.

She stayed like that for a long time, her eyes shut against the sun's bright rays, her limbs splayed, floating in the warm, sparkling sea.

"Look at you. I'm impressed."

Anna opened her eyes and saw James standing over her.

She turned over and stood up beside him, pushing back her long hair, slick and dripping with seawater.

"I feel like I should scold you for going out by yourself." James lifted one of Anna's arms and spun her around. "But you appear to be in one piece." He squeezed her shoulder, and she leaned in to his embrace.

"I wasn't going to go very far," Anna assured him. She ran her hand through the clear water.

"Your eyes are sparkling, Anna." James smiled at her.

Anna twirled in the water, splashing him and laughing.

"Can you come out, my little water sprite? I want you to meet someone."

Anna stopped twirling. She swallowed, her stomach tightening with nerves.

"Sure," she murmured.

James took her hand, and they walked through the water up to the beach where Topper stood, surrounded by a small throng of people. His bright blond head towered over them all.

"Maybe now isn't the best time. He looks busy," Anna hemmed.

At that moment Topper looked up and saw Anna and James emerging from the water. He moved toward them, the small group parting to let him pass.

"You must be Anna. I've heard a lot about you." Topper held

out his hand, and Anna took it. His smile was warm, his hand-shake firm but gentle.

"You too." Anna squinted up at him and found kindness in his eyes. She held on to his hand for an extra beat, making note of the softness of his palm. Her eyes locked on his, and she noticed small flecks of green among the glassy blue.

"All right then," James said cheerfully, breaking the spell between Topper and Anna.

"It's good to meet a fellow traveler," Topper said, letting go of Anna's hand. "I look forward to trading tales from the road."

Anna gave a small nod, not breaking eye contact.

James looked from Anna to Topper and back again.

"I forgot how charming you are, Top." James clapped a hand to his back. "We'll let you get back to this." He gestured to the people surrounding them and took Anna's elbow, leading her toward the water.

Anna glanced over her shoulder, hoping to get a last glimpse of Topper before the crowd swallowed him again.

"Are you doing anything right now?" James was watching Anna.

She turned to him, blinking. "Oh. Um, tons of things." She laughed. "What do you have in mind?"

"Would you like to join me at the cottage?" James asked. "I'm experimenting with dye for a project. Maybe you can take some of your fabric from the villa to test it out on?"

"Sure." Anna beamed at him. "I can't think of anything I'd like to do more."

"Fantastic." James clapped. "I'll get the horses."

Anna chanced one last look at the thickening pack surround-ing Cups's favorite traveler before squeezing the water out of her hair and running toward the villa.

When they arrived at the cottage, the early afternoon sun glinted brightly off the metal lanterns. The sea, washed from the rains, was green and calm. They tied up the horses, gave them water and carrots, and got to work setting up.

James gathered his collection of small animal carvings while Anna spread a cloth over his worktable in the garden. She found a box of glass jars filled with bold colors next to the table. Anna picked one up and examined its rich pink contents.

"This is a gorgeous color," Anna marveled. "How did you make it?"

James turned around. "Rebecca helped me with it." He walked over to Anna and took the jar from her. He shook it up. "It's made from strawberries, cherries, and roses, I think." He scrunched up his nose. "She knows so much more about plants than I do." He picked up another jar from the box, this one filled with a thick dark-green liquid. "Nettle and spinach. So brilliant, right?"

Anna leaned down and rummaged through the rest of the jars. There was purple from elderberries and mulberries, blue from red cabbage and blueberries, and yellow from marigold and goldenrod flowers.

"I bet we can mix them too," Anna said, gently swirling around the jar of blue dye.

"I bet we can," James agreed. "We just need to find something to put the dye in." He looked around the fragrant garden, then raised a finger and dashed inside the cottage, emerging with one of his beautiful wooden bowls.

Anna shook her head. "But won't we ruin it? The dye will stain. Do you have a bucket or a basin of some sort? Something less special?" James narrowed his eyes and ducked back inside. He emerged a minute later holding two tin buckets.

"The roof leaks." He shrugged.

Anna smiled at him. She twisted her hair into a bun and poured the jar of bright pink dye into one of the buckets. James did the same with the purple.

He reached for the statue of the elephant on the table. "I was thinking we could use these to stamp the dye," James suggested. "It's flat on one side, so I was hoping it would look as if they were walking across the fabric." He tapped the elephant across the cloth Anna had laid out on the table. "It might not work," he added, blushing.

"I love that idea," Anna exclaimed. "I've never seen anything like that." Anna scooted the bucket with the purple dye over to James. "You do the honors."

"Yeah?" James asked sheepishly. "Just cover it?"

"I think so." Anna nodded. "Let's see what happens."

James lifted the small wooden elephant, leaving a perfect purple print on the fabric. "Ha!" he said in triumph.

Anna's eyes lit up. "Let's do a whole row of them."

James dipped the stamp into each color dye again and again, until a line of multicolored elephants marched proudly across the fabric. He stood back to admire his work.

"It's so colorful." Anna clapped her hands. "Just gorgeous."

James put the stamp down and turned to her. "*You* are gorgeous." He picked her up in his arms and spun her around playfully. "This is perfect. Creating this with you."

He stopped spinning and held her to him. She slid down his body, feeling the muscles in his chest against her own, until they were face-to-face.

"I've never known anyone like you. You inspire me, Anna."

"Me too," she whispered.

Then he put his forehead to hers, and her whole body ached with desire.

He kissed her neck. Tiny kisses that let a million butterflies loose in her stomach. She let her head fall back as her hair tumbled from its bun and fell down her shoulders.

They faced each other.

"You make me nervous," Anna confessed.

"I know what you mean." James softly put his lips to hers, and Anna closed her eyes. They kissed, slowly at first and then with passion, stopping only to breathe and embrace each other tightly, letting waves of sensation splash over their bodies.

They ate lunch on the beach in front of the cottage. When the sun became too warm, they dragged their blanket beneath a bushy palm whose shade provided a haven from the heat. They sat next to each other, silence falling between them. Anna looked over at James, and when he caught her eye, she quickly turned back to the sand. She winced and opened her mouth to say something, but she couldn't think what, and closed it again.

"Nope," James said suddenly, nudging Anna's back. "We're done with these awkward moments." Then he placed his hands on her waist and squeezed.

She yelped. "James, that tickles!" Anna rounded on him and moved to grab at his waist, aiming to tickle him back.

He rolled backward in the sand.

"Fine," Anna said, putting her hands up. "If you promise to stop, I will not retaliate."

"Fair," James accepted, sliding back toward Anna.

Anna leaned against the palm. "You know, I come from a kingdom with skilled knights and deadly hunters. And if there's anything I've learned from their tales of adventure, it's that first"—Anna wheeled around and poked James gently in the ribs—"you catch them off guard. And then"—she leaned in and pretended to grab his neck—"you go in for the kill!"

James laughed and let Anna pin him underneath her.

"Ha!" she cried victoriously. She collapsed next to him, pretending the effort had exhausted her.

"You're a formidable opponent!" James admitted, catching his breath from laughing.

Anna pushed up on her elbow and looked down at him, her silky black hair curtaining her face from the sun. James raised his eyebrows and shook his head.

"There's something otherworldly about your beauty," he mused. "It's as if you were forged under the seas and then kissed by the stars themselves. A perfect blend of dark and light."

29

"Do you actually have a plan?" the Hermit said under his breath as he and the Magician walked with hurried steps from the buttery and through the deserted Whitehoof Hall.

"No," the Magician said plainly. "But I need to get to my practice session with Barda or he will become suspicious." She stopped beneath a large silk banner that held the King's family crest. The Magician stared up at the large horse with an eagle's head, standing on its hind legs. The creature stood hoof-to-hoof with a great white Pegasus, whose feathered wings were extended in flight. Above their heads was a crown and in its center, a large cross.

"What is it?" the Hermit asked, studying the banner, trying to figure out what was catching the Magician's eye. The symbol was displayed all over the castle—on banners, needlework pillows, even one of the King's rings.

"It reminds me of Anna's tapestries," the Magician said. She turned and squinted at the Hermit. "I think I've just figured out a plan." She tilted her chin up and rolled her neck, eyeing the banner once more. She lifted her hand and waved it in the loop of the infinity symbol, her face screwed up in concentration.

The Hermit shifted from side to side. He'd never experienced such impatience, but now two of the most important people in his life were in grave danger.

"I think perhaps the King's worst fears did indeed come true." The Magician cocked her head. "Anna's gifts have surfaced." She spun on her heel. "Come on. I'll explain everything on the way!" she yelled to the Hermit. "Call in a favor from Drake. We need Anna's tapestries."

30

Morgan had painted Anna's face in silver, blue, and white to represent the surface of the Moon. A large group of Cups girls were getting ready together in Lara's room. The night of the Full Moon Festival had finally arrived.

"Your face looks enchanting!" Lara declared. She braided Anna's hair into two sections and twisted them together down her back.

"So does yours," Anna said, spinning her head around to take another look. Lara's face had been painted to look like a blood moon, with red and gold makeup that complimented the color of her hair, which was teased at the crown and flowed in waves down her shoulders.

Lara nudged the back of Anna's head gently, signaling for her to turn forward so she could finish her hair. "What do you think about having a day where just you and I do something after all this is over? We've been working so hard!" Lara swept her arm over the room. The girls were all dressed in elaborate, colorful costumes made from the fabric Anna and James had stamped. Terra, Daisy, and Rebecca had made great assistant seamstresses. Their dresses were adorned with colorful ribbons and shimmered with sequins and metallic buttons. Looking around at the girls, Anna was reminded of the chimerical artisans in her Wands tapestry—an explosion of color, whimsy, and creativity.

"I would love that," said Anna.

Daisy bounded in from the bathroom. "What do you think?" she asked. Half her face was bare, while a crescent-shaped moon painted in sparkling white covered one eye and cheek, its bottom tip extending over her mouth and chin.

"Morgan is quite the artist," Anna said, remembering how she and Luke had painstakingly painted elaborate patterns on the garden rocks. "Hey," Anna said suddenly. "Has anyone seen Ivy?"

Lara tied off Anna's braid and scanned the room. "I don't know, now that you mention it. Maybe I should go find her?"

Anna hadn't seen Ivy around much at all lately, and she had a good guess why. She took a deep breath. "No, let me. Are you finished?" Anna asked over her shoulder.

Lara squeezed Anna's arms. "You're all done, Blue Moon."

Anna jumped up. "Morgan," she called across the room. Morgan was painting Rebecca's face all white to represent the Full Moon. "Can I take some of the face paint?"

"Sure," Morgan called back.

"Just don't let the boys see you," Lara whispered. "Bring her back here when you find her."

Ivy's door was closed, so Anna knocked lightly.

"Who is it?" Ivy called out.

"It's Anna," she called through the door.

Silence.

Anna slowly opened the door a crack. "Can I come in?"

Ivy was sitting on her bed, combing her long blond hair, dressed in a simple, plain frock. Her eyes widened when she saw Anna's painted face and dress of patterned elephants.

"Hey," Anna said gently.

"What do you want?" Ivy grumbled.

"Can I do your makeup for the night?" Anna offered. "I could do something that would complement the dress that's waiting for you upstairs." Anna held her breath, prepared for a biting reply.

Ivy looked at Anna squarely. "Why?" she asked softly.

"Because I want to include you," Anna said simply. "You're much more a part of Cups than I am."

Ivy laughed bitterly. "It doesn't feel that way. I used to see a lot more of James, sure, but did you know that Lara and I were close too?" Ivy tossed the comb onto the bed. "I know I drove her crazy sometimes, but I never thought she'd dump me for the first new girl who stumbled into Cups." She threw her arm toward Anna. "She made you come in here, didn't she?" Ivy asked.

Anna looked down at the floor, stung by Ivy's words, and embarrassed for thinking she was only upset about James.

"No, I wanted to come," Anna said quietly.

"To show off the fact that you've won?" Ivy glared at Anna, and Anna wondered if she'd made a mistake by coming in. The last thing she wanted was to drag Lara and Daniel into another mess she'd created. Anna took a seat beside Ivy on the bed.

Ivy crossed her arms and screwed up her face, her eyes shining with tears. "You've just swept in and become the sweetheart of Cups."

With shaking hands, Anna unscrewed the lid on a pot of paint, placing the rest beside her on the bed. "Turn toward me." Ivy wiped the tears from her face and shifted on the bed to face her.

"Close your eyes," Anna instructed.

"Wait," Ivy said. "Can you make me a star instead of a moon phase?"

Anna gave her a small smile. "Of course." She drew the first point of the star on Ivy's forehead in a light-green paint. "Would it make a difference if I said sorry? About James? About disrupting your life?" Anna frowned, holding the brush above Ivy's cheek. "About everything? I feel like I haven't even gotten to know you."

"No," Ivy said flatly.

Anna blew the air out of her cheeks. "Well then, how do you feel about glitter?"

Ivy hesitated. "I like it," she admitted.

"I am sorry that I've hurt you, Ivy. I didn't mean to."

Ivy opened her eyes and studied Anna. "It doesn't help because it's not really your fault. It is, but it isn't. I don't know—it's why I can't stand you. I mean, it's not that I can't stand you. It's just . . ." Ivy trailed off. She looked down at the little pots of face paint sitting on the bed. "I like that violet. Can you use some of it around my eyes?" Ivy asked.

Anna grabbed for the violet pot, looking at Ivy's hazel eyes. "Yes! This will make your eyes really pop."

Ivy closed her eyes again and Anna swiped the bright purple pigment across her lid, waiting for Ivy to finish.

"I've loved him for as long as I can remember," Ivy told her. "But I knew he wasn't mine to keep." She took a deep breath. "Even before you got here, if I'm honest with myself. I think that's why I haven't been the most welcoming. From the minute I saw him with you on the beach that night. You were like this little lost puppy he wanted to take care of," Ivy scoffed. "It kind of made me sick."

"Yeah, I could tell," Anna said.

Ivy opened her violet-lidded eyes and let out a yelp of laughter. She clapped a hand over her mouth and Anna looked at her, one eyebrow raised. Ivy shook her head and laughed harder, and Anna, in her utter surprise and relief, found herself giggling too.

Ivy pulled herself together with a long sigh. "I guess I was a little chilly," she said, another smile creeping across her face.

Anna snorted. "A little?"

"Don't push it." Ivy pointed her finger at Anna. "Now, where's that dress? I want to blow them away."

"Come on. It's in Lara's room." Anna gathered up the little pots of makeup with Ivy's help.

"Thanks for coming to get me." Ivy handed Anna the last pot of face paint. "You didn't have to do that."

Anna shrugged. "I know a little something about feeling isolated."

"I doubt that," Ivy challenged.

"You have no idea." Anna peered at Ivy. "I only ever dreamed of being as confident as you. Of being able to do all the things you can do. You make thriving here look easy." Anna smiled at her. "And I know from some pretty messy attempts at swimming and riding that it really isn't."

Ivy flicked her hands at Anna. "Oh stop," she said. "Let's just get out there and see who turns James's head first."

Anna's jaw dropped.

"I'm kidding. I'm kidding." Ivy held up her hands. "This was a good talk, Anna, but we're heading out of Ivy land into some really heavy territory. Too deep for me." She grimaced.

Anna rolled her eyes, laughing, and let Ivy lead her out of the room.

Paper lanterns were strung on each side of the villa's staircase, lighting the way as the girls floated down like a coterie of lunar creatures. Down on the beach, the boys gasped at the sight of them. The full Moon was high and round and the color of wheat, and the stars looked like powdered sugar sprinkled on the night sky.

As the girls walked down the steps toward the beach, arms linked, Anna noticed that the sea was glowing, as if it were lit from below by starlight.

"What is that?" Anna leaned into Terra, who was on her right, and pointed toward the water.

"It does that every now and then," she answered. "Beautiful, right?"

"I've never seen anything like it. The fish even look like they're glowing." Anna's eyes swept over the whole scene in front of her. Open canvas tents had been set up on the beach, and a sumptuous, sprawling feast had been laid on a large, heavy-looking wood table that was flanked by lit torches. The boys all wore white, their tawny skin glowing in the moonlight.

Someone let out a loud whoop, and Anna smiled when she saw James running toward her. When the girls hit the bottom steps, they dispersed onto the beach and James grabbed her hand, twirling her around.

They sat down as a group to eat. The table was overflowing with food: roasted chickens, crispy and browned; warm rolls and guava jelly; plates of rice and beans; bright yellow plantains; and slices of pumpkin glistening with brown sugar. Bowls of crimson pomegranate seeds filled carved-out pineapple husks. Carafes of wine lined the length of the spread.

As Anna sat down next to James, Topper approached the table, sitting down across from them, next to Daniel and Lara. Anna helped pass around trays of each delicacy and watched as

the wine traveled endlessly from person to person. Except the carafes never reached Topper, Anna noticed.

"He's the guide tonight," James whispered in her ear, his
own eyes glossy from drinking.

"Guide?" Anna asked.

James pointed to his glass "This isn't just wine tonight," he
proclaimed. His voice was becoming louder the more he drank,
and he kept grabbing at Anna's hand throughout dinner, squeezing it with vigorous affection.

Anna sensed her own body becoming warm, but there was
something different than the feeling the regular wine had given
her the night she and James had drunk at the cottage. She felt her
thoughts slowing and her muscles loosening as everything around
her seemed to take on a glowing sheen.

"Just don't drink too much of it, since it's your first time."
James leaned in and kissed her passionately. Anna found that
all of her senses were heightened, and she gasped when the
sound of rhythmic drumming filled the air and James finally
pulled away.

He leapt up from the table and others followed suit. Anna
scrambled out of her seat, clutching her wine goblet, as people
began clearing the plates and food. Two tall, muscly boys Anna
hadn't met yet lifted both ends of the table and carried it around
to the other side of the tent.

"Feeling well, little Anna?" Lara tiptoed up to her side,
wearing the green dress Anna had made for her when she'd first
arrived. Her hair looked almost like it was aflame, and her green
eyes glittered behind the red makeup.

"You're the most gorgeous person I have ever seen, Lara,"
Anna said with admiration, the wine pushing her thoughts out
from her lips.

"Be careful of that." Lara nodded to Anna's cup.

"James warned me." Anna moved her eye in what she hoped was a wink.

"My beautiful Lara," Daniel boomed as he ran toward the two girls. "Come dance with me."

Anna and Lara giggled. "You'd better go," Anna said, waving to Daniel.

"Come find me if you need me. And no swimming tonight." She poked Anna's arm lightly. "For anyone."

Anna watched them disappear into the crowd of dancers that had gathered where the table had been. She turned around and saw that James had gone.

"Don't you dance, Moon girl?" Ivy snuck up behind Anna and grabbed her hand, pulling her into the crowd. Anna spun around, feeling the pulsating beats in the sand. Everyone in the crowd was lost in their own worlds, moving their bodies in time with the beat. Ivy stood in front of Anna, her eyes shut, making small circles with her hips, completely absorbed in the music.

Anna started to sway, awkward and slow at first. She'd never really danced, but it didn't take long for the thump of the drums and the heat of the wine to take over. She moved her shoulders and her chest from side to side, her head bobbing to the beat. Her hips swayed and her bare feet shuffled in the sand.

The drumbeats started to increase in both volume and tempo, and everyone screamed with joy. Anna found herself yelping along with them, adrenaline and exhilaration surging through her. She felt like she was underwater, the barriers between things and people softening into a dreamlike fuzziness. Even gravity bowed at the feet of the sea. It could have been minutes or hours. She felt suspended in time.

She was free.

Then, all of a sudden, there he was. The kind smile, the unruly chestnut hair.

"James!" Anna yelled as if she hadn't seen him in a year. They grabbed each other and kissed passionately, Anna's hands working their way under James's white shirt. His body swayed beneath her touch, and they broke apart, shaking their heads and jumping up and down to the beat.

When Anna finally slowed down, she realized how thirsty she was. By then James had traveled into the middle of a small circle of dancers and was too far away for her to call his name. Anna stumbled away from the crowd and looked up, the Moon distracting her from her quest for water. She felt someone's hand on her shoulder.

"Are you all right, Anna?"

Anna's eyes stayed glued to the Moon. "That's my father," she announced.

"It feels like that sometimes, doesn't it?"

Anna blinked slowly and turned to see who she was talking to. Topper looked down at her with gentle, sober eyes.

"But he really is," she slurred.

Topper chuckled and creased his brow. "How about we get you some water?"

"That's what I was on my way to do!"

Topper gestured to the largest canvas tent.

"I don't need a break." Anna waved her hands. "Just water."

"Just water then." Topper took Anna's hand, and they squeezed through the throng of people, some dancing, others just standing and talking to one another. He towered over most of them, and his blond hair shone like a beacon. In that moment she could only think about how badly she wanted to weave him.

He led her to a tent that was closed, and opened the flap for her. It was lit by soft candlelight, and cushions littered the floor. Henry was there, handing out water and coconut milk. His face lit up when he saw her.

"Anna!"

"Henry." Anna rushed up to him. "Don't you want to dance?"

"I was! Right behind you." He laughed. "But I needed a break, so I thought I'd come help out in here."

Anna collapsed onto the fluffiest-looking cushion she could find and drank coconut milk straight from the shell. She set the coconut down on the floor with a clatter as the room spun around her. Topper and Henry both winced.

"Have some bread. It helps the stomach," Topper said.

Anna ate the bread and drank more of the milk. As the room steadied, she found herself wishing that James were beside her. But perhaps she could rest here for a while and find him later, and they could dance together.

She watched as Topper crossed the room and picked up a guitar that was resting against the center tent pole. He sat down and started strumming a soft tune. Anna, her eyelids feeling heavy, curled up on the bed of cushions. She'd only close her eyes for a second.

She dreamed she was walking on the beach, but as she got closer to the sand, she felt something sharp cut her feet. When she looked down, she wasn't standing on sand anymore, but a carpet of broken cups. They were scattered as far as the eye could see. Broken glass, porcelain, chunks of hot silver—broken cups everywhere.

Anna woke with her heart beating wildly, and when she sat up, she clutched an aching head. It took her a minute to figure out where she was. The room was still dark, but the lilac of dawn broke through the cracks of the tent. All around her, people were sprawled out on the cushions, sleeping soundly.

"Hey." Topper was sitting up across from Anna, drinking a cup of something steaming. Anna smiled at the way his hair stuck up in the back.

"Hey," she said, squinting. "Is this what it means to be the guide?"

"It does," he whispered.

"Do you have any more of that?" She pointed to his cup. "I just had the weirdest dream." She rubbed her hands over the cracked paint on her face and the mess of tangled hair that had come loose from her braids.

Topper handed her his cup. "Hot water," he said.

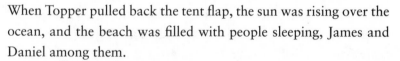

When Topper pulled back the tent flap, the sun was rising over the ocean, and the beach was filled with people sleeping, James and Daniel among them.

"I think I need a bath," Anna said. Topper lifted his chin to the sea in front of them, to which Anna wrinkled her nose. "I've only just learned to swim."

"Really? That's quite an accomplishment."

Anna stared at him to gauge whether he was making fun of her, but his expression was sincere.

"You seem different from the others here," Anna said without thinking.

"How so?" Topper's expression was open, curious. This time

Anna chose her words more carefully.

"Well, you didn't drink the wine last night, and you didn't wake up looking like this"—she pointed to herself—"for one thing."

Topper laughed.

"You travel, and you just have a more thoughtful . . . Is that the right word?" Anna's head felt cloudy with sleep and the aftermath of the wine. "You just seem more calm, more grown-up."

"Ah." Topper shoved his hands in the pockets of his white linen pants. "Well, I might say you seem quite thoughtful yourself, at least from what I've gathered in our few encounters."

Anna grinned. As they approached the water, she knelt down, scrubbing her makeup off in the water. She wiped her face on the hem of her dress and looked up at Topper.

"James said you keep a library," Anna suddenly said. "But no one has mentioned it since. Where is it?"

Topper nodded. "I can show you."

Anna followed as Topper led her to the beach where she had entered Cups. She'd meant to return there, but she'd never worked up the courage. It felt like it might change everything, and she wasn't ready for the possibility of giving up life in Cups. Her heart caught in her chest and she stopped abruptly.

"Are you all right?" Topper asked her. It was the first words they'd spoken since they starting walking. Anna had been too nervous to say anything, sensing from the focused look on his face that Topper could go hours without speaking.

"I'm fine," she said quickly. "Just a little unsteady from the wine." If she said what she was thinking, it would open a door to a conversation she didn't want to have. Couldn't have.

Topper nodded his chin up the beach. "It's just up there, but we don't have to go farther if you don't want to," he assured her.

Anna studied him. He indeed seemed perfectly happy to turn back. "Let's keep going," she said.

They walked up the beach to a trail that led into the mountains, stopping at a small cave set into the cliffside.

It was fairly small, but there was a clear view of the sea through the arched entrance, giving the space an airy feel. Just inside, the rough black rock gave way to a smoother, sanded surface where a handful of stone shelves lined with books stood out from the walls. There was a table set up in the very back of the cave with two chairs and a large candle melted halfway down.

"Why keep the books here?" Anna asked, looking around. "You could have built a larger structure closer to the villa, no?" Topper pulled a chair out from the table and turned it around, offering it to her. Anna declined and he took the seat instead, resting one impossibly long leg across the other.

"I didn't build this, Anna. I found it."

Anna looked at him, puzzled. "Just like this? With the books inside?"

"Just like this," Topper repeated.

She fingered the spines of the books, reading each title. As she circled the room, she felt her stomach tighten. This library contained every book she'd *ever* read, books the advisors had brought her, and no others.

Anna whipped around to face Topper. "Why are you the only one who has ever left Cups?" She narrowed her eyes, observing him.

Topper sighed and leaned his elbows on his knees. "I'm searching for something. Daniel and Lara have always encouraged people to pursue their passions, and since this was my chosen focus, they let me go. Not right away. They said no plenty of times. But this last time they finally relented."

"What are you searching for?" Anna asked.

"It's complicated." Topper sat up again, studying her face.

"I can handle complicated." Anna thought of the King, Marco, and the legend of the Moon. She knew she was prying, but she had to know how, or if, she was connected to this place.

Topper eyed her, brows knitted. "We have no history here."

"Here in Cups?" Anna asked, cocking her head to the side.

Topper rose from the chair and joined Anna next to the shelves of books. As he moved closer, he brought with him the smell of lime and sandalwood. Despite being tall herself, Anna had to tilt her head back to look up at him.

"Yes, here." Topper paused. "No one knows where we came from as a people, and no one knows where they came from as individuals. As you know, in Pentacles, there are parents and children and family lineage," he explained.

Without thinking, Anna grabbed Topper's arm. They both blinked down at her hand, and she quickly removed it. "I asked Lara about it," she said, recovering. "But she doesn't seem to know much either."

Topper cleared his throat and moved toward the entrance of the cave.

Anna watched him as he stared out at the sea.

"I need to know why we are here, where we came from," he said, leaning against the arch. His long, lithe figure was silhouetted against the sun shining in from the cave's mouth. "This library, for instance. The collection is seemingly random. I've studied it for as long as I can remember, but it has no real pattern. It's like someone lived here for a while, someone from another land, and then just left it all behind."

Anna wanted to tell him about her education, about why her advisors had chosen these particular books. Perhaps if they worked together, they could unravel this mystery. She thought of the book at James's cottage, how he said he'd taken it from this library.

"What about the books in Pentacles?" Anna pressed.

"That's what is so strange." Topper shook his head. "They are the same as these. I thought there would be other books in other lands—it would seem so, right?" he asked Anna. "But then, I have hardly explored all of Pentacles. I'm sure there are manors with great libraries."

Anna felt her breathing quicken. She hadn't seen them herself, but she *knew* other books existed—books her advisors had read, studied, and then talked to her about.

"Another thing about Pentacles," Topper continued. "They measure time in years, and a physician there calculated that I have lived eighteen of them."

Anna nodded, her mind wandering to the lines she had scored into the floor of her Tower, illustrating sixteen years of isolated existence.

"My memories from the past, the short past I have, are fading." Topper clenched his fists and slid down the wall of the arch, sitting in the hard-packed sand. "I believe that all of our memories are fading, but I'm the only one trying to hold on to them."

"You're a historian." Anna knelt beside him at the cave's entrance.

"Yes, but even the idea of history or culture—it's nonexistent here. I had to learn about those concepts in Pentacles."

Anna wiped a hand across her face. "This reminds me of one of those drawings where the artist has placed a hidden image within the scene, but the closer you look, the harder it is to find." She leaned her head against the wall. "It almost makes my brain hurt."

Topper smiled at her. "When I was traveling, I heard about

something called the Akashic Records from an old man who owned an inn where I stayed."

Anna sat down and leaned her back against the wall next to Topper, tucking her knees under her dress.

"It's a library that contains every event, thought, and emotion that has ever occurred, is occurring now, and will occur in the future," Topper elaborated.

Anna's mouth dropped open. "How can that possibly exist?" As she uttered the words, she thought of the Magician, of her own father possibly hiding as the Moon, and her disbelief waned. "Is it supposed to be a place? A structure?"

Topper shook his head and shrugged. "I don't know. No one I've met so far does, but it is my life's purpose to find out."

"So you'll leave Cups again?" Anna stood back up and paced the length of the cave. Topper rose from the sand and met her in the middle of the small space. She stopped and they stood face-to-face.

"I will. I won't find anything new here." He peered down at Anna.

"Does it bother you?" Anna met Topper's blue-green eyes. "That you're the only one with these questions? With this quest? Isn't it lonely?" She wanted to reach out and touch him again, grab his hands, run her fingers up his arms, but the thought of James stopped her.

"That's a lot of questions," he whispered.

Anna was willing herself to back away from Topper when suddenly the ground shook so violently, she was thrown against one of the shelves. Topper ran to Anna and threw his arms around her, huddling against the wall until the quaking stopped.

When, after several minutes, an eerie stillness fell over the cave, Topper unwound his arms and took Anna by the shoulders.

"Are you all right?"

Anna nodded, rubbing her arm where she had collided with the stone.

"Daniel told me you experienced an earthquake last moon cycle. Did it feel like this?" He asked, breathless.

Anna looked up at him, her eyes wild with fear. She motioned for Topper to follow her as she crawled toward the mouth of the cave, bracing herself for the next rumble, but it didn't come.

"We should get back," Topper said, "and see if the others are okay."

They clambered up from the ground and ran down the path back to the beach. Anna dashed in front of Topper and, stopping near the water, tried to inconspicuously feel around the air for a wall or a sticky sensation—anything that might signal that the entrance to the Hierophant's Kingdom was still there. Nothing.

When Topper reached her, he turned his head to one side, just watching her. Anna spun around and winced sheepishly. He was looking for a library of souls for stars' sake, Anna reminded herself. He was probably not one to pass judgment easily. She blew out a big breath and set her shoulders.

"Okay, let's go."

The wind started to pick up as they made their way back to the festival, and they had to shield their faces against the swirling sand to spot the group in the distance. When Anna and Topper reached the site, they saw that people were running panicked from the flapping canvas tents.

"Inside, everyone! Now!" Daniel yelled. He and James were corralling the swarm of confused people into the villa. The wind was so strong, it was starting to lift the stakes from the ground one by one. Anna watched as the huge recovery tent flew into the air and out over the beach, the brightly colored cushions tumbling down the shore behind it. She clapped her hands over her ears to block out the buzzing sound that had descended upon the beach, and fought through the wind to get to safety.

Through the crowd of fleeing people, Anna saw Lara limping up the beach. She sprinted over to her.

"I think my ankle is twisted!" Lara had to scream above the horrendous noise. Anna put her shoulder beneath Lara's and helped her reach the villa's staircase. She handed her off to a girl with short dark hair who was ushering people through the door.

There were partygoers from the night before frozen in the garden. Anna could see them from where she stood. A small group of them, looking dazed and scared as dirt and wind pummeled them from all sides.

She ran toward them, the dark-haired girl screaming after her not to go.

In the distance Anna could hear the animals of West Farm screaming in their various tongues, creating an ominous cacophony of sound. She had to duck to avoid being hit with flying shovels and rakes as she neared the garden.

"It's not stopping!" Suddenly James was at her side, shouting. They were thrown toward each other as the earth quaked violently beneath them. James linked arms with Anna, and they careened toward the group of people huddled in fear at the edge of the garden. Just before they got to them, the garden's earth began to rise up at their feet.

"Run!" Anna and James shouted at them. The group broke apart and bolted toward Anna and James seconds before the earth split in a thin, jagged line.

A deafening rumble muted the sounds of stragglers screaming on the beach. She saw the terror on their faces as they ran in the direction of the sea.

"Anna, this way!" James shouted, trying to reach for her hand. Anna lifted her arm but stopped abruptly as something caught her eye. Instead of more earth in the ever-widening crack, she saw what looked like sky. She inched closer and dropped to her knees, crawling forward to get a closer look.

"Help them, James! I'll be right there!" she screamed over her shoulder.

He shook his head violently. "No, Anna! It's too dangerous!"

Anna held up her hand. "Listen, it's stopping." The ground had ceased its shaking, but the wide crack down the garden's center remained. "Go. I promise, I'll follow you."

Torn, James looked from her to the panicked people of Cups and back again.

"Right away, Anna."

James ran off, looking distraught, while Anna crawled closer to the rupture, painfully aware that the quake could start up again at any second.

She peered over the side and gasped. It was small, almost minuscule from this vantage point, but she'd recognize it anywhere. Anna looked down onto the stone towers and turrets of the world she'd fled, the world of the Hierophant's Kingdom.

31

It was midnight when Drake rode out of the castle gates and into the woods under cover of darkness to meet the Magician and the Hermit. He arrived at a small deserted clearing surrounded by oak, hazel, and birch trees. He dismounted and took a lantern from the satchel tied to his saddle. As he was about to light it, he felt a hand on his shoulder and jumped in surprise.

"It's only us," whispered the Hermit. He held up his lantern and saw that Drake's eyes were red-rimmed and puffy.

"Did you bring them?" The Magician emerged from the darkness. Drake tilted his head toward his horse. The three of them walked over and untied the heavy tapestries. "Thank you, Drake. You are a good friend to the Fool and you've done well."

"You *will* get him out?" Drake's voice caught as he spoke.

"We're doing our damnedest," said the Magician. "You should go. We've put you in enough danger." Drake looked as if he wanted to say something, but he decided against it and mounted his horse.

"Be careful," the Hermit said under his breath as he watched Drake ride back into the blackness of the forest, leaving him and the Magician alone in the small clearing.

"What do we do?" asked the Hermit.

"I've been thinking this through. Anna was being chased," the Magician explained. "She was scared and alone."

"I've always taught her to breathe through her fear," the Hermit stated. "Maybe she stopped to collect herself for a moment and the bridge appeared?" He shook his head as if chasing the thought away. "No, that wouldn't explain it. . . ." They hemmed over the tapestries at their feet.

"Let's lay them out," the Magician suggested.

Together the two began to roll out what was left of Anna's tapestries. They were tattered and mostly just depictions of landscapes now, with people dotting them here and there, missing the areas where Anna had sliced through them.

When they had covered a good portion of the forest floor, the Magician grabbed the lantern and examined them carefully.

"Where do we begin?" the Hermit said, feeling overwhelmed by the four vast lands before them.

The Magician took her wand from her robe, the quick movement causing the Hermit to gasp.

"Where did you get that?" he asked.

"I switched it out with a decoy when that beast Barda wasn't looking," the Magician said proudly. "I've been taking things here and there each session. A little at a time, so he won't notice."

The Hermit smiled at her. "Clever. But I thought you didn't need it anymore."

The Magician crouched over the tapestries. "I don't *need* it, but it certainly helps things along," she mumbled under her breath.

The Hermit followed the Magician as she knelt in front of the Pentacles tapestry. The Magician took a small vial filled with iridescent powder and uncorked it. She placed a little on her hand

and blew it out onto the tapestry, muttering a long incantation.

Epanfatheo, genimaintos, therapinatos . . .

The landscape in front of them was patchy, but the pieces began to mend under the Magician's spell.

The Hermit nearly put his hand on the Magician's shoulder but then thought better of it. "It's like you're healing them. Restoring them to their original forms." He knelt down next to her to watch.

But it was more than that. The figures that had been cut from the tapestries were coming alive beneath the watchful eyes of the Magician and the Hermit. The King was back on his throne, but now the peach thread in his face morphed into flesh, and he walked from his seat, taking the Queen's hand. Soft music echoed around the court, and the figures within the tapestry began to dance. The sound of waves crashing and a brackish smell wafted up from the sea at the tapestry's base.

"I don't believe it," breathed the Hermit.

The Magician moved to the Wands tapestry next. Warm sands kicked up at the Hermit's feet as he peered into the desert land. The mountains looked like flowing chocolate beneath the light of a moon sliced into a sharp crescent from Anna's scissors.

"Look for Anna." The Magician scrutinized the miniature worlds before them. "Do you see her?"

The Hermit squinted and walked around the tapestry. "I don't."

"Neither do I," the Magician huffed.

The Magician performed the same spell on the city of Swords. It was hard not to forget their purpose as the Hermit watched people rush to and fro among the strange silver buildings towering over the land.

"I've found her," the Magician yelped. "Over here."

He tore his eyes away from Swords and joined the Magician in front of Anna's land of youth—her last tapestry, unfinished and not yet named. The Hermit gasped and put his hand over his mouth. There was Anna, walking along a white stretch of beach with a tall blond boy.

"How do we get there?" The Hermit leaned forward to touch the tapestry before the Magician could stop him. The moment his fingers touched the threads, a great force sent him stumbling backward. The tapestries went dark and lifeless. The figures froze, the tide of the sea stopped flowing, and everything went completely still.

The Hermit got to his feet slowly, dazed from the impact. "What was that?"

"We can't use the tapestries to get to her. They're protected, and I believe it's Anna's magic that's doing it. Whether she knows it or not," the Magician added. Out of habit, she reached for the chain around her neck to study her infinity charm, but when she found only bare skin, she remembered that she had given it to Anna. "But I think I might know another way in."

32

Before Anna could react to what she'd seen, the fissure in the land slammed shut with immense force. She scrambled away, afraid of being sucked back into the kingdom she had run from.

"Anna!" Daniel dashed toward her, screaming her name. She got to her feet, wiping dirt from her legs.

"I'm okay," she reassured him. Her body trembled with shock.

"Why didn't you flee with the others?" Daniel asked, putting an arm around her shoulders and leading her back toward the villa.

Anna felt a dark pit in her stomach. She wondered briefly if she should offer him the truth. He might think she was being absurd, but she was more afraid of what might happen if Daniel believed her. She had history with the people of Cups now; unfortunately, not all of it was built on the truth. Which was the very reason why she couldn't tell him what she'd seen. Anna had placed them in grave danger by associating herself with them, but she also couldn't bear the thought of losing the friends she'd made.

No, she had to discover exactly what was happening and

exactly how to fix it. She would figure out how to protect the people of Cups from the Hierophant King. To tell them the truth now would only scare them.

"I was trying to see what was happening," she finally answered quietly.

"That was incredibly dangerous and foolish," Daniel said.

Anna shrank back, feeling cowardly for not being honest with him.

Daniel sighed and dropped his arm from her shoulders. "I think the villa is the safest place for us now. We can all gather there and try to work out what's going on," Daniel said comfortingly. "Something is terribly wrong." He took Anna's elbow and steered her toward home.

Daniel halted just before they reached the door. "I have this feeling, this heavy feeling in my gut, that you are hiding something from me. From all of us." He looked deep into Anna's eyes. "Do you know something about what's happened here today?" He clenched his jaw, waiting for her to respond.

Anna stopped breathing for a moment. She longed to tell him the truth, just unburden herself, but instead she crossed her arms and waited for Daniel to speak again.

"If you say it now, Anna, we can help each other. If there is something I need to know as the leader of my people, you have to tell me."

She pulled her arms closer to her body. "There's nothing, Daniel." Anna hated herself as she said it.

"What were you looking for in the split in the ground?" Daniel wasn't giving up. "I saw you leaning into it. Why would you put yourself in danger like that?"

Anna felt trapped. "I thought if I could examine the crack, I might find something out about what has been happening lately."

Daniel pressed his lips together.

"That I would see a clue of some sort," Anna continued. "There was the disturbance at sea, then in the jungle, and now this. I'm scared, Daniel."

With Daniel's silence, and the stiff set of his jaw and shoulders as they walked, she decided her best bet was to stop talking.

"We're all a little traumatized." He slumped and then reached for the front door. "I'm just trying to work it out myself."

When they entered the villa, Anna was not prepared for the scene before her. The people of Cups were clustered in groups in the main room, crying and holding one another, the girls' faces still cracked with last night's makeup. Lara and James were flitting from group to group, trying to calm them. The doors and windows had been shuttered, and the normally cheerful room was dark and stuffy.

Terra and James spotted Anna at the same time and flew toward her, wrapping her in a tight embrace. How could she have caused these people, these people who she loved, this sort of pain and fear? She saw Topper watching her from the corner of the room where he was talking to Luke and a curvy girl with dark red hair. He tilted his chin at her and then returned to his conversation.

"What can I do?" Anna asked James. "I could make tea for everyone."

"Henry is in the kitchen." James gestured to the room off the main common space. "I'm sure he'd appreciate the help."

Anna took a step toward the kitchen, but James grabbed her hand. She spun to face him, and he brought her in close. She felt safe, pressed against his warm chest, his arms tight around her.

"I was so worried about you," he whispered in her ear.

She lifted her face to his and they pressed their foreheads

together briefly before she headed off to the kitchen.

She found Henry inside, placing a huge tray into the oven. His movements were slow and drawn out.

"Oh, hello, Anna." He wiped his brow with a rag and leaned against the oven, pointing her to a large ceramic bowl filled with a thick dark-orange batter.

"What is this?" she asked, picking up a long wooden spoon and beginning to stir.

"I'm making sweet potato bread. It's all I can think to do right now." Henry turned around and leaned his elbows on the counter. "I hope it will comfort people."

"I'm sure it will." Anna stirred while she watched Henry prepare ingredients next to her. He grated sweet potatoes and zucchini until they formed a towering pile, cracked eggs into a bowl and added sugar to them, whipping the mixture into a cream.

"Anna, I want to talk to you about something." Henry dusted his hands off on his apron.

Anna kept stirring, hoping she didn't have to face another confrontation.

"I saw you walk off this morning with Topper." He rubbed the back of his neck.

"Yes," she admitted freely. "He showed me his library." She stirred a little faster.

"It's just strange that the winds picked up right as you were returning. Did something happen there?" Henry rocked on his heels.

When Anna didn't answer, he waved at the air. "I don't know what I'm getting at." He took the bowl from Anna and dumped it into an empty pan. "Maybe Daniel's putting ideas in my head. I'm not saying you're to blame for any of this—how could you be?"

Anna's chin trembled as she watched Henry smooth the batter.

"I almost forgot," Henry said suddenly, spinning on his heel. "The baking powder." Anna sidestepped out of his way, allowing him to add the white powder to the pan of wet batter. "It'll probably rise unevenly now, but it would just fall apart without it."

Something hit Anna like a bolt of lightning. She stood frozen to the spot, afraid that if she moved, she would lose her thought. She needed to talk to Topper. She needed to articulate this to someone, and he was the only one who might give her a chance to explain it.

"Henry, will you excuse me?" she said, not waiting for his answer. She dashed out of the kitchen, scanning the common room for Topper's bright blond head. Anna was about to go upstairs when Daniel approached, Lara limping behind him, her ankle swollen and a deep shade of purple. James spotted them from his station by the front door and came to Anna's side.

Daniel looked furious.

"Anna, I need to talk to you." Lara put her hand on Daniel's elbow, but he shook her off. "Now." His eyes were shining and his hands shook. "How exactly did you come to us, Anna?" he demanded.

"I've t-told you," Anna stammered. "I ran away from my home in Pentacles." She tried to meet Daniel's wild gaze.

"Did you walk? Did you ride a horse?" Daniel took a step toward Anna. "How? And why here?"

"Daniel," James said, but Anna put her hand on his arm.

"I told you, some friends put me in a boat, and after that I can't remember what happened. I must have blacked out. I just woke up in Cups."

"How did you find us? Our villa?" Daniel asked, his posture tensing.

"I came across James on the beach that night. You know that."

"What friends helped you? You said you had no one." He clenched his fists in frustration.

"Daniel," Lara cautioned.

"What's going on here?" Topper rushed up to the small group.

Daniel waved him into their circle. "Topper, you've traveled from Cups to Pentacles. If she was unconscious, floating on the sea, could she just end up here? Is that even possible?" Topper looked from Anna to Daniel.

"I don't know what you want me to say!" Anna shouted, feeling backed into a corner, her face reddening from a combination of anger and embarrassment.

A gust of wind slammed at the boarded windows and everyone jumped.

"How far is that exactly?" Daniel barked, now looking positively manic after the scare from the wind. "We've never seen anyone from any other land, and you are able to just drift here? It doesn't make sense."

Anna took a slow step back, scared of Daniel's rising anger. James pushed his way in front of her.

"I can't believe I'm saying this to you, but calm down, Daniel," James reproached him. "What is this even about?"

"I'll tell you what this is about." Daniel pointed a finger at Anna. "She is the only thing that has changed since we've been having these horrific accidents." He let that settle in the air between them. "I've been going over and over it in my mind, and she is the only variable. How long have we lived here? Our whole lives." Daniel threw up his hands. "Nothing like this has ever happened!" he shouted.

A heavy silence fell over the room. Anna felt tiny seeds of

doubt being planted in every person whose eyes she met. Tears spilled down Lara's cheeks as she leaned into Daniel. Terra stared at her from a corner of the room. People gaped at her, their mouths half-open, but not one of her friends came to her side.

"Why don't we take a break?" Topper said. "Let our heads cool."

Anna needed to do something to gain their trust back. If the Hierophant King was coming after her, she couldn't leave these people unprotected. Not to mention the heartbreak she would endure if they cast her out. And where would she go? She had no place to run now.

"You asked me when I got here if I was mistreated," she said. "I was. I was locked in a room and made to stay there. You saw how pale I was when I got here, how weak. I was never even allowed outside." Everyone was watching her. "It's the reason why I could not swim or ride a horse or cook when I arrived." She wrung her hands as she spoke, choking back tears. "I wish I could tell you more about where I came from, but I just can't." She addressed the whole room now. "I can never repay all of you for what you have given me. I've never experienced anything like the joy I have felt these past few weeks. I'm sorry for what's happening. There aren't words for how sorry I am." She made a move to head up the stairs, and James did not try to stop her or follow. Like the others, he simply stared, shock clear on his face.

As Anna's foot hit the first step, Lara broke away from Daniel and grabbed her arm. "We'll get through this. Whatever it is," she whispered. Anna gave her a weak smile and headed up the stairs to her room.

She threw herself on the bed, arms and legs spread wide, feeling utterly bereft. After a few minutes she heard a light knock on her door.

"Come in," she said, hopeful that one of her friends had come to check on her. Or better, that Daniel would burst inside and tell her that it was all a misunderstanding. But when she looked up, it was Topper who stood towering in the doorway.

33

"Can I help?" the Hermit called out to the Magician, who had been conjuring a series of objects with her wand for what felt like hours. She was surrounded by twenty tall white candles; a giant bunch of fragrant sage; dried rosemary; a tall jar of seawater, sloshing in its glass bottle as if it were alive; and a thick tangle of cabbage root.

The Magician examined the pile at her feet. "Find a bird feather."

The Hermit hopped off the rock where he had been seated. "May I use one of your candles for light?" he asked. The Magician nodded, pointing her wand at one of the candles. It lit at once.

He beamed and took it. "I really like you having your magic back. I wish you didn't have to hide it."

"You and me both," she said. She was starting to drag her supplies in front of the tapestry where they had seen Anna walking on the beach.

The Hermit poked into the surrounding trees, at first finding nothing but cobwebs, sticks, and branches. But then there it was, hanging off yet another branch. A sage-green tail feather from a

Dartford warbler. It was long and velvety soft and tipped with apricot.

"Will this do?" the Hermit asked, spinning around to show the Magician. "Ah!" he gasped.

The Magician had shaped the ingredients of her spell into an infinity symbol six feet wide. It was stunning, the light from the tall candles flickering in the night, casting shadows on the palms and sea in the tapestry. The Hermit joined her and offered her the warbler feather.

"Very good," she said.

The Hermit tilted his chin toward a space that was obviously missing the candle he held. "May I?" he requested.

"Yes, but do it quickly. Place the bird feather in the middle, and be careful not to knock anything over!"

When the Hermit was finished, he gingerly stepped from the center of the second loop.

"Stand back," the Magician ordered, waving the Hermit behind her. "It's a spell to break barriers and bind those who love one another." She took the vial of iridescent powder that brought Anna's tapestries to life and threw the whole thing at her infinity symbol without even opening it. The vial hit the ground, smashing into thousands of tiny pieces and scattering shimmering dust. An iridescent light swam through the loop of the infinity pattern, coiling back and forth, purple with sheens of gold and green. The ground around them began to vibrate.

"My love for Anna is infinite, as is my love for my brother. Break the barrier between us so that I might reach her. Unite our familial blood, a tie that binds us regardless of dark or light, earth or heaven, stone or water, fire or ash." She swayed as she whispered the words. Then, quite suddenly, she pulled her wand back as if drawing an arrow in a bow and shouted, *"Anoixahtaye!"*

She thrust her wand at the glowing infinity loop.

"Look!" the Hermit said, pointing and leaping from foot to foot.

At the edge of their small clearing, the mossy, green bridge was materializing.

The Magician scurried around the infinity symbol, rolling up the tapestry frantically. She didn't know how long the bridge would stay there, so she motioned for the Hermit to grab the stack of the other now tightly bound tapestries.

"Let's go! We may not have much time." The Hermit stuffed the stack into his knapsack, hurrying after the Magician. Once in the middle of the bridge, overcome with feelings of exhilaration, the two looked over the side as Anna had, and discovered a vast expanse of nothingness. They giggled like giddy children.

The Magician grabbed the Hermit's elbow, and together they ran across the bridge and smack into a wall of viscous goo.

She grimaced.

"Keep moving! You can push through it!" called the Hermit, his body sinking through the wall.

The Magician pressed herself into the sludge, and in a moment they were gone.

"Should we go after them, Sire?" Senator Bassett appeared from behind the bushes, ready to follow the two double-crossing traitors across the bridge. The King marched out from the brush.

"No. Not yet. They'll be back, and we'll be right here waiting for them when they do." The King clenched his jaw. "With an army this time. We need to be prepared for whatever comes back out or whatever might wait for us on the other side."

Bassett sucked his teeth. "But, Your Majesty, what if they don't return?"

"They'd never leave the Fool behind to rot in the dungeons," the King assured him. "Guards should be posted here around the clock, and have the general make sure the troops are at the ready." The King glanced back at the bushes. "You can come out now, boy."

Drake emerged from the brush, his face dirty and tearstained.

"You've done well, young man. Your loyalty will be rewarded."

34

Topper stood in the doorway for a moment, looking at Anna. She stared back at him, her big black eyes welling with tears, her cheeks and the tip of her nose flushed pink from crying.

"May I?" He gestured to the bed beside her, and she nodded. He sat down next to her and tipped her chin gently up toward him. "You look so sad, Anna."

Topper's tone was full of concern, and devoid of expectation. His compassion and thoughtfulness broke something free in Anna. She took his hand and covered it with both of hers, shifting so that her body faced his.

"I *have* been lying." She scanned his expression to see his reaction.

He nodded but held her gaze. He put his hand over hers and squeezed gently.

Anna told him everything. Her story came spilling out, gaining momentum as she spoke. The Tower, the King, Marco, her advisors, and her tapestries.

They dropped hands and Anna began to wring hers. She cried as she spoke, and every now and then she turned to him to make sure he was still listening, still there.

He was, his bright blue-green eyes trained on her, shaking his head and taking deep breaths as she came to the worst parts in her tale. He dropped his head into his hands when she spoke of the King's order to execute her, but he did not interrupt.

When she finally reached the part where James found her on the beach, she stopped and melted into Topper's thin frame. She shook with the violence of her tears and a rushing feeling of release. Topper held her tightly and stroked her hair. He wiped her tears with his sleeve, and when he rolled it up, Anna noticed the base of a black goblet tattoo just like Daniel's. They sat like that for a few minutes, Anna's truth hanging in the silence between them.

"I really want to meet your aunt," Topper said quietly. "But she sounds a little scary." Anna laughed, her shoulders shaking beneath his embrace.

"She is." Anna took a deep breath and sat up, smoothing her hands over her hair and glancing down at her dress. "Stars, I can't believe I'm still wearing this."

They both laughed lightly. Anna bit her lower lip, feeling new tears brimming in her eyes. She let out a long sigh and turned to him. "Thank you for listening," she said, smiling sadly.

Topper shrugged. "I imagine that's a very large burden to carry alone."

"I was so scared that if I told anyone who I really was, they would make me leave." She grabbed his hand. "I felt like you were the only one who might understand. Your mind is open to new things, new ideas." She thought of James as she said this, and wondered if she was being fair to him. Perhaps he would be just as open if given the chance.

Topper bowed toward Anna. "I'm honored to have your trust." They interlaced their fingers and stared down at them. "I'm so sorry you were treated that way, Anna. That the King hurt you, that he hid your talents from the world. That he went back on his word and your tapestries weren't celebrated the way they should have been, that you were not given your freedom."

Anna blushed.

"It makes me angry just thinking of you being confined like that. The injustice—you were a child, an innocent caught up in other people's conflicts."

Anna smiled at him, her body filling with warmth. "Thank you." She rolled her shoulders back.

"What do we do now?" Topper squeezed Anna's hand.

"Are you going to tell Daniel?" She took her hand away and smoothed a piece of his blond hair behind his ear.

"I think that's a decision we should make together." He rubbed his hands back and forth over his thighs. He started to say something and then stopped.

"What is it?" she asked.

Topper ran a hand over his face and sighed. "I don't think now is the time to bring it up."

She wrinkled her nose. "I just exposed the deepest, darkest corners of my soul—you kind of have to tell me. It's only fair."

Topper gave a shaky laugh and took a deep breath. "It seems like there's something happening between us. I felt it in the library, and I feel it now . . . again." He arched an eyebrow at her. "And I fear it might be one-sided."

Anna wanted to assure him that it wasn't, but then she thought of James and felt a heavy sludge of guilt slide into her chest.

"There you two are."

Anna jumped.

James stood in the doorway. "I brought you some sweet potato bread, Anna."

Topper shot Anna a quick look and hopped up from the bed. "I should probably go," Topper said.

"You don't have to," Anna said, unnerved at the thought of him leaving. James set the tray down next to Anna and took Topper's place on the bed.

"Don't leave on my account, Top," James chimed in.

Topper stood tall and stiffened his posture. He gave James a small nod. "We'll pick this up later, Anna?" he asked hopefully, stepping out the bedroom door and into the hallway. Things heavy and unfinished hung between them. Anna stared at him an extra beat before he turned around and disappeared from the doorway.

Silence followed Topper's absence.

"Hi," James said, nudging Anna's elbow lightly. Anna turned away from where Topper had stood and looked at James. His light-green eyes were rimmed with red and his brow was creased with lines of worry. "Do you want me to go?"

"No," Anna said, studying his face, devoid of its usual brightness. "Yes. I don't know."

James raised his eyebrows. "You're angry with me."

"You didn't defend me when everyone was turning against me down there." Anna shifted slightly away from him on the bed. When she did, she felt James stiffen beside her.

"Can you see things from my side? Daniel's my brother, and I was in shock. We've all been through a lot in the last day. Look at this place." He gestured outside to the patio. "It's destroyed."

Anna put her face in her hands. She knew she wasn't being fair, and right now, Topper's confession made her feel worse. She gazed at James, and felt her heart soften toward him. She could tell him the truth like she had just told Topper, but something stopped her. It was like he'd said: he was Daniel's brother. That was where his loyalty lay. And really, how could she blame him for that?

"I don't think we can resolve this tonight," she said. She rested her hand on his back. He turned to her.

"I never want to have to choose between the two people I love most in the world."

"You shouldn't have to," she said quietly. Suddenly she had a strong desire to be close to him. To put aside their overwhelming problems and just touch him, have him touch her.

Anna moved over to James and leaned into him, resting her head on his broad chest. James wrapped his arms gently around Anna, the two of them breathing softly.

Anna looked down and realized they both still had their festival clothes on. "Do you want to take a bath?" she asked him. "I'm filthy, and I think it would feel really good." He raised his eyebrows. "I just want to feel close to you."

James nodded.

She took his hand, and they walked through a light mist on the patio down to her bathing room. Silently, they lit candles all around the tub and heated the water. James got in first, and Anna stepped in after him. She sat back against him, his chest hard and strong and comforting, the warm water seeping the tension out of her body. Her mind was not at ease, and she still felt the distance between them, but when James began to pour warm water over her shoulders, moving her hair aside so that he could plant light kisses on her bare shoulders, she tried to forget her worries and let herself melt into the moment. They stayed like that for a long time, until the water grew cold, and then went up to bed and fell asleep in each other's arms.

Anna bolted awake. James was beside her, eyes shut tight. She threw the covers off, quickly dressing and tiptoeing to her satchel. Carefully, Anna reached through her tapestry squares until she touched upon the silk linen where she hid her infinity necklace when she wasn't wearing it. She placed the chain around her neck, tucking the golden symbol into her dress. She hoped that the charm really did have a magical connection to her aunt, to her father.

Anna didn't even have to look for Topper. When she got to the bottom of the stairs, he was sitting in a big chair in the main room, a lantern lit at his feet. They didn't say a word as they stepped softly through the villa's front door, closing it quietly behind them.

The Moon, high over the ocean, lit their path along the beach to Topper's library, the sea a dark purple beside them. Anna felt like it was the one place where no one would find them.

She sat on a chair while Topper paced the length of the library, his face drawn in concentration. Anna watched him, wondering what James would say if he found them together here.

Topper stopped and looked down at her. "It's like there are two different worlds running parallel to each other. There doesn't seem to be a normal land border to your Hierophant Kingdom, a place you can cross with a horse or sail over in a boat. Nonetheless, these two worlds exist," Topper continued. "And you probably are a magician, like your father, but you don't know how to use your powers. Yet."

"You are a very good listener," Anna said, impressed with his recall of the details she had thrown at him earlier. "And do you think these two worlds are affecting each other?"

"It seems so," Topper said. He tucked his blond hair behind his ear and looked up, as if the answers lay somewhere above.

"The tapestries." Anna opened her palms in front of her on

the table. "If I open my mind to the possibilities of magic, then maybe . . ." She paused.

Topper turned toward the entrance of the cave. "Then what?" he asked.

"Then perhaps there is some connection between my un-finished tapestry—the unbound threads—and the fact that Cups seems to be unraveling."

"What is that?" Topper said suddenly.

"I know. I can't make sense of it either—"

"No, not that." Topper waved Anna over. "Look. There are people down on the beach."

As Anna came closer, she saw that the figures were cloaked. The light from the Moon shone down upon them, and she noticed that one of the cloaks was a dark crimson.

"It couldn't be." Anna gasped. She pushed past Topper and ran down the sandy path to the beach.

Anna couldn't believe her eyes, but there, struggling in the shallow water, was the Magician, her long braid of brown hair winding down her back and her red robes flowing in the tropical breeze. She was bent over trying to help the Hermit, who was flailing his arms and shouting. The sea was quiet and dark, and the Hermit's hair shone silver under the light of the Moon.

"I'm drowning! Help!" he said breathlessly, his gray cloak billowing around him like a storm cloud.

"Calm down! You are in shallow water. If you just stay still, I can help you." The Magician looked like she was circling a wild animal as she tried to grab hold of the Hermit.

"I can't swim!" he gasped.

Anna and Topper ran to them, Anna's heart beating madly in her chest. They reached the beach in seconds, their feet kicking up sand as they went. Topper grabbed the Hermit underneath his arms and pulled him up in one fluid movement, holding him upright until he was sure that the Hermit had his footing. The Hermit, shocked, craned his neck to get a look at Topper. When he was sure the Hermit was steady on his feet, Topper took a few steps away.

"Anna?" the Hermit said. His chest rose and fell quickly as he tried to catch his breath.

"My dear Hermit." Anna took the Hermit's hand and led him the few steps out of the water to the beach. She squeezed his hand tightly, fearing he might disappear. She remembered how it felt to be scared of the water. The Magician followed them, pushing her wet hair off her face, her robes heavy with seawater.

"Is it really you?" Anna said. She cupped the Hermit's face in her hands and looked into his amber eyes. Before he could answer, she turned to her aunt and ran into her arms. The Magician wrapped Anna in a firm embrace.

"You're safe," the Magician whispered into Anna's ear, stroking her hair. "Thank the stars you are safe."

They hung on to each other for a long moment before breaking apart.

"Things are going to be okay now," Anna whispered. Her heartbeat had slowed, and she squeezed her aunt more tightly. She wasn't alone in this anymore.

"The tapestries!" the Hermit suddenly shouted. He started to run back into the water but stopped short at the edge of the shore. Topper and Anna looked into the water and saw a large dark shape bobbing along the surface. Anna dashed into the shallow water, but she struggled under the weight of the heavy package. The Magician and Topper quickly came to her aid, and together they dragged the large bundle out of the water and dropped it on the beach at their feet.

Anna walked to the Hermit and put her arms around his shoulders.

"You're okay!" The Hermit laughed. "She's okay," he said, turning to the Magician to share the news.

"I see that." The Magician nodded, but she understood that the Hermit was overwhelmed. She felt the same way.

"This is Topper," Anna said, tearing her eyes away from her friends. "Topper, this is the Hermit and the Magician. My aunt and friend who I told you about!"

Topper's eyes shone brightly. "It is an honor to meet you both," he said. "And I must admit, your presence here confirms that I am not crazy." He pumped their hands heartily, and the Magician looked at Anna, clearly uncomfortable. "I know, you must think I'm a bit mad." He dropped their hands. "I just knew there was more to this life than Cups, and for years I was alone with my thoughts and theories." He wiped his brow with the back of his hand. "I'll compose myself. I'm just stunned and delighted. And thrilled for Anna to have this reunion."

Anna had never seen Topper so animated. She smiled as she watched him, her own eyes glassy with emotion. She knew what a miracle the appearance of her advisors must be for him. It was a miracle for her to see them standing on this beach beneath the Moon.

"The enthusiasm of your spirit is a thing of beauty," the Hermit said, and placed a hand on Topper's shoulder.

"Anna! You look so different, so strong and healthy," the Hermit said with admiration, taking in Anna's tanned limbs and glowing complexion. "Oh, and the Moon!" the Hermit exclaimed, staring upward, openmouthed.

"We don't have a lot of time," the Magician interjected. She was twisting her hair back into its braid, wringing out the ends.

"I'd like nothing more than to have a good catch-up and hear everything that has happened since you left us, but we need to get back before we are found missing." She paused. "He's coming after you, Anna."

"I've known he would since the day I left." Anna pressed her lips together. "I don't want you to go, when you've only just gotten here." She smiled at them. "You both would love it here. There's so much to see, and it's so different from where we come from."

Anna paused again. If anyone would have advice on the recent events in Cups, it would be her advisors. "But strange things have been happening here since I arrived." She scrunched up her face. "Something isn't right."

"What do you mean?" the Magician asked. She shook off her wet slippers and wrung them out onto the sand. The Hermit watched her and then did the same.

"It started with a storm brewing over the water. The sea became angry and violent, which, as you can see, is not its natural state."

They all turned to look at the ocean. It stared back at them, smooth as glass, nearly still save for the gentle swell of low tide ebbing back and forth near their feet.

"Then there were the quakes where the earth itself shook, with terrible winds and a deafening buzzing sound." She shook her hands out in front of her. "And today the ground split in two."

The Magician eyed Topper. "This has not happened here before, young man?"

Topper shook his head vigorously. "Absolutely not."

The Magician took this in.

"But Anna has a theory," Topper offered.

"I was just thinking," Anna mused, "that this land is so similar to my tapestry—"

"The land of youth," the Hermit interrupted. "Yes, it's how we got here."

"What do you mean?" Anna squinted at him.

"We used your tapestry, or what was left of it anyway. Through our Magician's newly rekindled magic, we were able to make them whole again—at least temporarily." He pointed to the Magician. "We saw you walking along this very beach," the Hermit said, shifting from foot to foot.

"I don't understand," Anna said, trying to follow. "And, wait, where is the Fool?" she asked, spinning around, hoping to catch a glimpse of his blond curls on the beach.

"There's something I have to tell you, Anna." Her aunt looked up at her. "The King has imprisoned the Fool."

"No." Anna's voice trembled. "Why him?" But before her aunt could speak, the answer dawned on her. "Because he helped me."

"He would do it again if he had to, Anna," her aunt promised. "We all would. But we have to go back and figure out a way to get him out."

Anna tilted her head back, blinking away the tears that threatened to spill from her eyes. Topper put his hand on her arm to comfort her, but she shook him off. "How did you find me?"

"I performed a tracking spell," the Magician began carefully. "We saw you cross a mossy bridge and then disappear, so we knew you must have gone to another land."

"A bridge no one had ever seen in the Hierophant's Kingdom," the Hermit added. "The King himself even suggested you had crossed over to another world."

Anna gaped at them. "He has the Fool *and* he knows where I am?"

"No, no," her aunt reassured her. "I only let him see a

glimpse of you to make him believe I was on his side, that I was still loyal to him. Tonight I enchanted your tapestries, the worlds you created. Anna, they came alive. Right beneath our gaze."

Anna's expression was blank. "I still don't understand."

"The people got up and walked around," the Hermit said. "The trees swayed in the wind and the nobles feasted and danced."

"These were worlds I created in my *imagination*," Anna said, incredulous. "Created with thread and my loom."

The three went silent. She heard Topper suck in his breath behind her.

"Cups is a real world with living, breathing human beings! It's not a land I dreamed up and wove. It's real," Anna said, looking around at the sand, the sea, and the wall of black rock behind her.

"You were just saying yourself that you thought there was a connection between your tapestry and Cups, the fact that the yarns were not bound," Topper reminded her.

Anna stepped back a few steps, trying to take in what they were implying. There was the cove where she and James swam, the one she had woven before she'd ever seen it, the library filled only with books that she had read, the sea and the earth, which seemed to rage and calm with Anna's moods.

"This is your gift, Anna." The Magician put her hands on Anna's shoulders. "You do have powers, and they are formidable, my dear. Now you need to fortify this land, your land, and keep the King out."

"If what you say is true, there is nothing I'd rather do," Anna said. "But how? All I can do is weave!"

"Exactly," the Hermit piped up. "That's why we've brought your tapestries."

Anna looked at the large wrapped package that lay on the sand next to where they stood.

"We think the key to barring the King from this land has something to do with your tapestries—perhaps if, like you said, you were to bind your last tapestry, he would not be able to enter." The Magician paused. "Or perhaps . . ."

Anna looked straight at the Magician, eyes saucer-wide. "Changes to the tapestries change the world."

"You are Marco's daughter, Anna," the Magician said breathlessly.

Suddenly the beach went black. The silver strip of ribbon reflected on the sea had gone, and they were left with a very familiar darkness, heavy and total. The four looked up at the sky.

The Moon had disappeared.

35

The King tossed and turned in his bed, unable to sleep, his bedclothes wet with sweat from a grinding anxiety. His mind whirled, listing off everything that needed to be done. He had his armor prepared, his swords were sharpened, and the general had the soldiers at the ready, sleeping in shifts and prepared to fight at any second.

"You're a fool, John." The voice came out of nowhere and the King jumped, his heart hammering in his chest.

"Who is that? Show yourself!" The King squinted in the darkness, trying to untangle himself from his sheets. His heart pumped with adrenaline. Where was his Guard?

"Hello, old friend." A match was struck, and the smell of a pipe floated into the room. "Ah. How I have missed this."

The King could just make out a figure sitting in the chair by the window.

"Guard!" he yelled, now out of bed. He shoved his feet into his slippers.

"They can't hear you, John," the man spoke from his table by the window.

"Where's the damn lantern?" the King muttered angrily,

fumbling around in the dark. So it was finally happening. Some-one had gotten past the Guard to assassinate him in his sleep.

"I see you've become just like your father—a helpless old king. Here, let me help you." The man snapped his fingers, and the room was illuminated by candlelight.

The King gasped.

"You? But how?" He put his hand to his heart, which felt like it might burst from his chest with the shock of seeing his old friend Marco sitting at his table.

"Oh, really now, John. You can't be that surprised. You're about to launch an attack on my daughter. You thought I wouldn't show up?"

Recovering, the King moved to sit in the chair across from Marco.

"But you have no power here, Marco." The King took a seat. "I made sure of that a long time ago when I stuck a knife through your heart."

"That's true," Marco said, taking a long draw off the pipe. He offered it to the King, who took it and inhaled from it deeply, then handed it back. "But I thought I would appeal to you now. As an old friend."

"It's disgusting how you haven't aged." the King said, look-ing at Marco's hair, still thick and black, his skin taut around his long white neck.

"She'll beat you," Marco said, suddenly serious. "You will lose everything."

"So you've come to warn me? Is that it?" the King demanded.

"To warn you, make a request of you. Whatever you want to call it." Marco set the pipe down on the table and peered into the orange embers of tobacco in its bowl. He looked up at the King. "Do you remember when we were boys and we used to fight with wooden swords? Do you remember how we'd go sailing with your father and pretend we were pirates?"

The King reached for the pipe again, and Marco handed it over to him.

"Of course I do," the King answered thoughtfully. "Some of my best memories."

"Simpler times." A higher, softer voice had replaced Marco's.

The King's head jerked up and he found himself looking into Anna's face.

This was no pale, sickly youth. Her skin was deeply tanned and covered in black tattoos. A goblet was inked into one of her bare forearms, a long sword on the other. She swept her long black hair off her neck, revealing a pentacle symbol, and she was nearly exposed but for a thick red silk scarf wrapped around her body. On one arm, she held an eagle; with the other, she stroked a large lion seated on the floor beside her.

The King bolted up in bed, drenched in sweat, his heart galloping in his chest. The room was dark and quiet.

"May the heavens help us," he gasped. "Guard!" he shouted, and this time they came at once.

36

"That is the strangest thing," Topper said. He lit a lantern and several candles in the library, and then peered out at the blackened night sky.

"It's all we know," said the Hermit. "We have no moon where we come from."

"Yes, Anna told me about that. This would all be very exciting if we weren't in mortal danger." Topper grimaced.

The Hermit chuckled. "It's all about perspective."

"It's probably just behind a cloud," Topper said, blinking up at the inky black sky.

The Magician sat on the stone steps outside the library, feeling too claustrophobic in the small room, while Anna sat beside her.

"We'll hold the King off as long as we can, Anna, but you should focus on binding the tapestry."

Topper and the Hermit came and joined them on the steps.

"But it's just a theory. What if I'm wrong?" Anna bit her lip.

"Anna, how did you get here?" the Magician asked suddenly.

Anna cocked her head at the Magician. "Like you, over the bridge. I was running from the King's men, cornered nearly, and this bridge appeared."

The Hermit and the Magician exchanged a look.

"Think, Anna. Think back to that night and tell us *exactly* what happened," the Magician urged her.

Anna recalled hearing the King's men approaching and then running for her life, only stopping for a moment.

"I pulled out pieces of my tapestries." She closed her eyes and thought back to that night in the dark, with only the Hermit's lantern to guide her. "I felt like I couldn't go on, and I wanted to remind myself why I had fled. I threw the tapestries on the ground: there was a Page, a Queen, and a King. There was a girl having a tea party and a boy swimming in a turquoise sea. . . ." Anna trailed off. "I need my satchel." Anna stood up suddenly.

"What is it, Anna?" Topper took a step toward her.

"We need to go to the villa," Anna urged. "Now."

The Magician rose from the steps. "Then this will be where we leave you, Anna."

"How will you get back?" Anna asked the Magician. "There is no tapestry for the Hierophant Kingdom."

"I don't think our return trip will be an issue. The King has never even thought to place a barrier spell around the kingdom. There was never a need," her aunt said.

"I wish you didn't have to go." But Anna thought of the Fool. They needed to go back for him.

The Hermit put his arms around Anna. "We thought it was goodbye once before," he whispered in her ear.

Anna stood tall and set her shoulders, but the tears still rolled down her cheeks. "Take care of our Fool," she said. "I can't stand the thought of him in the dungeons." Her voice caught. Topper stood next to her. He brushed his hand near hers.

The Magician strode over to Anna and kissed her on the

forehead. Topper took a step away to make room. "Do you still have your necklace?" the Magician asked.

Anna pulled it out of her dress.

"We are never really apart, right?" The Magician looked Anna in the eye and plucked her wand out of her robe. "Hold on to me," she instructed the Hermit.

The Hermit kissed Anna's cheek once more and then held on to the Magician's robes.

"Wait!" Anna called. "What if binding the tapestry doesn't work?"

The Magician gripped her wand and leaned down, encircling herself and the Hermit with golden light, starting at their feet and moving toward their heads. As the light traveled up their bodies and they began fading from sight, the Magician gave Anna one last look. "Then you'd better weave an army."

Topper wrapped Anna in a tight embrace. Tears spilled over her cheeks, and she buried her face in his neck. Just then the Moon returned to the sky, and the beach lit up once again. Anna and Topper looked up, blinking against the sudden brightness.

"We have to get the tapestries back to the villa," Topper said.

"What is going on here?"

Anna and Topper jumped apart.

James pulled up on his horse, watching as the Hermit and the Magician disappeared into the golden light, leaving behind only the impressions their feet had made in the sand.

"James." Anna's voice shook. "How long have you been there?"

"Long enough to know that Daniel was right. You have been lying to us all along."

Anna started to run to James, but he pulled on the reins and dug his heels into the horse's sides, turning back toward the villa, the sun rising behind him. Seeming to change his mind, he gave the reins a tug once more and slid off. He stalked toward Anna, raising his finger to point at her chest. "You are nothing but a liar, and you've put my family in danger."

The sea, which until then had been still, reflecting the pink light of dawn on its surface, began to stir.

"James." Topper tried to step between them, but James gave his shoulder a rough push, and Topper stumbled backward.

"Oh no," James said. "I don't want to hear a word from you. I think it's pretty clear where your loyalties lie, and they are not with me."

Topper tensed. "I know you're angry, but if you'd just give us a chance to explain—"

"Since when did you two become an us?" James was seething, his face reddening and his green eyes shining.

"James, stop this." Anna took a big step forward and placed a firm hand on James's chest. She needed to get to the villa, and they were running out of time. "Let me explain everything to you." Waves were erupting in the sea now, gaining strength in its center and building until they came crashing onto the shoreline in an explosion of white foam.

James jammed his finger toward the sea. "*That* is because of *you*. The earthquake that could've killed all the people I love was because of you. I get it now. I've had enough of your explanations for a lifetime, Anna." He stormed off and remounted his horse. "I'm going to tell the others," he spat, kicking his heels into his horse's sides and tearing down the beach.

Topper sighed, rubbing his hand over his face.

Anna stared at the sea. "Is that really because of me?"

"The stirring of the elements does seem to match your moods," Topper offered gently.

Anna told herself that she would need to stay calm if they wanted to reach the villa in one piece. She tried to mimic the Hermit's deep breathing, attempting to distract herself from the anger and sadness warring inside.

"We need to go tell Daniel the truth ourselves. He'll believe you," Anna said. She jogged down the shore, and Topper followed.

They ran for as long as they possibly could, but the heavy, cumbersome tapestries slowed them down. They trudged in silence for the second half of the trek, dread bubbling up in Anna's stomach.

When they finally reached the villa's steps, they were faced with the whole of Cups. Daniel had his arms crossed, his mouth a tight line of anger. James stood on one side of him, his chest puffed out, and Lara stood on the other, her fists clenched at her sides and her eyes bloodshot and puffy. They were all there: Terra, Henry, Ivy, Morgan, Simon, Rebecca, and Luke, along with people Anna had seen every day but whom she hadn't yet gotten to know. Looks of betrayal were plain on all their faces.

"Are you ready to tell us the truth now?" Daniel challenged her. "Who were those people who disappeared into thin air? Did they come to do us harm?"

"No." Anna shook her head. "They are friends, advisors of mine, come to warn us."

"Warn *you*," James hissed. Anna avoided his eyes. She understood his anger and hurt enough to know that she could no longer comfort him. She had lost his trust.

"Please, give her a chance," Topper begged.

Daniel's eyes flitted to him. "Fine. Go on."

How could one explain the Hierophant King to people who had only known freedom? Anna chose her words carefully and launched into her explanation. "I come from a very faraway land ruled by a tyrannical and immensely powerful king.

"This King believes in order, rigid rules, and hierarchy. He controls everyone and everything—when his people eat, sleep, who they marry, and what they do for work." The group listened, rapt, as if she were telling a strange bedtime story. "He believes that free will and our ability to make our own choices lead to chaos and destruction."

"What does this have to do with us?" Lara asked softly. "Why did you come here?"

The question stung, and Anna had to take a few breaths to steady her voice. "I came here to escape him. He is the one who locked me in a tower for my entire life. Those people, the people who came here today, they helped me escape. He was going to kill me on my sixteenth birthday."

"This is preposterous," Daniel said, shaking his head. "Just more lies."

"She is telling the truth, Daniel," Topper interjected. "You have to listen to her. If you will hear her out, everything will make sense to you. Please open your mind and your heart, Daniel. This is life or death."

Anna took another step forward, pleading with the people of Cups. "He is coming after me, and he will show no mercy when he gets here. He will not just take me; he will destroy Cups in the process. This land, this amazing, wondrous land, stands in direct opposition to everything he believes in."

"Why would you put us in this sort of danger, Anna?" Terra called, eyes shining.

"I am so sorry." Anna's voice trembled. "I didn't mean to come here. I was just running, and I was desperate to get away from him."

"Then why didn't you tell us the truth immediately?" Daniel wondered. "Or when I asked you at South Farm?"

"I didn't want to lose you. Any of you." She locked eyes with James. "You can't know how much you mean to me. I would never put you in harm's way on purpose. We can fix this. We just need to—"

Daniel cut her off. "You must go, Anna. That is how we fix this. Go, and don't come back."

Anna rushed toward them. "We need to work together to stop him. If you send me away, you will be more vulnerable."

A light rain began to fall. Anna felt the drops and tried to steady her breath.

"You have every right to be upset, Daniel," Topper said. "But you can't turn her away. She can help us." His eyes swept the crowd. "I know this is scary, and you think if you send her away that you will be rid of the problem. But you have not seen what I have seen. There is magic out there, and powers so great that they could easily destroy a land like ours."

"We lost half our livestock, and our friends are wounded, Anna. The very land is being torn apart, all because of you," Daniel said, unmoved. "You are a sickness, destroying our way of life," he thundered. He held up his hand, revealing the angry red scar that now ran down the length of his palm. "I will always have this to remind me just how dangerous you are."

Anna recoiled at his words. A boom of thunder smacked the air, and the rain fell in fat drops. She looked up at James and saw pain flicker in his eyes. He was staring at the ground, his arms crossed over his chest.

"James, you know me. Better than anyone ever has. Please tell them."

A jagged line of white lightning tore through the sky.

"I can't, Anna. I think it is best that you leave." Regret tinged his voice. "We have no way to trust that what you say is true."

"Lara." Anna turned to her friend.

"I'm sorry, Anna," she said, choking back tears.

"Topper, come join us now," Daniel commanded, making space between him and James. When Topper did not move, Daniel continued. "If you do not stand with us, then you, too, will be banished from this land."

"If we don't help her, there will be no Cups to come back to. Don't you see?" He threw his long arms out wide.

"Then you've made your choice," Daniel said.

37

"What the hell is going on here?" The King stared in disbelief. "Why has this hall been opened?"

A line of people snaked through the halls of the castle, ending in Whitehoof. Barda watched from the doorway and stood to attention when the King approached him.

"Next!" Senator Bassett was seated in a large, ornate chair with two guards at his side, receiving the most motley group of people the King had ever laid eyes on. The room reeked of rotten garlic and sweat and who knew what else, and it was filled with a cacophony of chatter as people spoke to one another to fight the boredom of waiting in line.

Gathered near the front of the line were three young women with long, tangled hair and pentacles charms worn defiantly on ribbons around their necks. A bastardization of the symbol the King wore to indicate his wealth and power.

Witches, the King thought.

Throughout the line stood men with gnarled fingers carrying sacks that gave off the foul scents. Potion makers.

Children with dirt smudged on their faces ran circles around the crowd as their mothers and fathers tried unsuccessfully to contain them.

"Bassett better be rounding these people up to imprison them," the King grumbled to Barda.

"This is in case the Magician doesn't come back," Barda said. "Or can't come back. In case we need to find another way to the girl."

"I trust someone is posted at the bridge in the wood."

"Of course, round the clock."

". . . and these people?" The King waved a hand around the room.

"Medicine men, witches, alchemists—dirty frauds, if you ask me," said Barda. "Senator Bassett offered a reward, and they came oozing out of every crevice like vermin. Makes my job easier. I'll take the whole lot to the dungeons when this business with the girl is done."

"Vermin, indeed," echoed the King. "This is a waste of time."

"How can you be so sure? That lot, the Hermit and the Magician, they already betrayed you once, Sire. Why would they come back, and who's to say they will help you if they do?"

"They won't leave the Fool behind," the King repeated for what felt like the hundredth time.

"The Magician has grown quite powerful." Barda didn't want to let on that she'd fooled him and gotten her wand back. "Are you so sure she'll still help you?"

"I'm not asking your opinion on the matter!" the King shrieked. He rubbed at his beard and then opened his mouth to shift his jaw, which was tight with anger.

"Are the troops ready?" the King asked.

"Yes, Sire."

"Show me," he commanded.

"Right away, Sire."

The two men turned on their heels and walked down the hall, their heavy boots stomping as they went. The peasants farther down averted their eyes when they saw the King coming. He glared at them as he passed.

"And have the Senator shut this down," the King said, jamming his thumb over his shoulder as they walked outside into the courtyard that bordered the Keep. The King thought of his visit from Marco that morning. "The two traitors will be back soon."

Seemingly infinite rows of knights on horses, Drake now among them, glittering in chain mail, stood as far as the eye could see outside the castle walls. The King walked through the throng, nodding to his soldiers, each glance a boost to their morale. He was making his way back to the spot in the wood where the Magician and the Hermit had disappeared, knowing with everything in him that their return was imminent.

He would wait for those two to come back. And when they did, *he* would put an end to this disaster, once and for all.

38

"Anna!" Anna looked up to see Ivy running down the beach. "Your satchel and some of your things."

"Thank you, Ivy." She was so surprised, she could barely get the words out. "You didn't have to run all the way down here."

"Well, it doesn't mean I like you or anything." Ivy choked out a laugh, tears springing to her eyes. Her hair was plastered back from the rain, and she hugged the bag protectively.

"Of course not." Anna smiled, feeling her own vision blur with tears.

Ivy shoved the satchel into Anna's arms. "I'm still glad you came, and I know I'm not the only one," she murmured, and then ran back up the beach toward the villa.

Anna squinted at the villa in the distance, with its turquoise shutters, many now damaged and hanging loosely from the windows. The bright red roof tiles that had caught her eye when she'd first arrived were now cracked, with patches missing where they had been swept off in the high winds.

It was only now that Anna really took in the damage: the contrast of this battered villa with its boarded-up windows to the bright and happy paradise she'd originally come to. She turned to Topper.

"Let's go."

He nodded, his eyes filled with sadness, his shoulders slumped.

They walked down the beach until they were out of sight of the villa.

"I know of a place we can go," Anna said, guilt creeping into the pit of her stomach before she even mentioned it. "Think anyone would mind if we borrowed a couple of horses?"

The sun was setting by the time they reached the cottage.

"What is this place?" Topper asked as they rode up.

"You have your library; James has this."

"It's enchanting," he said.

"It is," Anna agreed. "I feel guilty bringing you here, but I don't know where else to go."

Topper tied up the horses quietly.

"A lot has happened today," Anna said, kicking the sand with her feet. "A lot to take in."

"Yes." Topper stood at the door of the cottage.

Anna respected his choice to give her space, but in that moment she realized that she and Topper hardly knew each other. She felt a pang for James, for Lara, and her other friends back at the villa.

Anna found Topper sitting on the beach near the water with his knees tucked under his chin, staring up at the sky. Darkness had fallen quickly, and a million tiny stars sparkled above them. The Moon was resplendent and as white as snow. She took a seat next to him.

"It's as if he is trying to cheer us with the sheer beauty of night," Topper said.

"That's a lovely thought."

"He'll come around," Topper said.

"Who?" Anna asked.

"James."

Anna ran a finger through the sand. "Oh, I'm not so sure about that."

"I've known him a long time." Topper let out a long, deep sigh. "He loves you. He wouldn't be so torn apart if he didn't."

"And I love him," Anna murmured. "I should have confided in him."

Topper shrugged. "Things might have not gone any differently if you had."

"But at least I would have given him a chance. A chance to trust me." Anna reached for Topper's hand. She paused and looked at him. "I know there's something here"—she gestured between the two of them—"but I don't know what it is, and right now, with everything going on, I can't process it."

"Then it can stay on hold for now. We've got more important things to take care of anyway." He leaned over and kissed the top of her head.

She blinked up at him, and he returned her gaze for a moment before she stood up. "Help me roll out the unfinished tapestry? At least now I can put it back together."

They worked in the sand near the cottage's front door, choosing the driest patch they could find. While huge chunks were cut from it, it was still a formidable piece of work, with its bright blue-green sea and massive swaying palms with their gold-tipped leaves, the sand stretching out like a big silvery-white blanket.

"Wow!" Topper stared down at the tapestry. "You made this?"

Anna smiled.

"It's so detailed." He ran his fingers over the great black cliffs of the cove while Anna reached into her satchel, pulling out her tapestry squares.

"We have to match these up with what's missing here."

They sat on the porch and made five piles: Swords, Pentacles, Wands, the land of children, and another for all of the pieces Anna had woven since she'd arrived in Cups. Anna sorted through the pieces and handed them to Topper to place in each stack.

"Ready?" he asked her.

"I think so." For a second the task seemed daunting. But Anna quickly realized that she still remembered exactly where the pieces belonged. Topper stepped back and watched as she began to piece the land back together.

When Anna put the Queen in place and looked at her long, flowing strawberry-blond hair and green eyes the color of emeralds, she gasped.

Lara.

She laid down the King, with his long chocolate-brown hair and broad shoulders.

Daniel.

Anna added vibrant, youthful figures lounging in hammocks and swimming in the shimmering sea while Henry with his curling red hair stirred a large simmering pot.

She held a final piece in her hand. Chestnut hair, light-green almond-shaped eyes. When she placed it onto the tapestry, she felt as if James himself were staring back at her.

"Is it time to name it?" Topper peered at Anna with bright eyes.

Anna cleared her throat. "This"—she swept her hand over the tapestry—"is the land of Cups."

A cold wind swept over the beach and Anna shuddered, her face draining of color. "I've created a world of children, completely defenseless against a king."

39

The Magician and the Hermit seemed to fall from the sky, landing with a loud thud in the clearing where they had crossed the bridge. The King, who was waiting with the others, snapped to attention and squinted, making sure he was seeing what he thought he was seeing.

Barda was already moving. "Seize them!" he shouted. "Bind the woman's arms so she can't get to her wand," Barda then whispered to a pair of foot soldiers, out of earshot of the King.

"They just dropped from the sky!" the King exclaimed. The King was surprised to find that there was no bridge in sight. He was supposed to be able to walk his troops over the bridge so that they could storm whatever was waiting for them on the other side.

"Don't worry," the Magician said to the Hermit under her breath. Just before they had entered Cups, she had ripped off a small remnant of Anna's tapestry and shoved it into her pocket. She had considered it a failsafe of sorts, and now she was grateful for the forethought. She reached into her pocket, making sure the small piece of fabric had not been lost on the journey. It was there. She unclasped her hand and let it fall into her pocket as a tall guard rushed her and held back her arms. The Hermit gazed wild-eyed at the army winding out of the wood as far as the eye could see, and spotted Drake sitting upon a white horse, dressed in full battle regalia behind the King, his eyes blank.

The Hermit narrowed his eyes. "When did Drake become a knight?" he muttered to himself.

Within seconds the Hermit's arms were bound too, and they were being shoved toward the King. Neither struggled, the Magician's face alarmingly calm as she stared at the King in defiance. The Hermit shook with fear. He cast his eyes downward.

"Welcome back. Did you have a nice trip?" the King asked, his voice dripping with sarcasm. "Look, I don't blame you. It's my doing, really—I charged you with raising the girl. She's like your child, and no parent wants harm to come to one of their own."

The Magician raised an eyebrow.

"But Anna is a darkness in this world that needs to be destroyed."

"Your Majesty . . . ," the Hermit began, the mention of Anna giving him courage. But the King held his hand up.

He looked at the two empty-handed prisoners. "Where are the tapestries?" he asked.

"We gave them to their rightful owner," the Magician spat.

The King huffed. "I don't believe that you would leave Anna with no way to get back here, sealed in a strange land."

"Strange, yes, but one of her own making." The Magician relished these words.

"Is that supposed to intimidate me?" the King snapped. He walked toward the Magician, leaves crunching beneath his heavy boots, until they were inches apart.

"You'd be a fool not to be intimidated." Now the Magician was stalling. She knew how this would end, and she needed to give Anna as much time as she could.

The King felt his cheeks redden. "You know how to get to her. What's it going to take to get you to share that information?"

The men on horseback watched the scene unfold, their breath tight in their chests. Their horses shuffled their hooves and whinnied, as anxious from waiting as the knights were.

"I thought you'd never ask." The Magician smiled wickedly. "The first thing you're going to need to do is go get the Fool and bring him here—alive."

The King knew he had lost his leverage, and was now losing face in front of his army. He should have rushed in after these two imbeciles when he'd had the chance.

"Bring the Fool," he barked to one of his guards. "Quickly!" The guard took off at a run, his sword rattling at his side.

"Once he is here, safe and sound, I'll grant you entrance. At that point, we are free to go."

"Fine," the King relented. It was a small price to pay in the grand scheme of things. "But tell me how you will do it. How will you get us there, to this other land? And tell me what I'm up against. I know you've warned her."

"An army of giants and monsters," the Magician lied.

The Hermit's eyes flitted to the Magician.

"The ground is made of hot lava, and most of your men will die trying to ride over it," the Magician continued.

The King swallowed hard, trying to keep his expression neutral. He glanced over his shoulder at the young boys on their horses, their faces growing wary, but the soldiers were still so eager to serve him. He felt a stab of worry.

The Magician hoped she appeared calm on the outside as she tried to intimidate the King, but once again she felt for the piece of tapestry she'd taken before they left Cups. It still sat, soft and warm, in the pocket of her robe.

40

"I need to get to my loom so I can bind these threads." Anna was still kneeling before her Cups tapestry in front of the cottage. She picked at an unraveling seam. "There's been so much damage, and there are sections missing, pieces I trimmed." She paused.

"What?" Topper's eyes narrowed.

"You heard what the Magician said. I need to weave an army." Anna ran her finger over the tapestry. "This is how you got to Pentacles," Anna said, thinking out loud. "When I cut the tapestries apart, the borders opened up."

Topper came closer. "Do you think so? That is why I was able to sail to Pentacles?" He fingered one of the tattered spaces in the landscape of Cups.

"I don't have any proof, so I can't know for sure. . . ."

"But if you weave an army, it will come here, to Cups?" Topper scratched at his chin. "Can you do that?"

"Changes to the tapestries change the world," Anna repeated.

The sun was shining brightly now and a cool breeze danced off the water, carrying the scent of a nearby jasmine bush into the air.

Topper stretched his arms out wide. "Let's weave an army!" He laughed. "As crazy as that sounds. I'll start figuring out how we're going to sneak you back into your old room."

She grinned at him. "Thank you, Topper. Thank you for believing in me."

Anna cleared a space on James's worktable, knowing she had very little time. The stains from their stamping project spilled across the table in deep gashes of color that made her heart catch in her chest. She began by working out her thoughts in sketches.

She did not want any ordinary army. There was enough violence in the King's infantry for the entire world as far as she was concerned.

No, this army would embody the most powerful parts of being. Each might stand alone—she thought of her illustrations of Strength and Death—but together they would make up a sort of counsel for the soul. She would imbue them with great wisdom and great power, and they would be the protectors of her worlds.

The Magician, the Hermit, the Fool, Strength, the Hanged Man, and Death. She thought of their offerings: creativity, quiet contemplation, innocence, spontaneity, fortitude, and rebirth. It was a strong start.

If only she were weaving as she went instead of sketching. Her loom was like an extension of her hands and her mind.

The High Priestess was next, a strong feminine figure who, to Anna, depicted the idea of knowing one's own voice and not having it clouded by the opinions of others. Next came the Empress, representing nature, beauty, and fruitfulness, and with her, the Emperor, an icon of wisdom and power. Anna drew them while thinking of the tales she had heard of her own parents, a similarly strong pair.

It felt like building a staircase, each figure a step toward truth. The figures were representative of all she knew. There was the surface knowledge—information from books that she had gleaned during her imprisonment, and everything she'd learned from her time with her advisors. There was her personal history, because there were important lessons there. From it, she drew the Tower and the Hierophant King.

She was culling from every emotion she'd ever experienced and those she had witnessed in others. All the parts of her that had developed since she had arrived in Cups. The pain she had caused, the joy she had known. She accessed all of it, and in turn she was also scratching beneath the surface for the wisdom that was pooling there. Because weren't these the things that made everyone human? Daniel's anger, her anger, the King's anger—was it all that different in the end? When one thing died within and another sprouted there, hopefully something good, but sometimes something evil. She wove an image of the Devil.

She paused and tapped her pencil to her forehead. All the experiences she had had since she'd arrived in Cups. She began to sketch them, too. The bonds of friendship and what happened when those bonds were threatened. How did people heal from pain?

Anna thought of James and how it felt to explore another person, body and mind. Her feelings for Topper, strange and confusing, and how talking to him seemed to stretch her consciousness—she sketched that, too. The Lovers.

She drew the darker side of things. The look on Daniel's face when he sent her away. The King's fear of losing control.

Back in the Tower, she had wanted to weave things, concepts

that were not quite ripened enough to manifest, and now she was able to pluck them, utilize them to protect the people of Cups. The Wheel of Fortune. The Star.

Perhaps one day they would be called upon to protect the people of Wands and Swords and Pentacles, too. Justice.

The sun was rising by the time she stepped back, surveying her work. Finished.

An army of twenty-one.

For Anna, it was a physical representation of everything she had learned, as well as all that was on offer for her to learn in the future. On offer for every human being to learn. But today it was an army she hoped would be more powerful than any the world had ever known.

Exhausted, Anna put the heels of her hands to her eyes and studied the sketches. "Are these just mad ravings?" she whispered aloud.

"For all our sakes, I sure hope not."

James.

Anna spun around.

"Hello," he said.

Anna froze. "Hi," she croaked, her voice rusty from hours of disuse.

"Can you ever forgive me?" he asked quietly.

Relief flooded through Anna's tired body and, without thinking, she ran into his arms and held on, tight.

"You?" Anna cried into his chest. "Can you ever forgive *me*? I lied to you."

He took her hands in his. "Topper told me everything, showed me the tapestries."

Anna realized she hadn't seen Topper all night and hadn't even thought of where he might be. While she'd frantically sketched, Topper had gone to find James and had convinced him to come back to her. Her face flushed.

James studied her sketches. "It's like nothing I have ever seen. It makes me feel so small." He leaned in, meeting Anna's eyes. "I hate that we turned you away like that. I hate myself for it. I'm ashamed of the way I acted."

"I understand why you did it," she reassured him, placing one hand on his chest and the other through his hair, making sure he was real. She had lied, she hadn't trusted James enough to tell him the truth, and she was confused about her feelings for Topper. Things just didn't seem so black and white anymore. She gestured toward the pages on the table. "We're complicated beings. We have many layers."

James surveyed her work. "I'm a little scared of you, Anna," he said.

A flicker of worry crossed her features, and she let her hands drop to her sides.

James smiled at her, but his eyes were serious. "You wove all of us before you even met us. It explains things—like why we have no past, no parents." He took her hand again. "If I hadn't seen your friends disappear like that on the beach yesterday, I might not have believed it. The night you arrived makes sense now. You really did come out of nowhere."

He kissed her, the gentle softness of his lips quelling her anxieties. When he pulled away, Anna felt dazed.

She rolled her shoulders and leaned forward to collect her sketches from the worktable, and James bent down to help her.

"I've created an army to protect Cups from the King," Anna explained. "But I have to get to my loom to weave them into the tapestry."

James picked up the sketch of the Tower. "Is there where you were held prisoner?" Anna nodded as she shuffled the rest of the sketches into a stack she could manage, preparing to sneak back to the villa.

"I asked the Magician to level it before we left the Hierophant's Kingdom," she said somberly. She felt a pang of guilt for the guards who had lost their lives.

James let out a low whistle. "Now I really am scared of you."

The three of them let the horses free on the beach once they reached the villa. James assured Anna and Topper that they would make it back to the stables on their own.

They crept up the stairs and onto Anna's patio. James went first in case they ran into anyone, but when he tried to open the door, it was locked.

He scrunched up his face and tugged harder on the knob. "Damn it," James said. "Why would they do this?"

In a place where doors were never locked, they had barred Anna's to make sure she couldn't try to come back.

"We'll have to break the glass," said Topper.

"Won't it make too much noise?" Anna whispered.

Before Topper could answer, James had taken off his shirt and wrapped his hand in it. He punched his fist through the window next to the door.

Topper and Anna jumped back.

James unwrapped his hand, shook it out, and then put his knuckles in his mouth.

He leaned over the patio to see if the noise had awakened anyone, but the rest of the windows on the villa's face remained dark. James waved for them to go inside.

Anna scrambled through the window, careful to avoid broken glass.

It was gone.

Anna grabbed at the air with her hands and pulled them into tight fists, shaking them in front of her chest.

"This is ridiculous!" she hissed. "How am I supposed to help them if they keep stopping me at every turn?"

James and Topper came up behind her in the darkness and glared at the piles of yarn and fabric where Anna's loom used to be.

"I told you not to come back." Anna jumped at the sound of Daniel's voice behind them, Dragon at his side, a low growl moving through his throat. He held up a bright lantern in front of his face, nearly blinding them.

"Where is the loom?" Anna demanded, panic rising in her chest. She didn't know if they had hours or minutes before the King and his army arrived.

"I burned it," Daniel said, lowering the lantern so that it lit his face in eerie shadows.

"Why would you do that?" Now it was James's turn to be angry.

"To rid Cups of this witchery!" He sounded like the Hierophant King.

Topper threw down the Cups tapestry, ignoring Daniel, and rolled it out on the floor. He jabbed his finger at the long-haired, broad-shouldered King.

"Look, we are all here. You, Lara, Terra, Henry—all of us."

"She could have woven this while she was here," Daniel argued.

"Her friends brought these to her yesterday from the Hierophant's Kingdom," Topper said. "I watched as they handed them over to her." His voice rose. "I was standing right there."

"I know it sounds unbelievable, but think about it, Daniel. What's your first memory? Twenty-four moon cycles ago? If that?" James looked to Topper for help.

"It explains why we have no parents or children of our own. No history. We came from Anna's imagination," Topper explained.

Anna took a step toward Daniel. "I wove a world just like this one. I wove you, Lara, James, that sea out there, those mountains before I saw any of it. I wove a whole world with four lands, and we are in one of them." Anna rubbed her dress between her fingers. "I know that's not an excuse for lying to you." Anna paused. "But whatever you believe or don't believe, the King is coming, and we need to protect this land."

James stepped in. "She's created an army to protect us, and we were sneaking back in so she could weave it into the tapestry."

"I burned the loom in a rage," Daniel said slowly.

James's face set into a deep frown. "Dan, you didn't."

Topper covered his face with his hands and groaned.

"How was I supposed to know?" Daniel said, his voice defensive. "Maybe you could have told me that our fate rested on the existence of the loom!"

Anna bit her lip, thinking. She inched toward him and carefully placed her hand on his arm. He flinched at her touch, but she did not remove her hand. Daniel might be the King, but she was their maker. "You need to go wake Lara and everyone else and tell them what's happening. Then gather anything we can use as weapons—rakes, brooms, knives."

The three young men stared at her in horror.

"But we are not soldiers." When Daniel opened his eyes, they were glassy with tears.

"Today you might have to be," Anna said, giving his arm

a squeeze. "Get creative. Boil hot water to throw from the roof, collect any sharp objects."

"We could throw rocks at them," James suggested.

"And sand in their eyes to blind them," Topper added.

"Keep thinking like that," Anna said. "He's got a bigger army, but he's on the wrong side of this battle. That's got to count for something."

41

Drake was hungry and cold, still stationed in the forest with the rest of the knights and growing more restless by the minute. But when the soldiers pulled their horses to the side to make way for the guard, he was not prepared for what he saw in front of him.

His Fool. He could barely walk. The guard half carried, half dragged him through the path between the soldiers. Drake put his gloved hand to his mouth, sure he would be ill.

They walked the Fool past Drake. His eyes were swollen and bruised, and he was weighed down by chains, struggling to keep his feet on the ground. When he finally reached the Magician and the Hermit, Senator Bassett shoved him forward.

"Unchain him!" the Magician shouted.

At the sound of the Magician's voice, the Fool felt a warmth bloom in his chest. He attempted to smile, but his jaw was tender and the smile dissolved into a twisted grimace.

The Magician continued, her voice booming over the army. "Unbind us, and then I will manifest the bridge and you can do your worst."

"What? No!" the Fool started to struggle, and that was when he noticed Drake, sitting in shining silver armor on a horse behind the King. "He's been knighted!" the Fool yelped, excited that Drake had finally fulfilled his dream.

The Magician thought her heart would break inside her chest. If her arms were free, she would have had a very hard time deciding what action to take first—throw a rock at Drake's head or take the Fool in her arms to comfort him.

"Drake is no friend of ours," the Magician rasped to the Fool.

The Fool stopped struggling, his face blank.

"He betrayed you," the King said. He was as restless as his troops and eager to go into battle. "Drake was kind enough to let me know not to trust these two." He waved his arm in the direction of the Hermit and the Magician. "For which I am very grateful." He nodded at Drake, and Drake bowed back, but his face was pale and his body was shaking.

The Fool looked up at Drake and then back to the King. "This can't be true," he said. "I don't believe it."

Drake slid off his horse and ran to the Fool. The King narrowed his eyes but did nothing to stop him.

"I was trying to save you." Drake came face-to-face with the Fool. "I only betrayed them in order to get you out of the dungeons."

"But in doing so, you betrayed Anna, and you know what she means to me," the Fool whispered. He lifted his chained hands to wipe away his tears.

"Maybe it was misguided," Drake pleaded. "But I did it for you."

The Fool whispered something in Drake's ear that the crowd standing around them could not hear. Drake nodded, and the Fool touched his forehead to Drake's.

The King let out a sigh of impatience, and Barda looked away, disgust clear on his face.

"I forgive you," the Fool said to Drake, their lips inches apart.

Drake pressed his lips gently to the Fool's swollen, bruised mouth.

"I'm so sorry," Drake said.

"Take him to the dungeons!" the King called to Barda.

"No!" the Fool screamed as two guards grabbed Drake's arms and tore him away from the Fool.

"He is not part of the deal," the King said, pointing at Drake, who did not take his eyes off the Fool as they dragged him away. "If he would betray his lover, then he would betray me."

The Fool moved to follow, but the Magician shook her head fiercely.

"Unchain the other three," the King called to Barda. "We've wasted enough time."

Unbound, the Magician started for the clearing where they'd entered Cups, her hand in her pocket, the piece of tapestry clenched in her fingers. The King, Senator Bassett, and Barda followed her a few steps behind.

"Remember," she said. "Monsters and giants and lava that will melt your skin off."

The three men glared at her as she took her wand from her robes. She relit the candles and swayed slowly, uttering the words of love that had opened the bridge into Cups.

Barda grimaced. Senator Bassett leaned in close, while the rest watched from a safe distance.

The Fool stood by, his whole body shaking, while the Hermit rubbed his arm softly.

When the Magician finished reciting the poetic spell, she pulled her wand back and shoved it forward forcefully, shouting, "*Anoixahtaye!*"

42

Anna tried to pull one of her sewing needles through the threads of her Cups tapestry, but it had snapped in half, no match for its thickness.

She groaned and threw her head back. People were supposed to be looking for weapons and preparing for battle as best they could, but Anna could feel their eyes peering at her from all corners of the villa's common room.

Sitting in the middle of the Cups tapestry, pieced together again like a loose puzzle, she ran her fingers over another needle, imagining it gliding through the threads like silk. She squeezed her eyes shut and stabbed at her tapestry. The needle broke through the thick landscape. Anna's eyes flew open, and, as she pulled the needle through the other side, a golden light raced up the thread.

Her fingers darted and flew with an almost inhuman agility. Golden light filled every new stitch and seam and then slowly faded, like pulsing stars. Without the barrier of the loom's shuttle, her fingers and mind were able to move as one.

She bound up all the loose threads of Cups, and as she began on her army, her counsel of protectors, Anna heard the others whispering about strategy behind her.

Daniel had sent a team to act as lookouts at various locations, stationing a larger group at the cove below the library where she had entered Cups.

She stitched the Hanged Man and Death onto the beach of the tapestry. It would have looked to an outsider as if she were dancing, golden dust trailing her fluid movements.

In went the Magician, the Hermit, and the Fool. The friends who had taught Anna to learn her gifts and use them wisely.

Next, she wove in the Empress and the Emperor, followed by the icons of Anna's past and future battles, the Tower and the Hierophant King.

Then came celestial bodies of this world—the Sun, the Moon, and the Star. She wove the Lovers into the sea, the warmth of the Sun shining down on them. Anna thought of her and James splashing in the water during her first swimming lesson and smiled to herself.

On she wove until only three figures remained.

A loud banging rang out through the villa. "Something is happening at the cove!" a voice shouted from the other side of the front door.

Anna frantically wove in the final members of her army—the Wheel of Fortune, the Devil, and Judgment. An army of twenty-one, the army of the new world. The keepers of truth.

She leapt from the table as Daniel, wielding a rake, shouted for everyone to follow him out. Lara ran to Anna's side, and the two young women stared down at the tapestry. The enchantment had faded. Without the sparkling gold, the threads looked disheartening flat.

"Do you think it will work?" Lara whispered, taking Anna's hand, her eyes wide with fear.

"I'm not without hope," she said. But inside, Anna was not

so sure. "You stay here. I am going out there to fight."

"I won't!" Lara protested.

Anna looked down at Lara's ankle, still swollen. "I wish you didn't have to. But you are in no shape to fight." She kissed Lara's cheek, took one last look at the tapestry, and ran down the steps to the beach.

43

The sky turned black above them, and thunder boomed through the sky. Rain came down in sheets, pelting the knights' heavy armor.

"Move aside!" the King shouted, mounting his horse. Barda and Senator Bassett did the same.

The bridge had appeared.

The King donned his helmet and felt for the sword at his side.

A thick fog was creeping in, and the men might have lost sight of the bridge but for the electrifying light, jagged, angry bolts of lightning.

The Magician stepped aside, saying a silent prayer that Anna was ready on the other end. She noticed the bridge was different this time—what she could see of it at least. The moss had given way to a brown, stinking rot. It looked menacing, like the open mouth of something monstrous.

The King took a deep breath and dug his heels into his horse's sides. He half worried the bridge would collapse under the weight of his army. His men began to follow him two by two, squeezing onto the narrow bridge.

It was frigid. The King would be lucky if his army didn't freeze before they made it all the way across.

The King's horse quickly came to the thick, viscous sludge and whinnied in protest. He dug his heels deeper into the poor beast's sides, and he pushed through the sticky wall.

Suddenly the atmosphere changed, and the King felt suffocated in his heavy armor and helmet. The air was thick and hot. Was this the lava the Magician had spoken of?

The King took a deep breath through his nose and drew in the smell of salt and lush greenery. They were somewhere tropical. Senator Bassett rode up beside him, looking uncharacteristically stunned.

For a split second the men forgot their mission. The most beautiful body of water they had ever seen stretched out for endless miles in front of them. A blanket of shimmering turquoise, calm and nearly translucent.

They scanned the shore and saw, in the distance, a motley group of young farmers holding rakes like spears. The King's men were pouring through the opening now, hundreds of them, their horses pounding through the shallow water. They lined up behind the King.

He looked at the ragtag group barreling away from them. These were mere children playing at war. The Magician had lied about giants and monsters. The King looked to the Senator and let out a deep, uproarious laugh.

44

Down the shore, Anna watched with the people of Cups as the King and his army marched over the enchanted bridge. They should have hidden, in the jungles, at South Farm. They should have sailed away.

"Run!" she yelled to the people of Cups. They grabbed their makeshift weapons and ran back toward the villa. But they were no match for the King's horses.

The King gave the command for his men to charge, and soldiers on horseback galloped toward the people of Cups with sudden speed, swords swinging violently. They slashed and stabbed anything and anyone in their way, kicking up walls of sand in their wake.

Anna screamed as young people fell all around her, dead or writhing in pain. She watched in horror as they crumpled, defenseless with their pathetic rakes and their broomsticks, their pots and pans.

She saw Topper running toward a soldier with a shovel held like a spear. But he was no match. The soldier swung a metal ball attached to a chain and aimed it at Topper's head. The ball tore into Topper's skull, and he crumpled to the ground on the spot, dropping face-first into the sand, blood pooling beneath his body.

"No!" Anna wailed, dropping to her knees. She crawled through the hectic scene, dodging horse hooves and flying swords to get to Topper. She knelt beside him, trying to turn him over. She brought his limp palm to her heart, the pumping of her blood drowning out the sounds of clashing weapons and agonized screaming. Something hit the ground beside her and her eyes snapped up. James was standing over her, urging her to get up.

She squinted at him as he leaned down, whispering in her ear and pulling her to her feet.

Everything seemed to stand still. The soldiers ceased their onslaught and pulled their horses to one side, creating a path between them in the sand.

The King rode through on a giant black stallion. He looked regal, with a shining purple sash pinned over his armor. He removed his helmet, showing off a closely cropped head of salt-and-pepper hair. Even his horse was draped with flags, his mane braided carefully with ribbons and tassels.

Anna glared at him as he approached, but he had not yet noticed her among the wounded.

"Who is in charge here?" the King roared. He looked indignant as he took in the young farmers, some still gripping their scythes and makeshift weapons, others weeping over the bodies of their fallen friends. "You're a bunch of children, for stars' sake!"

Daniel stepped forward bravely. Anna moved to stop him, but James held her back.

"No one is a leader!" Daniel yelled. "Everyone is equal, and everyone is free."

The Hierophant King let out a deep belly laugh. Daniel stared up at the King, enmity forming a vein in his brow.

"We are not a joke for your amusement," Daniel said.

With this, the King's mirth vanished. "No, but see, you are exactly that. Your lack of leadership, your 'everyone is free' philosophy," he said in a singsong voice, mocking Daniel, "is the very reason my army will destroy you." The King leaned forward, wiping sweat from his brow. "I look forward to having this land under my jurisdiction. That sea of yours looks exquisite."

Daniel rushed at the King, and two soldiers grabbed him, pinning his arms back.

"Here's what's going to happen," the King snarled. "You are under my rule now. You will wake when I say, eat when and what I say, and sleep when I tell you to."

Daniel struggled against the soldiers, and one stuck his knee roughly into Daniel's spine, bringing him to his knees.

"I wasn't finished, young one. Anyone who tries to rebel will be put to death." He looked down at Daniel. "Understood?"

Daniel hung his head.

"Now, where is the girl?" The King's eyes swept the bloody scene.

Anna took a giant stepped forward, away from Topper's lifeless body.

"I am right here."

The King looked taken aback at the sight of her. "This way of life really agrees with you, Anna." he commented, looking her over. "Too bad I have to destroy it."

Anna lunged at his leg and tugged, attempting to pull him off his horse. "You are a monster!" she screamed.

"Seize her!" the King yelled, and a soldier with blood smeared down the front of his armor yanked Anna back by the arms. The King slid off his horse and walked toward her. He pulled a blade from the belt at his waist and held the tip to her chin.

"I created this world that you stand in. You are not welcome here!" Anna spat at his feet.

"Your point?" the King asked. He moved the blade just enough to prick her chin, blood blooming at the blade's tip.

"Anna!" James leapt forward.

"Oh, who is this?" The King waved the blade at James. "Did you find yourself a little love here?"

"James, stay back!" Anna commanded. "Why are you so full of hate?" she asked the King through gritted teeth.

"You are so naive, Anna. I don't hate you. Your father was like a brother to me—until he wasn't," he said. He paused, searching for the right words. "Whether I like you or not, whether I admire you or not, you are dangerous, and it is my job to protect our way of life."

Anna's plan had failed; no army was coming to save them. She knew she was about to die, but not before she gave the people of Cups hope.

"You are not all-powerful, and you cannot control people's destinies. I am living proof of that, and so is the entire world I've created. Every single person who breathes in the land of Cups is evidence that free will exists—" Anna gasped as the King brought the blade back to her throat.

"Are you finished?" he asked, grabbing both of her wrists with his other hand and twisting them tight behind her back.

"No!" James screamed.

"He'll be the first one to go, after you," the King whispered in her ear, nodding to James.

"I'm the first of many," Anna announced, despite the blade at her throat. "I may have failed, but more will come after me. You'll spend your whole life hunting us down."

"Enough!" roared the King. In one swoop, he pulled the

blade violently across Anna's throat, bright red blood following its path. Her eyes widened, and she slumped in his arms. The King threw her onto the sand in front of him and turned away from the crowd. He didn't want anyone to see the pain in his face.

45

At first, Anna felt nothing. She heard nothing. She saw James running toward her, his mouth torn open in what must have been screams, but she couldn't hear. Then, one by one, her senses turned back on, and the pain came, molten and suffocating. She grabbed at her throat, gagging and gasping for air that wouldn't come.

Her vision was spotty. She saw shadows approaching from all sides, dark and out of focus. Out of the jungle, down from the mountains, out of the water, and up the beach. At last.

Her army had arrived.

She let the pain take her, subsume her, until she was burned to nothing but ash.

"Seize them all!" the King yelled to his Guard. They stood with their mouths agape, staring at the phantom figures. "What is wrong with you? Why don't you follow my command?" The King pulled his blade once more, but the Empress put a hand on his shoulder, and he found he could not move. "What are you?" he whispered.

"We are the Major Arcana, Hierophant King, and we are here to protect this land," the Empress said in a voice like a song.

"There is no place for tyranny in this world, John."

The King startled upon hearing his given name.

"There are many paths," crooned the Lovers as they surrounded the King. He swatted at them as if they were gnats. "We are here to serve as guides."

The people of Cups watched in awe as the Sun, the Moon, and the Star surrounded Anna, raising her body and wrapping it in a blanket of luminescent starlight. The gash at her neck closed. The Moon pursed his full lips and blew new life into her crumpled body.

Anna's long black lashes started to quiver, and she slowly opened her lids, revealing not black, but eyes the color of amethysts.

James flew toward her, and the Arcana stepped aside for him.

"Can I touch her?" he asked. They nodded. He took her in his arms as tenderly as he could manage. "Thank you," he said. Tears rolled down his cheeks, and he covered Anna's face in kisses as she blinked up at him. "You did it." He kissed her more. "You did it, Anna."

Judgment stepped up. His face was cherubic, and his curls bounced yellow around his plump face. Angel wings sprouted resplendent and gossamer from his back, but his horn blared ominous, and when he approached, the King flinched.

"You have been so blind, John. You let your pain and fear run away with you all these years, and now you must pay the price for your misdeeds."

The King was speechless. Judgment waved his arm in a sweeping gesture, and the King and his great army were shackled, their weapons dropping to their feet. The King's faced drained of all color. He had lost in every way.

Anna looked on with wonder as the Arcana worked their magic. Judgment waved his arms once again, and the innocent rose up from the sands of Cups. The wounded were healed, the dead risen. Anna watched, joy blooming in her chest, as Topper rubbed his eyes, disoriented but very much alive.

The Wheel of Fortune, a being more sphinx than man, complete with an elaborate headdress, tossed a giant wheel with eight spokes into the sky over the sea with such force that the ground began to shake. He snapped his giant fingers and sealed the people of Cups in a silver bubble of protective light. While all around them the winds picked up into a tempest and sand blew violently into the eyes of the King and his soldiers, the people of Cups were untouched.

The wheel itself spliced the sea into two parts. A giant corridor now ran through the sea between two massive waves suspended in midair. At the end of the path through the sea sat a vast, gaping black hole, spinning on the horizon. A great wind blew the Hierophant King and his army down the wave-lined path and into the vast hole. When every last soldier was sucked into the blackness, the sea knitted back together and the hole slammed shut with a deafening crack. The Wheel of Fortune held up his hand and the wheel flew back to him. He smiled with satisfaction as he closed his mighty hand over the large disc.

A silence descended upon Cups, the silver bubble dissolved, and the sea twinkled, calm and bright blue once more.

"You came," Anna cried, her cheeks flushing with joy as she spotted the Fool, the Magician, and the Hermit standing among the Major Arcana. She sprinted up to them. "Are you real?" she asked.

"We are as real as anything here, dear Anna." The Fool threw his arms around her, his bruises now faded, his cuts now healed.

Bembo, following close at his heels, let out an excited bark. Anna scooped him up, her heart bursting with joy as the little dog licked her cheek. The Hermit and the Magician smiled at her and then swept her up in a tight embrace.

The Empress approached Anna, her feet floating just above the sand. She took Anna's hands in her own. At her touch, Anna's chest was filled with warmth. She took in her flowing gown, gauzy white and embroidered with red roses, her crown made of twinkling stars. Her skin was a deep brown, and her hair escaped her crown in glorious long, tight curls. "Dear girl, you've created this world from all you know, but now it will take on a life of its own."

"I'm not sure I understand," Anna said, blinking up at the ethereal creature before her.

"This land was limited to your own experience and your glorious imagination. But now that it has been birthed, it will grow in its own way. Within it, there will be people and places you've never dreamed of."

"It sounds magnificent," Anna answered.

The Empress leaned in and kissed Anna's cheek. "Goodbye for now, dear Anna."

The Major Arcana were fading as they began to walk into the water, up the mountainside, and down the beach. There was so much Anna wanted to ask them, but they were slipping away, one by one.

Anna grabbed her aunt's hand before she, too, headed away down the beach.

"Will I see you again?" she pleaded.

"We will watch over you, my dear," the Magician said.

"We will always come when needed," the Hermit said.

The Fool took Bembo from her arms and gently pressed his

hand to Anna's cheek before turning away with the others.

James walked toward her, pushing his hair out of his battle-worn face. He put his arm around Anna's waist. Topper approached from her other side and leaned into her shoulder. Even Dragon bounded up and licked her hand, followed closely by a beaming Daniel.

"I have so many questions," Anna said.

"I'm sure they will answer if you ask," Topper said. "You did create them, after all."

Anna studied Topper's face, thinking of his travels. With the Hierophant gone from her world, Anna, too, was finally and truly free to explore.

EPILOGUE

Silk flags, each decorated with an emerald-eyed serpent, graced every turret of the kingdom, welcoming visitors from near and far. The filth had been removed from the gutters, and the peasants found their homes stocked with food and baskets of dry firewood.

The Hierophant King sat in a dungeon cell. He wished daily that death would come early. After living in such padded luxury, the confines of the cell made him claustrophobic, not to mention incensed. Accommodations suited for rats, which he believed might be sharing his cell, judging from the ugly scratching sounds that kept him awake at night. The King's only comfort was the Senator, who shared the next cell over. They talked through the hours until the King grew tired of his ramblings.

The Magician, the new ruler, sat in a window high above the Keep. She smiled upon seeing the faint beginnings of a perfect crescent Moon as the sun began to set.

"How wonderful that you've come back," she whispered. She looked out over the kingdom, happy with her decision not to rebuild the Tower out of respect for her beloved niece. Moss glowed bright green over the pile of rubble that used to be the young girl's prison. Vines twisted and grew at a rapid rate, as if the soil were enchanted. Buried deep beneath the ground, in a small locked chest, was a small piece of tapestry.

It was one of those perfect days. The sun was shining, and the sea twinkled like a jewel. A warm, salty breeze blew off the ocean. The people of Cups had made inroads repairing their land, and their collective mood grew lighter with each passing day.

Anna and James ducked under the water like dolphins, laughing and feeling instantly refreshed. They held hands, floating on their backs, each thankful for the quiet, the peace. Anna dove under suddenly and popped up next to him, her black hair slicked back, her eyes, now bright purple, gleaming in the sun.

James flipped over and treaded water, looking her in the eye. "I'm so happy it's all over," he said.

"Me too." Anna smiled, swimming closer to kiss him.

He kissed her back.

"Race you to shore!" She broke into a breaststroke and glided back toward the sand. He shook his head, smiling, and took off after her.

Topper was sitting on the beach when they got out of the water.

"I'm going to go get a drink. Top, do you want anything?" James asked.

"No, I'm okay." Topper saluted James and he tore off toward the villa. Anna sat down next to Topper and hugged her knees to her chest.

"You look thoughtful," she said.

He tilted his head toward her. "I am," he finally said, turning away and looking back out to sea. "Do you ever think about going back to the Hierophant's Kingdom? I mean, now that the King is imprisoned."

"Sometimes," Anna said. "Only for a chance to see my friends. But I spent so much of my life there, and I can't stop thinking about what the Major Arcana said—there are many paths."

Topper inhaled deeply, leaned in close, and quietly said, "I know you've made your choice, Anna. And I won't interfere with that." He turned and tilted his head in the direction James had gone. "But I just want you to know, I'd follow any path you were on. If you wanted me to." His breath was warm on her wet skin. He pulled away, and sadness was clear on his features.

She drew in a quick breath, her heart racing.

Topper started to get up, but Anna grabbed his hand.

"Wait. When I was stuck in the Tower, I never dreamed life could be so complicated outside its walls," she said.

Topper lifted his chin toward the beach and the sea. "If you stay here, I don't think it has to be that complicated."

"But you know I will not stay here. I have to go see the rest of this world I created." She paused.

"Of course you do." Topper winked at her and nudged his bare shoulder gently against hers. "People like us. We can't stay in one place for long." His tone was lighter now.

Anna sighed.

James bounded back down the beach holding a coconut shell. He plopped down on her other side. "Here, Anna."

"Thank you, James." As Anna reached for the drink, his fingers brushed hers softly and a wave of warmth ran up her arm.

Anna looked out at the sea, the sun reflecting orange on its blue face. One day she was going to set off for another land; there was no doubt in her mind. But today was not that day. She leaned into James. There was still too much she needed to experience here. She'd only just stopped running.

Acknowledgments

First I want to thank Jessica Almon Galland for inviting me to the party. (Then and now.) Thanks for getting me on the playing field, dear lady.

Endless thanks to Ben Schrank and Alex Sanchez at Razorbill. What a joy it was working together with you two on this book. I loved our talks so much, and your insight and smarts helped me take the book and my writing to the next level. Thank you for pushing me to "beat this." Ben, you're a philosopher king. Alex—you have such a line on all things current and a true talent for adding a little fairy dust to scenes to make them truly come to life.

Thank you, Casey McIntyre and the entire team at Razorbill. I could not be more excited and proud to be a part of the Penguin Random House family.

Thank you to Danielle Noel for the gorgeous cover.

My deepest thanks to my agent, Taylor Haggerty, for always picking up the phone—even when you had just stepped off a plane. Thank you for all the good advice, the kindness, and being a "wonderful human."

Krista Gardner, thank you for my first tarot reading and for cleaning out and aligning my chakras. (That felt amazing!) Hats off to the Good Spirit in Vancouver for taking tarot and making it accessible and a little more user-friendly. Stephanie Pui-Mun Law and Barbara Moore—your Shadowscape deck was my first deck and a lovely intro to tarot. Butterflies and tarot—yes please. I could not have written this book without Skye Alexander's *The Only Tarot Book You'll Ever Need*. (Especially if you are writing a book called *Tarot*. Phew!) Same goes to Johannes Fiebig and Evelin Burger's *The Ultimate Guide to the Rider Waite Tarot*. All mistakes are mine and mine alone.

A giant thank-you to Maria Cavalieri and my Relentless Fitness family (Tom, Anya, Matt, Rosaria, Tina, Becca, Jonn, Steve, and Olga). I could not sit and write for the hours it takes to write a novel without our workout sessions. On that note, Claire Hartley—your yoga keeps me sane and my back working—you know what you do. I am forever grateful.

Laurie Gigliotti and Tiffany Rhine. My first readers—the people I go to when I'm anxious or over the moon. You are amazing writers and editors and friends. Writing has lonely moments, and knowing you are an email away means everything. To my online writing group, the YA Story Sisters: muah!

Rebecca Heller, Alicia Peterson, Morgan Bailey, ALL Neglias (Ashley, Dave, and Ross), Josh Tager, Amber Hartgens, Glen Wilson, and Clare Drysdale—I love you all so much it hurts. I feel like you are the ingredients for a magic friendship cake recipe—and I'm damn lucky to have it.

My in-laws extraordinaire—Paul Kennerson and Kathleen Snyder. I cannot express how grateful I am for your love and constancy.

Mom—thank you for being one of my best readers and sounding boards. A writer in your own right—thanks for all of the love.

Dad—thank you for always being my biggest fan. I love you something awful.

Herb and Deb—as stepparents go, you guys take the cake.

My brothers: Rodger—my brother here on earth and on a spiritual plane. Brad—you inspire, marching to the beat of your own (tabla) drum on the other side of world. Elliott—yeah, well, I won big in the in-law game. Wendy—my sis—our chats are legendary. I can't thank you enough for always being there for me and making me laugh my head off.

Last but not least—my boys. My husband and son, my heroes. You changed everything. Your love makes me better every day, and oh how we laugh. Greg—the world's best writer, editor, fashion director, and husband all in one. Shepard—you wow me. Thanks for letting me take over the kitchen table for months at a time, you two. This would never happen without you.